HIGH WIND

HIGH WIND

(*Ka Meikhar Ghar*)

TILOTTOMA MISRA

Translated from the original Assamese by
Udayon Misra

zubaan

ZUBAAN
128 B Shahpur Jat, 1st Floor
New Delhi 110 049
Website: www.zubaanbooks.com
Email: contact@zubaanbooks.com

First published by Zubaan Publishers Pvt. Ltd 2020

ISBN 978 93 85932 82 3

10 9 8 7 6 5 4 3 2 1

Zubaan is an independent feminist publishing house based in New Delhi
with a strong academic and general list. It was set up as an imprint of
India's first feminist publishing house, Kali for Women, and carries forward
Kali's tradition of publishing quality books to high editorial and production
standards. *Zubaan* means tongue, voice, language, speech in Hindustani.
Zubaan publishes in the areas of the humanities, social sciences, as well as in
fiction, general non-fiction and books for children and young adults under its
Young Zubaan imprint.

Printed and bound in India by Thomson Press India Ltd.

THRESHOLD

'Well! Now I know why my father had to leave this university. Clearly it was because of his views.' Arvind looked at Jeumon in surprise as she spoke the words almost to herself. Jeumon was pensive as she looked into the crackling flames of the log fire whose glow lent a mysterious sadness to her soft, rounded face. Seated in small groups around large empty drums with fires lit inside them, teachers and research scholars were busy talking in the front lawn of the guest house. They had come for a seminar at the university and were now gathered for dinner. Sitting by Jeumon's side were two scholars from Delhi University, Arvind Das and Rabindra Sinha, and a teacher from Guwahati, Prashanta Saharia. Jeumon Diengdoh herself was from Shillong. She'd done a doctorate from London and was now working at a research institute in Delhi.

Everyone was busy discussing issues that had come up during that day. History student Rabindra Sinha called attention to prevalent misconceptions about the traditions of written and oral literature, and then went off into a long discourse: 'Western scholars have long viewed written and oral literature in terms of a hierarchy. But when we look at the history of the Sanskrit language, we see that even around the third century B.C. when Sanskrit was accepted as a written language, contemporary poets did not discard the oral tradition. Rather, it was given a place of honour. The introductory verses to Valmiki's *Ramayana* show that they actually acknowledge the existence of an oral tradition which preceded the written epic. And the attempt to present the whole of the *Ramayana* through the oral renderings of Lava and Kusha shows that there were no barriers between the written and the oral at the time. But historians today quite often use nationalism as a tool in the writing of history and try to sideline the entire oral tradition. As a result, an important component of the nation's culture gets left out of its literary history. It's natural therefore that the educated class from the largely oral communities looks with suspicion, even a sense of hatred, at the nationalistic arrogance of the written tradition.'

Sinha's argument deeply touched Jeumon, who was listening to him with attention. His words, she thought, justified much of what she had said in her presentation at the seminar that morning. She'd talked about how one could improve one's understanding of the hill-valley relationship by looking at the folk tales of the communities living in the regions bordering the foothills. She had narrated some folktales which historians have long regarded as fanciful stories unfit to be considered as history. She'd pointed out that such stories, which spoke about the ties of friendship between the inhabitants of the hills and those of the plains, have always been vibrant in the people's imagination. One of these was the story of Watlum and Gadadhar. Known widely in the plains of Assam as the love story of Dalimi and Gadapani, the story of Watlum-Gadadhar was still very popular among the people who visited the rural haats and bazaars at the Assam-Nagaland border. For them it was quite a credible tale and many actually believed it to be true. Even today when the *O-Tashi* or the storyteller of the Ao Nagas narrates the story of Watlum-Gadadhar – of how suddenly a flock of birds from the plains took wing to the hills, of how flowers in the plains lifted their heads towards the hills as if to tell the spies of the Ahom king that Gadadhar was hiding in there, of how thunder and lightning broke out as soon as Gadadhar set foot in the Naga village and of how the villagers realized at once that someone of royal descent was among them – to groups of eager listeners sitting around the fireplace, they never for once doubted the veracity of the tale or made fun of it. Jeumon reflected that if the language of the streams and the trees and the wind could be believed, then folktales too were trustworthy. In her own way, she had tried to stress the importance of the shared oral tradition in fostering true peace and friendship between the hills and the plains.

That morning, as Jeumon was leaving the seminar room after presenting her paper, quite a few of the participants had walked up to her and congratulated her. Although she was already a known name in academic circles, many people had not had the chance to listen to her. Her clarity of argument, rational approach and pleasant manner of delivery had impressed everyone. An elderly person who had been listening with great attention, came forward and praised her warmly. He introduced himself somewhat self consciously as 'Dr Parameswar Deka, the former Vice-Chancellor of this university.' As Jeumon greeted him with folded hands, he asked. 'You must be from Shillong. What's your father's name?'

'Saratchandra Bhattacharyya. He was previously editor of the *Hill People's Daily*. Now he's the owner.'

'Oh! So you are *his* daughter?' asked the gentleman, giving her a quizzical look.

'My father once taught at this university. Do you, by any chance, happen to know him?' Jeumon asked eagerly.

'Yes, of course. I was the Head of the Department when he was here.' He walked away. Jeumon smiled and turned to Arvind, 'Looks like he wanted to avoid me. I wonder why?'

'Yes, I could see that. He looked somewhat uncomfortable when he heard your father's name. For sure, there must be some old skeletons hidden somewhere in his mind's cupboard.' Arvind had said this half in jest, without giving much thought to what had passed between Jeumon and the gentleman. But Jeumon's sudden outburst about her father now set him thinking and his curiosity was aroused. He had a strong urge to listen to her father's story from Jeumon's lips. As for Jeumon, she continued to speak, somewhat absentmindedly, keeping her gaze fixed on the fire, 'I think my father's views were not acceptable to the academic community of our state at the time. Assam was then a composite unit made up of both the hills and the plains. Maybe it was his concern for the future which had led him to oppose the very idea of one particular community extending its hegemony over the others. He had also suggested that the oral and the written traditions be treated equally. Also, his views on the reasons behind the growth of an insurrectionary mindset among the people in the frontier areas were very particular. He felt this was happening because these small nationalities had not been touched by the freedom struggle and there was little space for them within the mainstream of Indian nationalism. Once his departmental Head came to know that he had spoken to the history students in favour of Naga nationalism. He immediately wrote to the Vice-Chancellor seeking action against my father for his "anti-national" activities. But that did not deter my father, who continued to speak up according to the dictates of his own conscience. Some of his colleagues even wrote letters to the newspapers saying that my father was not fit to be a university teacher. Perhaps it was because of all this that the university found an excuse and dismissed him from service.'

Jeumon stood up abruptly and began to stoke the fire, throwing in some more wood. Once again the flames leapt up. Prashanta Saharia, who belonged to the host university, could not control his curiosity any longer. He gave Jeumon a sharp look and asked, 'So your father is the well-known Saratchandra Bhattacharyya who once taught in our department? I have a good collection of his articles with me. And your mother is a Khasi?'

'Without a doubt,' replied Jeumon with a smile.

The next morning Jeumon and Arvind left for Shillong in a taxi. On the way, Arvind talked about some of the funny aspects of the previous day's seminar, of how some of the participants couldn't make sense of his theoretical approach to certain issues and ended up changing the entire course of the discussion through their simplistic interventions. He said, 'This has been my experience in most seminars. At the end of it all, one feels so foolish.'

'There is always a sense of frustration in most academic events. Even so, we go to them in the hope that something will come of them,' said Jeumon with a smile.

Arvind suddenly changed track and said, 'I found out only yesterday that you are not fully a tribal in your roots. So, your father is a Bengali?'

'No, he is Assamese. But before you heard my father's name, all of you thought me to be a Khasi, right? Do you really think that our surname is our only identity?'

'I should have realized this earlier. After all, you look so much like *our* people,' Arvind said with a laugh.

'So, *now* you are speaking like a true Indian! "We", "they", all these have entered your thoughts. But let me tell you that I look exactly like myself. Maybe, others will judge from the shape of my eyes, ears, nose and face whether I am "pure" or "mixed"! But I am fully certain that I am the only one who knows for sure who I actually am, what my identity is, what the "me" inside me really is.' Jeumon's gaze was fixed on the distant hills as she said this.

'You seem to have taken my remarks to heart. Please don't mind. I was actually referring to the wonderful mix that characterizes the people of the northeastern region. Perhaps nowhere else in India is there such a mix.' Arvind used his researcher's tone to retrieve lost ground. At this, Jeumon smiled and tried to reassure him: 'That's all right. Actually, I am trying to write a novel so as to understand my own identity and existence. Naturally, my family's history will also be part of it.' Then, after a slight pause, she added: 'Would you like to hear the outline of the story?'

'Why, of course! But who is the narrator of the story? Is it you or someone else?'

'Maybe it will be a third woman whose own story will be intertwined with mine,' Jeumon said thoughtfully.

'Must be quite a complicated plot,' Arvind said in a light tone.

'Life itself is so complex that no story as such can really express its twists and turns. But I'll try to give you an idea of the entire story. I'll have to finish it quickly before we reach High Wind.'

'What language are you writing in? Shall I be able to read it?'

'No problem. I will write in the same language I speak. It is neither my mother-tongue nor my father-tongue. It is my own language, the language through which I like to express my innermost thoughts,' Jeumon replied with a smile.

'Please go on. I am now, by my own choice, your captive audience.'

The car began to make its way up the winding hill road.

2

Saratchandra Bhattacharyya's father, Banamali Panchatirtha was a highly knowledgeable Sanskrit pandit. A scholarship of ten rupees a month from the Maharaja of Coochbehar allowed him to study at the Girish Chatushpathi in Nabadwip, where he earned the title of 'Panchatirtha' because of his mastery over five branches of study. The high grades that he scored in his final examination had made him eligible for that scholarship. In those days very few bright students could really go through this difficult examination for which Banamali had not only read classical texts like the *Raghuvamsha, Uttara Ramacarit* and *Abhijnanam Shakuntalam*, but had also studied in great detail the complete version of the *Amarkosh*. After spending several years in centres of Sanskrit learning in Coochbehar, Rangpur and Kashi, Panchatirtha finally came to Calcutta. Here, he studied at the famous Sanskrit College but because of financial constraints he could not complete his course. Nonetheless, he carved for himself a niche in the academic circles of that city by dint of his mastery of the language, both written and oral. The then Vice-Chancellor of Calcutta University, Ashutosh Mukherjee, was said to have taken a liking to Panchatirtha after having heard the young man give a speech in flawless Sanskrit and would often invite him home where he would take part in many academic discussions. Later, on his return to his home state of Assam, Panchatirtha would often recall with pride his association with the intellectual luminaries of Calcutta; but the Assamese bhadralok always took his words with a grain of salt. They just couldn't believe that a pandit of a tol could make friends with the likes of Ashutosh Mukherjee.

Panchatirtha came from a small village situated on the banks of the Pagladia river in Lower Assam. While in Calcutta, a student friend, Shivaprasad, proposed that he marry his younger sister. At first, Panchatirtha didn't agree. How would a girl brought up in an Upper Assam town adjust to the rural surroundings of his village? But his friend continued to try and persuade him, saying that their father had a government job and a house of his own in Shillong and that, on his return home, if Panchatirtha needed governmental assistance to secure a job, his father-in-law would surely be able to help. Moreover, the girl was quite young and would be able to easily adjust to her new surroundings.

Eventually, Panchatirtha gave in. But when the marriage proposal reached his village home, there was a huge commotion. How would a girl from Upper Assam understand the Lower Assam dialect? It was swiftly concluded that since the girl's father worked in a government office in Shillong, all the women would invariably be 'bread-eating' memsahibs. How would such a bride be able to conform to the rigid practices of the household of an eminent Sanskrit scholar like Raghunath Bhattacharyya?

Banamali Panchatirtha's mother, Debeswari, was an accomplished housewife. As the mistress of a traditional Kamrupi Brahmin household she could deal efficiently with all the nitty-gritty of such a household. Easily the most important of her many duties was to prepare the sidha or the raw provisions for a meal for her frequent Brahmin guests. Even a minor lapse in this could affect the family's prestige and earn reprobation. Debeswari knew only too well how to separate and serve the sidha in her many small and large utensils and in the clean white donas made of plantain stems. Her Brahmin guests who cooked their own meals were always satisfied with her excellent arrangements. When a special Brahmin guest arrived, Debeswari measured out a portion of fragrant joha rice and placed the washed rice at the centre of a large brass plate with all the smaller sidhas neatly stacked around. There were portions of lentils, potatoes, brinjal, fish and vegetables. On another brass plate salt, turmeric, ground condiments and chillies were placed carefully on small pieces of delicately cut plantain leaf. The intricate arrangement gave the impression that the entire preparation was being made for some god to descend to their hearth and cook a meal. Before they got married and left home, Debeswari's three daughters helped her out in this rather complicated task, picking up all the details in the process. They had also learnt how to arrange the sidha for the vegetarian boram-bhoj or feast held in the month of Kati and the non-vegetarian boram-bhoj held during the month of Magh. Apart from their own house, Debeswari's daughters were much in demand when neighbours arranged for brahma-bhojan to feed Brahmins. It was because of these qualities, that Raghunath Bhattacharyya had received a substantial amount as bride-price when giving away each of his accomplished daughters in marriage. The youngest daughter was both fair and attractive. So, for her he had taken a thousand rupees in cash as her bride price. In order to pay back the mahajan's loan with which he had paid the bride-price, the son-in-law had to work for several years in the Goalpara region. This practice was known amongst the people of Kamrup as *bilaat-khata*, the word 'bilaat' signifying the foreign regions beyond the western borders of Kamarupa, comprising of Goalpara, Rangpur and Coochbehar. Debeswari's youngest son-in-law had to spend several years working as a priest in those areas so that he could collect enough cash to repay the loan taken from the mahajan for his bride-price. By the time he returned home, he was already much advanced in age. This, however, did not bother Raghunath and Debeswari at all. Rather, they were a bit upset that their son Banamali and his young friends were speaking against the practice of bride-price. They feared that even the slightest change in the accepted social practices could lead to a severe social crisis. That was exactly why the marriage proposal from a family from Upper Assam had created such a commotion in Banamali's family.

When Banamali Panchatirtha heard from the messengers who had gone to his village home that his family was not in favour of the match, he decided to go ahead with his resolve to marry the girl from Jorhat. So he rushed to Jorhat, stayed with a friend there and went to visit the prospective bride. The moment he saw the fair, beautiful girl of some nine or ten years of age, he decided to marry her and fixed a date for the ceremony. The bride's father, Sashikanta Barua, hurried home from Shillong for the marriage. Banamali assured the bride's parents that he would come to take the girl away once she attained puberty, and then he left for his village.

News about the marriage had already reached his home. So, the moment he entered his village, Panchatirtha knew that something was amiss. Instead of going straight home, he stopped over at a relative's. It was from him that he learnt about his father publicly disowning him because he had married a memsahib. It was as if someone had died in his family. His mother and aunts were in deep mourning and neighbours had come to join in and add to the atmosphere of 'bereavement'. With heavy steps Panchatirtha crossed the threshold of his ancestral home and approached his father who was sitting in his soraghar or outer sitting room. A solemn-faced Raghunath Bhattacharrya, seated on a borpira, was engrossed in his hookah. Panchatirtha pulled a low wooden stool, sat down beside his father, and asked angrily: 'Pray, for what crime have I been disowned as a son?' His father didn't utter a word and continued to puff at his hookah. 'I have married a girl from a good Brahmin family of Upper Assam. They aren't mlechhas as you think,' said Panchatirtha.

His father pushed the hookah aside and, wiping his face with a gamosa, declared in a magisterial tone, 'We are in the know of everything. We know which families eat bread and biscuits. In this house we will never allow such a memsahib to prepare sidha for Brahmins and sajjans. And, let me tell you that this house is out of bounds for anyone who has established links with such a family. Let me tell you that after death, we will never accept pinda from such a son.' As if to add some extra stress to his concluding words, Raghunath Bhattacharyya almost banged his hookah on the floor and left the room.

Panchatirtha jumped up and rushed to his bedroom. On a broad bamboo rack above his bed were his books tied up in a large cloth bundle. He looked at them and pondered for a while. He had a strong emotional bond with these books and manuscripts which he had collected over the years from different places in Nabadwip, Coochbehar, Kashi, Bikrampur and Rangpur. Some of them he had laboriously copied. He knew that even if he could have given up everything else related to his father's home, he would never be able to leave these books behind. In an instant he decided that he would take all the books with him. He carefully brought down the bundle from the rack and kept it on the floor. Then he made several small bundles of his books with old gamosas and sheets and whatever else was readily available and carried them outside.

Meanwhile, an old family hand named Ratiram came in and was watching the activities with some consternation. Ratiram was one of those peasants whose family had lived for generations on the rent-free debottor land belonging to Panchatirtha's family. There were several peasant families who lived on their land as was customary during the times of the old rulers of the pre-British days, and they were called golams or serfs. Ratiram was almost the same age as Banamali and they had grown up together playing village games and going for swims in the river. Hence, they were sort of friends. Ratiram had a bullock-cart and he suggested that since the cart was making a trip to Guwahati, the books could be transported in it. Panchatirtha readily agreed.

After a while, villagers saw a bullock-cart loaded with bundles of books and papers leaving the village and walking behind it with steady steps was Banamali Panchatirtha. Panchatirtha never ever returned to his village, not even when he got news, many years later, about the death of his parents. Throughout his life he continued to carry this enormous burden of self-pride and resentment which was thrust upon him in his youth. It was not as if there weren't other individuals at that time in his village who sympathised with him. But they lacked the courage to speak out against the harsh edicts of a deeply conservative society.

3

Getting a head pundit's job at the Sivasagar Government High School was quite easy for Panchatirtha. Normally, Sanskrit scholars who had a knowledge of *Nyayaya, Smriti* and the *Shastras* apart from grammar, *Kavya, Gita* and the *Upanishads*, would not move out of the chatuspathis of Kamrup and work in a government school where English occupied an important slot in the curriculum. It was the usual practice for degree-holding scholars like Panchatirtha to set up their own tols or chatuspathis in different parts of Kamrup where they would coach students for scholarship examinations or for higher degrees in Sanskrit. Generally, there were two levels of scholarship examinations. If a particular student excelled in both these tests, then along with the student, the teacher too would get a reward in cash and this greatly helped in the running of the tols. Meritorious students from the chatuspathis of Assam would go on for higher studies in the tols of Rangpur, Coochbehar, Nabadwip and Kasi and return with degrees such as Vidyabagish, Smritiratna, Tarkaratna, Kavyasmriti, Mimansatirtha, Tarkatirtha, Nyayaratna and Siddhantabagish. These tols usually subsisted on royal patronage or donations from the public and many well-off people considered it a virtuous deed to help students or scholars of the tol to meet their expenses.

Soon after joining the Sivasagar High School, Panchatirtha realized that his position was not at par with that of other teachers. Although on the face of it, everyone addressed him as 'Pandit Mahashai', 'Pandit Moshai' or 'Gurudev' and his students, whether in class or at the weekly 'Jnandayini' meets, listened to him with much attention, yet he felt that his English-knowing colleagues often looked upon him as an object of pity. Over time, this feeling became stronger. He noticed that whenever he came upon his colleagues in the middle of a discussion, they would immediately switch over to English, correct or otherwise, and would derive a lot of satisfaction at his discomfiture. Panchatirtha was much pained by such behaviour. He had never thought before coming to Sivasagar that his lack of English would reduce the relevance of the store of knowledge he had acquired with so much effort. In his moments of dejection, he would often yearn to return to Calcutta. The very thought of his days in Calcutta where he had pursued Sanskrit with his many friends, brought succour to his disturbed mind. But Panchatirtha could not take that step immediately because his family responsibilities had increased in the meantime. After he brought his beautiful wife Haimavati from her Jorhat home, Panchatirtha bought a piece of land in Sivasagar and built a small thatched cottage there to begin his new life.

Haimavati had read up to the seventh grade in the Girls' High School at Jorhat. Since she was a good student, her teachers had high expectations that she would bring credit to her school by doing well in the Matriculation examination. But that did not happen. After collecting the transfer certificate from the school and nursing hopes of taking the Matriculation examination in the future, Haimavati had to come to her husband's house to set up a family. While with her parents, she had read most of the Bengali novels which were there in her father's study. She had even read on the sly the romance of *Vidyasundar* which her brother had brought from Calcutta and had hidden under his mattress. Now, at her husband's house, she continued with her practice of reading books during her leisure time. The moment her husband left for school, she would quickly finish her household chores and sit down to read a novel either by Bankimchandra or Saratchandra. The women of the neighbourhood did not seem to be at ease with Haimavati's love for books. Nonetheless, they looked upon her with some respect as the pandit's wife.

Haimavati's two sons, Saratchandra and Bijoychandra, were both born in Sivasagar. With Panchatirtha and her two sons, Haima's family seemed complete. In the beginning, Haima, who had never met any member of her husband's family, found Panchatirtha's language a bit strange. But gradually husband and wife started to make fun by imitating each other's style of speech. Both the sons, however, spoke in the Sivasagar dialect and their father used to teasingly call them 'Rangpuria Apa', Rangpur being the name of ancient Sivasagar. There was a nice mix of the Upper and Lower Assam tongues in the Panchatirtha house. Sometimes when Panchatirtha slipped into his own dialect and complained about something, Haima would promptly reply in her Upper Assam idiom. The boys loved to take part in this banter and often teased their father about his Kamrupia dialect. When Panchatirtha went to the market, they would ask him to bring *sumthira* and *kamala*, *jalakia* and *bhajluk or madhuriaam* and *saphuriaam*, though both sets of names stood for the same thing! Like their friends, the boys called their mother 'bouti' but addressed their father as 'pita'. When it came to food, there was a wonderful mix of the cooking habits of the two parts of Assam in Panchatirtha's house. While Haima prepared the dishes she had learnt at her mother's place such as the different tangy fish curries made with tomato, lime and herbs, she had also learnt to cook her husband's favourites where mustard and black pepper were freely used. Panchatirtha too would often cook for the family, with his sons always insisting that he was the better cook.

Panchatirtha had put both his sons in a Sivasagar primary school called Dukhiya School or Poor School. The older son, Saratchandra, who was called Borbaap at home, was of a quiet nature. He was always punctual and went to school neatly dressed. But the younger son, Bijoychandra, or Sarubaap was of a different temperament. He would get up early in the morning and, after reciting a few pages from his school text at the top of his voice, would quietly slip out of the house to explore the back yard for fruit and berries. Sometimes he even went to the riverfront to watch the boatmen at work. As a result, he was often late for school. Once, when he was late for the morning prayer the teacher made him stand apart, holding his ears. His brother was deeply embarrassed by this. But his affection for his younger brother prevented Saratchandra from speaking of this at home. Thus, two brothers shared a close bond from an early age. The younger one always rose to the defence of the older. If any of his classmates tried to play a prank on Borbaap, Sarubaap invariably took his elder brother's side and fought his little battles with the classmates.

Panchatirtha always jokingly referred to his elder son as 'Sahabar Bapa' or a sahib's son because of the his love for discipline and the rules. His wife was fond of narrating the story of how when Borbaap was a baby, he spent hours happily looking at a timepiece. Panchatirtha, however, never liked the idea of being a slave to clock-time. He saw the large clocks at the court and at the Orunuday Press as symbols of British rule. It was as if these clocks were a constant reminder that people's lives were now governed by a powerful and all-conquering force. Panchatirtha put up his own feeble resistance to this unchallenged power by refusing to obey the clock and always went to the school a few minutes late. His colleagues commented wryly that the pundit could not submit to the discipline set by the clock because the time followed in the tols was not the same as that in their school. Panchatirtha tried to ignore such jibes and focus on his teaching. He'd enter his class with measured steps, and start imparting lessons to the boys. He taught from the great classics, his world controlled by the concept of timeless literary creations. In that world it was not necessary to put the past, present and future into specified time-frames. That was why Panchatirtha was often irritated when the school bell rang to mark the end of class and he had to cut short his lesson. He found it really strange that his students had to learn a different subject every hour. He would often ask himself: can knowledge be actually gained through such a mechanical process? This often triggered off memories of his own schooldays. Their classes in the tol would start according to the convenience of their guru and lessons were smoothly imparted without any heed for the clock. As a young student, Panchatirtha could never imagine the claustrophobic environment of a classroom where the students would be in a constant state of being terrified by both clock-time and the cane. At the tol there had never been such pressure and the students were always guided by traditional ideas of respect and devotion. Theirs, he felt, was a life-style built on the intellectual discipline that had emerged out of such an environment.

Though Panchatirtha was not happy with the manner of functioning of the English school, yet keeping in mind his situation, he tried to follow its rules and regulations. But, just as he was beginning to adjust to his new environment, a fresh challenge suddenly surfaced. A person named Taraknath Sarma, who had a degree in Sanskrit from Calcutta University, joined the school and was entrusted with the task of teaching the higher classes as a class teacher. Despite his eight to ten years of service, Panchatirtha was yet to gain this status because to be a class teacher you had to be proficient in what was considered as the most important of all subjects, English. Taraknath Sarma had this advantage: he had both Sanskrit and English. The moment Sarma joined the school, it was presumed that because he was a graduate from Calcutta University he would soon be appointed as Headmaster of some government school. Panchatirtha had meanwhile realized that in the new educational set up, there was little scope for promotion for a pundit like him who did not possess a university degree. He couldn't help being a bit envious of Sarma. A person who had spent just two or three years at a college had now been placed above him, ignoring the fact that he had earned his knowledge of the Sanskrit texts through laborious effort over more than a decade. Panchatirtha found it hard to accept such a situation. But, not having any other way out, he swallowed his pride and continued his work without coming into any direct confrontation with Taraknath.

One day, news arrived that the Chief Commissioner of the province was visiting the town. A number of eminent citizens got together to organize a felicitation programme for the sahib. Some of the government school teachers were entrusted with the job of arranging the meeting and fixing the agenda. This meant that they would decide upon the speakers as also those who would render the welcome song. Panchatirtha was requested to prepare a felicitation address. On earlier occasions too, he had prepared such addresses and when he read them out in flawless Sanskrit with clear intonations, the audience, not all of whom understood the language, would always listen in rapt attention and enthusiastically applaud. This time too, Panchatirtha carefully wrote out the address which he embellished with some of the choicest slokas. He then wrote it out a sheet of paper in his beautiful calligraphic handwriting which greatly resembled that of old manuscripts. In preparing this address, Panchatirtha had drawn from the many felicitations written by well-known pundits of the past for their patron kings and emperors. He read it through several times to see if there were any mistakes, and then kept it ready to be handed over to the Commissioner on the appointed day.

A few days before the meeting, Taraknath Sarma sent word to Panchatirtha that he would like to have a look at the felicitation address. Panchatirtha handed it over to him somewhat unwillingly. Maybe he will find some fault with it, thought Panchatirtha. But, a day or two later, he was quite relieved when Taraknath returned the paper with a smile. 'Quite well written,' he said.

The meeting took place with a lot of fanfare in the town hall. The front row seats were occupied by the leading citizens of the town and behind them sat Banamali Panchatirtha, Taraknath Sarma and the other teachers of the government high school. Following the bandana song presented by students, the felicitation was about to begin. But just as Panchatirtha stood up to perform his role, he saw Taraknath Sarma move towards the dais with quick steps. Taraknath then eloquently read out Panchatirtha's address in English. Shocked, Panchatirtha looked at the organizers. A teacher sitting next to him whispered, 'It's just a translation of yours. Thinking that the sahib would not understand Sanskrit, it was decided to have the address in English. But, you will also be given a chance to read yours.' Though filled with shame and insult, Panchatirtha went to the dais when his name was announced and read the address and returned to his seat. The meeting continued without a hitch. But Panchatirtha took this as a grave insult and stopped talking with Taraknath from that day onwards. The entire episode continued to be discussed in the gossip corners of the town for quite some time. Many were highly amused by the fact that Panchatirtha and Taraknath were not on speaking terms any more. Some would approach Panchatirtha and try to find out his response by speaking ill of Taraknath. If Panchatirtha responded, they would quickly go and present a completely different version to Traknath. This went on and like the ceaseless croaking of frogs in dark roadside drains, the people of the town continued to talk about this incident for days to come.

Those were difficult days for Banamali Panchatirtha and he desperately wanted to resign from his job and go off somewhere. But where would he go? With his limited qualifications, the only job that he could think of was that of a pundit in a tol. There seemed to be no other alternative. Sometimes he also thought of moving to Samarkuchi, Gamerimuri, Dhaniagog, Keihati or some other unknown village in Kamrup and starting a chatuspathi there. But he realized how difficult it would be to make ends meet with the meagre income of a tol if one didn't have enough land to fall back upon. Moreover, wouldn't it mean a defeat in life's struggle if he were to return to the same environment of obsolete customs and narrow prejudices against which he had rebelled and left? Troubled deeply as he was with all these thoughts, he couldn't think of resigning his job and leaving Sivasagar. Until one day, quite unexpectedly, a somewhat strange opportunity presented itself.

That day too, just as on other days, Panchatirtha was entering the school, umbrella in hand, when the headmaster, Mr Chakravarty, called him over to his office. A clerk from the Bar-sahib's office was already seated there. The moment Panchatirtha entered, the clerk greeted him with great respect and then said in Bengali, 'Mashai, our Bar-sahib wishes to meet you. It would be nice if you could go and see him once.' Reacting to Panchatirtha's surprised look, he added, 'There is nothing to worry about. It seems there is good news.' He didn't elaborate. Panchatirtha was both confused and worried. Why should the Bar-sahib ask for him? He did not possess any skill or knowledge that could be of use to the foreign rulers, and he didn't also have any such powers which could harm the almighty British government. He had last met the Bar-sahib at the meeting held to felicitate the Chief Commissioner and he couldn't recall any such incident which might have caught the sahib's eye. However, he fixed the date and hour of the visit with the clerk and told him that he would come and see the Bar-sahib at his bungalow.

On the appointed day, dressed in a clean white dhoti-kurta and a seleng sador with guna motifs thrown over his shoulder, an uncertain Banamali Panchatirtha set forth for the sahib's bungalow. But neither his appearance nor his gait gave any indication of his troubled mind. Even as he entered the sahib's bungalow he gave the impression that this was an everyday thing for him. Seated in the broad, airy verandah of his house, the sahib was smoking a cigar and reading. He politely greeted Panchatirtha, offered him a chair and, without further ado, promptly broached the subject, 'Pundit Babu, do you know how to read old stone and copperplate inscriptions?' As the question was quite an unexpected one, Panchatirtha took some time to think it over and then answered, 'I have deciphered a few inscriptions written in the ancient Kamrupi and Devnagri scripts. But, I am sorry, I will not be able to read those written in other languages.'

'Where have you read such inscriptions?' the sahib asked him.

'I have read the inscriptions at the Hajo-Haigrib Madhav temple and have copied these on paper. Apart from this, during my days in Calcutta I had the opportunity of reading a few copies of the Tezpur copperplates which were with the much revered Padmanath Bhattachrayya Bidyabinod. I had heard that the copies had been sent to Calcutta's Asiatic Society by Colonel Jenkins sahib. I am a member of that Society. The description of the Brahmaputra in those copperplates is really enchanting. I still have by heart some of those lines.'

The sahib nodded in approval and then placed a proposal before Panchatirtha, 'Edward Arnold sahib who is in Shillong has been preparing a very important report on the stone and copperplate inscriptions of Assam. He needs a Sanskrit pundit to help him. Will you be able to do this work?'

Panchatirtha, with head bowed, was silent for some time and then said with the utmost regard, 'Sir, my knowledge is very limited. I know little else apart from Sanskrit language and literature. My knowledge of English is extremely rudimentary. How will I be able to perform such a heavy task? Especially, how will I communicate with Arnold Sahib?' With a smile, the sahib gave a direct reply to Panchatirtha's direct question, 'Pundit babu, don't worry. The language in which you have been speaking with me just now, that language will do. Of course, Mr Arnold knows a little more Assamese than what I have picked up for my official work. Otherwise, he would never have taken up such a task.' After this, Panchatirtha was left with no more excuses. It seemed that in a totally unexpected manner the Almighty was about to fulfil his urge of all these days to finally leave Sivasagar. No more would he be pricked by the subtle barbs and derogatory comments of his colleagues. Whatever it might be, the new job would at least carry some respect for his knowledge. His pay would also increase fourfold, which meant forty rupees a month. On his way back home, Panchatirtha recited the gayatri mantra three times and bowed to the all-powerful Parameshwar for his good fortune.

The students and staff of the Sivasagar High School bid farewell to Panchatirtha as per tradition. Flower garlands, a plaque with compliments, a farewell song, gifts, everything was there. However, on this occasion Panchatirtha didn't even try to find out how many of those present that morning really possessed some genuine goodwill towards him. He was already feeling free and liberated. He was now prepared to forgive and forget all the envy and prejudice of the past. So, as he finally left, he walked up to Taraknath Sarma and warmly greeted him with folded hands.

The evening before he left Sivasagar, as he was sitting star gazing with his sons in their courtyard, Sarubaap Bijoy suddenly said in a voice filled with emotion, 'Pita, when you go away, won't all those ghosts around us – the jakhinis of the bamboo groves, the kandhs of the Dikhow embankment and all the jakhs – come over to eat us up?' Panchartirha realised in that instant that the darkness enveloping this small town had left a deep impress on these young minds. As for himself, he had long banished the fear of ghosts and spirits from his mind. Having travelled in different lands, he now knew that it was only when the darkness outside mingled with the darkness within that the human imagination got tangled in the world of ghosts, spirits and demi-gods. At the same time, once the lamp of modern scientific knowledge succeeded in illuminating the outside world, then the mind too became clear and free. As he walked through the dark alleys in his neighbourhood, he would often wonder why people in cities like Calcutta and Banares weren't obsessed with kandhs, jakhs and bura-dangorias and such other spirits. Panchatirtha was now a bit worried at the fear that had gripped the mind of a smart and active boy like Sarubaap. It was natural that the pitch dark bamboo grove near their backyard and the firefly dotted undergrowth in front of their house would throw up images of a primitive world. So, he tried to reassure his family, 'I have bound the four corners of our compound with the gayatri mantra. Nothing evil will ever be able to enter these precincts.' But it was the not the fear of ghosts but that of harmful humans that made Panchtirtha request an uncle of Haimavati's to look after the family while he was away. Deciding that he would go alone to Shillong, Panchatirtha set forth on his journey to the distant hills, planning in his mind that once he managed to make living arrangements there, he would bring his family along.

4

On his way to Shillong, Panchatirtha decided to stop over at Guwahati for a few days. His old friend Ramdutta Vidyavinod was there, busy with his work in the Kamrup Anusandhan Samity and in giving shape to the Assam Sanskrit Board. Panchatirtha stayed as his guest and both friends spent a lot of time discussing the future of the Anusandhan Samity and the Sanskrit Board. Vidyavinod also gave Panchatirtha news about his village on the banks of the Pagladia. He told him about his father Raghunath Bhattacharyya's deteriorating financial situation, although he was still quite strong both in body and mind. 'He comes to Guwahati quite often in order to fight court cases for his neighbours,' he said. 'Right now it seems he has spent a lot of money fighting a strange case. He is firm on helping a eunuch of his village secure rights to paternal property. It is certain that he will lose this case,' said Vidyavinod firmly.

'But I know that Pita will never learn to accept defeat. If he loses this suit, he will move the Calcutta High Court and then, if need be, the Privy Council too! Just because of Pita's obstinacy, we'll finally end up losing all the family property. As it is, the Pagladia river has been eroding our cultivable land every year,' Panchatirtha said with a sigh.

'Would you like to go home once?' Vidyavinod's voice was full of expectation.

'There is no need for that. If I miss anyone there, it's only my mother. I think of her often,' Panchatirtha replied in a voice bereft of any emotion.

'It seems you really have your father's blood running in your veins,' Vidyavinod said with a smile.

Preparing for his Shillong journey, Panchatirtha got a warm kurta stitched for himself and bought a pair of shoes and socks. Wearing his first ever pair of shoes, Panchatirtha practised walking within the house. He quite liked the squeaky sound the shoes made. Suddenly, he felt as if he was endowed with some new sense of authority. After the staid and monotonous life at Sivasagar, it seemed that the time had finally come for him to move swiftly towards his charted goal.

In those days there was no arrangement for a quick journey to Shillong. It was only some ten years after Panchatirtha's first journey to Shillong that the Albion buses with hard rubber tyres started to ply on the Shillong-Guwahati road. Once these buses, with their loud stuttering engines and frequent jerky movements, got moving on the narrow winding hill road, droves of people from the plains started taking the journey to Shillong. In the beginning, towards the end of the nineteenth century, it was the Ghulam Haidar Company which had started plying bullock-carts and horse-drawn carriages. Later, having secured government permits, the same company also ran horse drawn mail-carriages. In subsequent years, Ghulam Haidar's son, Kasimuddin Molla started the first motor service on this road. Because of their sharp business sense, Ghulam Haidar and his sons had secured a hold on almost all the commercial concerns of Shillong and had built up a considerable business empire there.

It was in one of these slow-moving bullock-carts of the Ghulam Haidar Company that Panchatirtha made his first journey to Shillong. The fare for a cart was twelve rupees and only three persons could travel in it. But in order to reduce costs, five of them jointly hired a cart and it was agreed that they would take turns at it: three of them would ride the cart while the other two would walk along with it. Of the four co-passengers who were with Panchatirtha, two, Indu Chaudhury and Tarabhusan Debnath, were from Dacca. Both of them were government employees in Dacca which was the former joint-capital of Eastern Bengal and Assam. Now that Assam had been made a separate province, they were moving on transfer to its capital, Shillong. Indubabu was a Brahmo by faith. He had a somewhat detached temperament and spoke very little throughout the journey. Although the other Bengali gentleman kept everyone entertained with his continuous flow of jokes and funny anecdotes, he could elicit only a semblance of a smile from the sombre Indubabu. The third co-passenger was a Christian gentleman from Nagaon, Mr Goldsmith. He was the manager of an Italian bakery in Shillong. His wife too was accompanying him to Shillong. But like all the other women passengers, a Khasi labourer was carrying her on his back, in a long cone-shaped bamboo basket or thapa. At Panchatirtha's evident surprise at this mode of travel, one of his co-passengers explained, 'Don't be surprised, Dangoria. This contraption has been there for quite some time. Such an arrangement has been made for the travel of the wives of the European sahibs and babus who live in Shillong. If you look closely, you will see that these baskets or thapas are not like the ones in which goods are usually carried. Here the lower part of the bamboo basket is kept open and there is a small footboard to rest one's legs. There is also a bamboo seat for the passenger.'

'One can also travel like this from Cherrapunji to the Surma valley,' the person who joined the conversation was Rabon Roy, a coal trader from Cherrapunji or Sohra. Sartorially, this Khasi person very much resembled an Assamese gentleman. With an endi silk turban on his head, Rabon Roy was in a dhoti with a large endi shawl known as a bor-kapor wrapped around him. But his sleeveless jacket didn't seem to go with all this. On the first leg of the journey, Rabon Roy and Panchatirtha followed the bullock-cart on foot. Rabon's company made the journey somewhat less rigorous for Panchatirtha who had taken a liking to the Khasi gentleman right from the time they had first met.

After travelling on the plains for some distance from Guwahati, the cart started slowly moving up the hill road. By then, the passengers who were walking behind, as well as the bullocks, were getting tired and hungry. Shortly after, once they'd climbed a small hill, they stopped for lunch at an open space from where the plains on the lower reaches as well as the outline of the Kamakhya Hill were hazily visible. Pointing in that direction, Rabon Roy commented, 'It is believed that our forefathers crossed the big river and came over to this side. They too had once worshipped Kamakhya Devi. The name "Kamakhya" is said to have come from the Khasi language. It was only later that the powerful kings of the plains pushed our people up the hills.' Rabon Roy kept up a discourse about his people throughout the journey. He could speak Bengali fluently and Panchatirtha too spoke to him in that language. At one point, Rabon began singing a melodious verse in his own tongue. When Panchatirtha, surprised to hear this unknown song which struck him as somewhat familiar, asked Rabon about it, he replied, 'This verse is a Phowar. There are lots of such Phowars in our language. The villagers themselves compose these Phowars and sing them.'

'Don't you have written texts of these songs?'

At Panchatirtha's query, a shadow passed over Rabon's face. Gazing at the distant mountains, he said, 'We too once had our script. Like all other people on earth, God had also given us our own alphabets. But our ancient forefathers lost it – washed away in the water or eaten up by some large animal. Unlike us, the people of the plains carefully preserved their script. Now the missionaries are trying to give us a new script. But our people prefer word of mouth to that which is written on paper. If there is a mistake when something is spoken, it can always be corrected by someone else. But if there is a mistake in the written word, that error persists, does it not?'

Rabon Roy's words set Panchatirtha thinking. It was only with the coming of British rule that people had started accepting the printed word or whatever was written in black ink as the unquestionable truth. But weren't the customs and practices that rule the day to day life of the common people all based on word of mouth? The world that existed outside of the courts and government offices had long been running without any written script. He wondered why no one had ever reflected on the fact that the world run on people's collective memory and oral wisdom was so marvellously complete, rich and full of possibilities? Rabon Roy saw that Panchatirtha's thoughts had wandered far away, so he tried change the subject, 'When you come to our place what will surprise you most is our women.' Rabon took out some ground betel nut from his cloth pouch and put it into his mouth. He looked at the confused and curious expression on Panchatirtha's face and then burst out laughing. The laughter touched every part of his face, spreading quickly over his eyes and cheeks. As he laughed, his eyes crinkled until they turned into two lines drawn across his face. When his laughter subsided he said, 'Well, you'll see for yourself when you come there.'

Panchatirtha had seen some hill women before. But, he'd never been particularly interested in the Naga women who came to the village markets or haats near Sivasagar or even the Mikir women who sold rice or pounded paddy in people's houses. So, he had no idea whatsoever of the special qualities of the Khasi women that Rabon had mentioned.

During the initial stretch of the journey, Panchatirtha felt quite exhausted as he walked up the winding hill road. Though it was the month of Ashwin, the sun was still quite strong and as they approached the plains near the Barnoi river, it was almost afternoon. In an open space on the bank of the river a large number of people were doing brisk business in a village haat. This was the famous Barnoi Haat where traders from the hills and the plains mingled. Rabon Roy exchanged greetings in his own tongue with some of the traders and replenished his stock of areca nuts and betel leaves. He even pounded a few nuts and leaves in the small wooden pestle which he carried in his bag. Tempted by the golden yellow betel nuts that were being sold, Panchatirtha was about to buy a few when Indu Chaudhuri intervened, 'You will not be able to digest these betel nuts. They produce a lot of heat. If you are not used to them, your head will reel with the intoxication.'

When he saw Panchatirtha had not bought any betel nuts, Rabon Roy laughed aloud: 'Don't be so scared! Only these betel nuts will be able to save you from the Shillong cold.'

The journey resumed from the Barnoi Haat. Bullock-carts, horse-carts, labourers carrying their thapas and those travelling on foot, all started moving slowly up the narrow hill road. This part of the journey was especially difficult, for the road through the thick forests was dark and slippery. Panchatirtha walked with cautious steps, listening to the heavy breathing of the load-carrying labourers, the jingle of the cart bells and the sweet choir of birdsong and cicada calls floating out of the forest, when Rabon Roy suddenly remarked: 'This road is much better than the other one.'

'Where was the other road?' someone from inside the cart asked.

'It passed some distance west from Raani Gudam to Nangkhlow and then through the territory of U Tirot Singh. The British tried to build their first road through that side. But because of the resistance put up by the Khasis under the leadership of U Tirot Singh, David Scott sahib had to abandon the idea of linking up Cherrapunji with Guwahati by road.'

'Do tell us about that battle. We Assamese do not know much about all this,' said Panchtirtha with some regret.

'Pray, how will you know? Why will the struggles against the British ever figure in the school texts? But in one of his reports, Major White wrote in detail about this struggle between the Khasis and the British,' Indu babu intervened.

'Then, let's hear about it from you,' said Panchatirtha, eager to know more.

'Ever since the British entered Assam, they were waiting for an opportunity to build a link road through the Khasi Hills to connect the Brahmaputra and Surma valleys. There was already a road between Sylhet and Cherrapunji. What was needed now was a road from Cherrapunji to Guwahati. Even before coming to the Khasi Hills, the shrewd British administrators had already collected all the details about the region's flora and fauna, its mineral resources, rivers and streams and, of course, its people. It was when the king of Nangkhlow, U Tirot Singh, approached the British government for some cultivable land in the plains, that David Scott got the chance he was waiting for all these years. He proposed to Tirot Singh that in lieu of permission to raise crops in the valley, he would have to allow the British to build a road through his territory and also set aside some land in the upper reaches of the hills where arrangements could be made for rest and recuperation of the British officials. Once Tirot Singh agreed to this proposal, the struggle between the Khasis and the British could be said to have begun,' said Indu babu with a tone of finality.

Rabon Roy, who had been listening quietly all this while, showed some signs of irritation and said, 'Gentlemen, certainly things weren't that simple. A Khasi syiem or king can never hand over land to anyone because in our society land is community property. Even the king does not consider himself to be the exclusive owner of the land. That is exactly why, after receiving David Scott's proposal, Tirot Singh invited all the neighbouring Khasi syiems and their subjects and held a big conference. In that meeting for two full days and nights the leading citizens of Khasi society deliberated and gave their views in an absolutely free and frank manner. It was only after this that everyone agreed to the British proposal.' Indu babu realised his mistake and he changed his tone and said, 'It seems that even the British had respect for the age-old democratic traditions that governed Khasi society. In his note to David Scott, Major White described how in that huge people's assembly everyone listened with patience to each speaker and the entire proceedings were carried out in a highly disciplined manner, there being absolutely no scope for heated arguments or raised voices. Since foreign guests were not allowed to take part in the deliberations, they observed the proceedings from a distance. At one point, an exasperated Scott sent some bottles of English whiskey to distribute among the delegates. But the Khasi leaders politely sent these back, saying that it wasn't their custom to drink before the meeting concluded. The foreigners were astonished on seeing these practices of the tribal people.'

Rabon Roy nodded in approval and said, 'The brave Tirot Singh allowed the British to build a road across his territory. But as soon as the people realized that in the name of building roads the British were planning to snatch away their sovereignty, they became rebellious and fought stubbornly to drive out the foreigners. After having fought for two months, Tirot Singh was finally defeated by the British. But this wasn't in a straightforward fair combat. Tirot was suddenly attacked treacherously when he was at a meeting and taking part in a discussion.'

Panchatirtha was simply amazed while listening to Rabon Roy and Indu babu. It could be said that he hadn't really met any hill folks before. Rather, all these years he had nourished strange ideas about them. On the face of it, Rabon Roy looked like a simple villager. But having listened to his observations, Panchatirtha was now convinced that beneath his disarming simplicity Rabon possessed a modern mind capable of expressing itself in fine language.

As they negotiated the last few turns up the Nongpoh Hill, the passengers seemed totally exhausted. Shillong was still some thirty miles away and as Panchatirtha looked down from the hill top, he could see on the winding road below an endless procession of bullock-carts, horse carriages and groups of labourers on foot carrying their loads – it looked as if this was a new version of the Mahabharata's *Swargarohan Parva*.

Nongpoh was a village situated on the flat land atop a plateau. Things brightened up once the passengers reached the plateau. The weather too began to change with the cool breeze from the south acting as a balm to the tired, sweating bodies. The caravan finally stopped in a clearing in the woods adjacent to the road and everyone got busy preparing to cook a meal. At this point of the journey, a new pair of bullocks would be attached to their cart. Meanwhile, Panchatirtha started searching for dry twigs and fallen branches to start a fire, when Rabon Roy placed on the ground a small bundle of finely cut pinewood sticks bought from the Nongpoh market. Panchatirtha made fun of this and said, 'If we try to cook our food with that small bundle of freshly cut wood, maybe we'll have to spend the entire night here.'

Rabon Roy smiled and struck a match to one of the sticks and within seconds it caught fire. Taking on the posture of a magician showing his tricks, Rabon said, 'Do you understand now? These twigs aren't freshly cut firewood. These are dhoop-khari. Because they have plenty of oil in them, they catch fire very quickly. When you come to Shillong, you will see Khasi women selling such bundles of sticks from house to house.' It was only later that Panchatirtha would discover that these strips of wood were actually cut out with sharp blades from the standing pine trees.

Following the meal, the journey began afresh. After a few miles, the surroundings on both sides of the road took on a new appeal. The thick sal and bamboo forests of the first part of the journey were now replaced by rows of dense verdant pines. The breeze itself was full of the fragrance of the pines, cool and refreshing, quickly soothing their tired bodies. Soon, the passengers in the bullock-cart broke into song, one after another, in Bengali, Assamese and Nepali. Even the cart-drivers started whistling their own hill tunes. As evening approached, camp was set up on the bank of a fast-flowing mountain stream. Here, the bullocks would be changed for the last leg of the journey and the next day they would reach Shillong. As they all sat around the fire, Panchatirtha and his co-passengers talked of many things. Goldsmith's wife too joined in the conversation. She had finished her studies in the Nagaon Mission School, and was now on her way to join as a teacher at a girls' school in Shillong. Both husband and wife would be staying in a house on the banks of the Umkhra river.

'Where will you stay in Shillong?' Namita Goldsmith asked Panchatirtha.

'To begin with I will stay with an Assamese family at Laban. They are old acquaintances of my father-in-law. I don't know them personally myself.'

'Did your father-in-law live in Shillong?' asked Indu babu with some interest.

'Yes, he used to live there a few years ago. But he gave up his job and moved to Jorhat after our capital was shifted from Shillong to Dacca. Sashikanta Baruah is his name.'

'Oh, Baruah babu! I know him quite well. After he left, it was on his post that I went on promotion to Dacca.' said Tarabhusan Debnath with a laugh.

Panchatirtha kept quiet. Lots of Assamese people like his father-in-law opted to stay at home rather than go to Dacca on transfer. Relatives and friends also considered this 'return to the fold' mindset of the Assamese as quite normal.

The moment the conversation veered to rented houses, Tarabhushan babu came out with many suggestions. He described the different localities of Shillong where the Assamese and the Bengalis lived. Then he spoke at length on how the Bengali Brahmos had set up their own 'Brahmopally'. Sensing that Panchatirtha was a bit confused at all this, Rabon Roy quietly intervened,

'There is a house that belongs to my wife in the Mawkhar locality of Shillong. No one lives there at the moment. If you wish, you can stay there. Later you can get a house built for yourself.'

'You said your wife's house? Isn't it yours as well?' asked Panchatirtha in surprise.

Rabon Roy, Indu babu and Tarabhusan babu smiled. They then tried to acquaint Panchatirtha with some of the customs of Khasi society where the families were matrilineal. The children took on their mother's surname and, when women married, the wife did not move to the husband's house. Instead, the husband moved to the wife's house. The youngest daughter of the house was called 'khadduh' and it was she who inherited all the maternal property. But the father and the maternal uncles were all held in respect within the family. Panchatirtha was astounded. He wondered how he had not even had the slightest idea about such a society which lay at a distance of barely two days from the plains.

Panchatirtha didn't want to reject Rabon Roy's friendly offer outright. Rather, he gave the impression that he was agreeable to the suggestion. At least he now knew where he would stay in Shillong. As they were retiring for the day and getting ready to sleep, Panchatirtha, who had been mulling over a question for the past two days, finally asked, 'Dangoria, I hope you don't mind my asking you, but who gave you the name Rabon?'

For Panchatirtha this was like a riddle. The person was a Khasi and yet his name had been drawn from Valmiki's epic. Being well acquainted with the *Ramayana*, Panchatirtha was convinced that Valmiki wanted to show Sri Ram's adversary as someone endowed with uncommon courage and wisdom. But, thus far, he had not heard of any Hindu parent naming a son after Ravana.

Rabon Roy seemed hugely amused by Panchatirtha's query. 'You find the name Rabon quite strange, right? Perhaps you're thinking that my parents were ignorant or otherwise why would they give such a name to their son? But the actual story is somewhat different. They had named me Ramchandra. Once, when I was very young I fell seriously ill. When no medicine seemed to work, the elders of the village suggested to my mother that my name should be changed so that the spell, on me, of the evil spirits, could be broken. Accordingly, Ram was replaced with Rabon. But no one considered it necessary to seek my approval.'

'So, Ram and Rabon are known names in your society?' asked Panchatirtha.

'Our people love to listen to the stories from the *Ramayana* and the *Mahabharata*. But these days younger people prefer to listen to stories from the Bible. Sita, Ram, Rabon, they all figure in our ancient folklore. Sita was much revered by our old people as Ka-Lakhumi. The leaves of some plants that grow here have names such as "Sita's paan" or "The leaf on which Sita ate her rice"', said Rabon Roy as he wrapped himself up in his large barkapor.

'You mentioned Ka-Lakhumi. That sounds like our goddess Lakhimi. She is the goddess of wealth.' There seemed to be no end to Panchatirtha's queries.

'Ka-Lakhumi is the goddess of crops. In our region, wherever paddy is grown, this goddess is worshipped. Someday I will sing to you the songs that are sung for her. Now, please go to sleep.'

As he lay down to sleep, Panchatirtha thought of Haimavati. Would she like this place? Would the customs, practices and superstitions of the plains be able to grow roots in this hilly soil? Would the ghosts and spirits of Sivasagar continue to frighten his boys even here? Soon, he fell asleep. Unnoticed, the clouds from the hills silently came down and slowly enveloped the small hut where the tired travellers lay.

5

On the third day of the journey, the group arrived at the lower reaches of the Shillong hill. Through the tall thick pine groves that encircled the hill, a few houses were still visible in the mist. All of a sudden, a sheet of thin cloud covered the entire hill, as if it were wrapping itself in a big blanket, readying to go to sleep. Pachatirtha spoke as if to himself, 'It's the sleeping hill.' Rabon Roy nodded, 'Yes, we also call this hill by that name, Riyad Sumthiya, the sleeping hill!'

'Very appropriate,' Panchatirtha smiled at his own clever observation. The other passengers, however, did not catch the word play.

The travellers were now moving on with brisk steps. The road was quite undulating, rising and falling at intervals. Once, when Panchatirtha looked up at the distant hill, he could see through small openings in the cloud cover, some lights sparkling like stars, as if the sky itself had come down to meet the earth. Enchanted by these sights, which seemed to mingle with the pleasant tinkling of bells hanging from the necks of cows, and the glow from rows of lamps swinging from the carts, the travellers finally made their entry into Shillong. But Laban, where Panchatirtha planned to stay, was quite far from the place where the carts finally stopped. Meanwhile, Rabon Roy had taken leave of his co-travellers and started walking towards his home at Mawkhar. Before leaving, he told Panchatirtha that he could have a look at the Mawkhar house with the help of the woman who supplied tea at the Commissioner's office. Since both Indu babu and Tarabhusan lived in Laban, Panchatirtha now started walking with them towards Dwarka Sarma's house there. A Nepali porter, a 'dai' followed, carrying his luggage.

Dwarka Sarma was an old resident of Shillong. He lived with his family in a house built on the raised bank of a stream. A clerk at the revenue office, Sarma had contributed a great deal towards creating a miniscule Assamese society out of the handful of Assamese residents who lived in Laban. He was from Sivasagar, while his wife Ambika Devi came from Dergaon. Every morning after she sent the kids to school and her husband to office, the carefree and ebullient Ambika loved to visit the Assamese families and pick up all the gossip. Her cheeks always flushed pink, Ambika would chatter endlessly, and alongside, chew tamul-paan which produced a deep reddish film on her lips. Unlike her, her husband Dwarkanath was of a somewhat sombre nature and seemed deeply concerned about the moral health of the Assamese in Shillong. He was especially worried about young Assamese men from the plains who easily got carried away by their newfound freedom. Some of them had taken to drinking the local brew while others were in relationships with Khasi women and had even quietly set up homes with them despite the fact that several of them had wives and children in the plains. Concerned at such developments, Dwarkanath and some others set up an Asom Sangha and a namghar at Laban. The menfolk would gather twice a week at the sangha to spend their evenings discussing literature, reading out their self-composed essays or playing chess, carom or cards.

On Wednesdays they would gather at the namghar for nam-kirtan while Thursdays were reserved for women's nam. By keeping the members of their community engaged in this way, Dwarkanath and his colleagues felt that they were helping to safeguard the moral and intellectual life of the tiny Assamese society of this hill town.

Once he settled in Shillong, Panchatirtha was immediately made a member of the Asom Sangha. But experienced observer of life that he had become, it did not take him long to see through the drawbacks of such a collective. Strange thoughts would often pass through his mind whenever he sat with the small Assamese group in their makeshift meeting room on the premises of an Assamese resident. It seemed to him that each one of those present in the room was carrying with him a baggage of culture from his distant home in a village or a small town of the Assam plains to an entirely new environment. Each one appeared overburdened by the weight of what he carried. The memories and experiences of places like Hajo, Tihu, Nalbari, Kalaigaon, Mezenga, Jagduar, Da-dhara and the many small villages scattered all over the nooks and corners of the Brahmaputra valley, would float around the room like wisps of confused clouds. The people inside the room, however, would make no attempt to understand the language of the wind roaring outside. Quite often Panchatirtha felt that the very atmosphere of the teachers' room of the Sivasagar school had been transported here – the same self-centred priorities, the same narrowness of thought. But the moment he stepped out of the room into the open, to be almost blown off his feet by gusts of strong, cold wind, he was filled with new hope, hope that the world would always provide opportunities for the mind to expand and grow.

Once he joined his new job, Panchatirtha was exposed to an entirely new environment. It was quite a relief for him that he was no longer subject to any hard and fast rules about time. Moreover, his new boss, Edward Arnold, seemed to be a serious and dedicated student of history, his house itself giving the feel of being a small museum. Apart from specimens of old sculptures, copperplates and sanchi-leaf manuscripts, there were plenty of books in Assamese, Bengali and English which had been carefully preserved and arranged in a neat and orderly manner. For Panchatirtha, such a tidy arrangement of the manuscripts and books in one's own house was quite a new experience. It reminded him of his visits to the Indian Museum at Calcutta and the Asiatic Society where he had seen how old manuscripts and writings that used to be kept in smoke-filled kitchen racks or artefacts abandoned in forests and jungles, had been preserved with the utmost care as if they carried great value. But till then it hadn't struck him that one could do the same in one's own house. It took Panchatirtha quite a while to understand why this person, who had come from the distant shores of England, was giving so much importance to the ancient artefacts and manuscripts of this region. It was only later when he read Arnold sahib's report which was published in the form of a book, that he realized how all this material from history greatly helped the British administrators to work out ever new policies to rule a vast and alien country. He could now see that these wily and intelligent rulers knew only too well how to put to use the knowledge and wisdom acquired over the years by scores of pundits like him. Yet, he reflected, if this were not so, perhaps the keys to this great treasure house of knowledge would be lost to posterity.

A deep sense of satisfaction filled Panchatirtha's mind as he walked every morning to his workplace through the pine-covered avenue that skirted the Government House. Once he reached Arnold sahib's bungalow called Whispering Pines, he immersed himself in his research work. It was the practice that after each copperplate or stone inscription was rendered by him into Assamese, it would be translated into English by a Bengali scholar and then Arnold himself would make the necessary modifications after due consultation with both of them.

In the evenings, as he walked back home, he would come across droves of government employees leaving their offices. The more inquisitive amongst them would often ask him. 'Bhatta (almost everyone had started addressing him thus) we never see you in the office. Why are you asked over to the Sahib's house to look at the files?' Initially, Panchatirtha would try to explain to them the exact nature of his work. But gradually he gave up and simply said, 'Well, my job is of a confidential nature. That's why I do it at the sahib's bungalow.' He never tried to find out what they actually made of this excuse. But, after a time, the queries stopped altogether.

6

Panchatirtha now began to search for a place to rent so he could bring Haimavati and his sons to Shillong and start his family life afresh. Initially, he thought that it would be nice to be a neighbour of a local gentleman like Rabon Roy. But once the members of the Asom Sangha got wind of this idea, they raised a storm. How could one even think of living with Khasi neighbours when there were so many Assamese families in Laban? They refused to listen to any of Panchatirtha's arguments and insisted that it would only be proper for his wife and kids, newcomers to Shillong, to live amongst the Assamese people. Eventually, Panchatirtha gave in to the advice of his compatriots and took a house on rent in Laban. All the doors and windows of the house were made of pine wood and no bricks whatsoever had been used in its construction. Even the pillars on which the house stood were made of stone. Beneath the house there was enough space to store firewood and charcoal. There were wooden verandahs both in the front and at the back and at the end of the rear verandah there was a small kitchen. Unlike in Khasi houses where even the kitchens had wooden floors, this house had a mud floor. Assamese people were hesitant to use kitchens with wooden floors, thus this house, which had been built by an Assamese gentleman, had a kitchen with a mud floor.

When Haimavati finally arrived in Shillong with her sons she was quite excited by her new surroundings. Theirs was the last in a row of five houses built on a narrow strip of land which lay by the side of a small, rippling stream. What Haimavati really liked was that all the sides of the house had open spaces and there weren't any bamboo groves at the back or undergrowth in the front, as there had been at Sivasagar. Moreover, the ground underneath the pine trees was always neat and dry and sometimes Haima and her sons would pick up the strange-shaped pine cones and bring them home to light the kitchen fire.

All the residents of that locality were Assamese. As the men were all employed in different government offices, the women had little to do in the afternoons. Unlike in their homes in the plains, there was no need here to fetch water from the pond or to pound paddy on the dhenki. None of these houses had a loom which otherwise was a must for every family. Hence, for these women the only way to spend their afternoons was by visiting one another or gathering in someone's house to play a game of carom or cards. In the beginning, like the others, Haimavati too would visit her neighbours and try to get to know them. But gradually she started disliking the idea of wasting her time thus. She had always loved to read books or weave new motifs at her loom. When they were about to leave Sivasagar, Haimavati's eyes were filled with tears when she had to give away her loom to a neighbour. Not having a loom at Shillong, she had taken to embroidering her clothes with the thread and needles she had brought with her. Often, when she sat down in the pleasant afternoon sun to read a book or do some embroidery, the other women would look at her disapprovingly. Initially, a few of them approached her to learn to stitch and sew, but unable to match her fine hand, they soon drifted away.

After having finished with the books she had brought with her, Haimavati started visiting her neighbours in the hope of getting something new to read. But each woman had the same tale, 'Well, books are the preserve of the owner of the house. I don't have the faintest idea where he has put them.' Haimavati gradually realized that maybe her love for books wasn't actually considered to be a feminine quality. So, she grew hesitant to ask for books on loan from her Assamese neighbours. However, when she shared her experience with her husband, Panchatirtha helped Haimavati to spend her leisure time meaningfully by borrowing the works of Bankimchandra and Saratchandra Chatterjee from his Bengali friends.

In their Assamese neighbourhood, Panchatirtha and Haimavati's days passed off quite peacefully. The government high school for boys at Mawkhar was some distance away from Laban, so they decided to put their sons in a nearby Assamese primary school. It was only about two years later that the elder boy, Saratchandra, started going to the high school. Meanwhile, Haimavati had become the mother of two more children. Both were girls. They named them Bhabanipriya and Gauripriya. And as the numbers in the family grew, Panchatirtha also felt the need to move to a larger, more spacious house. After a lot of searching, they finally rented a house situated on top of a hill. The owner of the house lived in Dacca while a relative of his who stayed in Laban was in charge of the house. The neighbours were almost all Bengali Brahmos. The members of this community living in different parts of Shillong had come together and started this neighbourhood almost exclusively for themselves. They had also set up a Brahmo temple in one of the houses. Bereft of idols, the people would gather here to sing Brahmo sangeet or listen to their Acharya read out from the Vedas and the Upanishads. The melodious notes of the devotional songs would often drift up to Banamali Bhatta's house and Haimavati would be seized with the urge to join in the prayers. But she hesitated because she wasn't sure whether the others present would approve. As the days passed, her reluctance faded. Her neighbours Subarna didi, Labanya didi, Saradamanjari and Loknath Kaviraj's wife whom everybody addressed as Kakima, had all grown fond of Haimavati and they started to take her along to the Brahmo prayer meets. Haima would quite often hum the songs that she heard at the Brahmo temple and would also try to teach them to her children.

Just across the road from the Brahmopally, lived a Khasi family in a high and spacious compound surrounded on all sides by tall pine trees. Behind their house there were the dwellings of a few other Khasi families and together they constituted a separate locality of their own. Though this Khasi locality was quite adjacent to the Bengali and Assamese ones, yet there was little interaction between them. Except for wishing each other with a 'khublei' whenever they crossed on the road, there wasn't any other conversation. The main reason for this was that the Assamese and Bengali residents could rarely speak Khasi. They had mastered a few Khasi words and mixed them with broken Hindi to create a peculiar language which they used chiefly for haggling at the market. But no one would dare to speak in such a gibberish tongue with the members of the elite family that lived in the big house which everybody called the house of Kharkongor. But one of the Bengali ladies, Labanyaprava, was quite fluent in Khasi. Her father had once worked as a physician at a village near Cherrapunji and his family had lived in that village for a long time, because of which they could all converse in fluent Khasi. The person who appeared to be the head of the Kharkongor family had a fair pinkish complexion, which gave him the appearance of a European. His name was Thomas Rynjah and since he worked at a government office, several of the residents of Brahmopally happened to know him. But he always kept to his Khasi circle and never visited any of them.

Sitting in the front courtyard of her house, Haimavati sometimes imagined the goings on in the Khasi house opposite theirs. She seemed especially attracted by the dress and appearance of the women who flitted in and out of the neat and tidy compound. Whenever these women went out, they discreetly covered themselves from head to toe in several folds of warm cloth, most of it made in some western country. Hence, the colour and tone of their clothes matched that of the European women and they would always wear fashionable shoes. While at home, the women wore regular, ordinary clothes and kept themselves busy with different types of housework. From cleaning the house to cooking and washing clothes and hanging them up to dry, almost everything was done by them. Haima had heard from her husband that the social status of Khasi women was much higher than theirs and that they were owners of all the property while the children took their names from the mother's side. Haima, however, couldn't help but think that if they were so well placed, then why, over and above all their housework, did they engage themselves in running small businesses? Instead, they could have easily whiled away their time at home, with their men looking after all their needs. But, it did not take long for Haima to understand that the dignity and independence of Khasi women sprang from their right to do all sorts of work and that the status of the men was not in any way compromised or lowered because of this.

Haima learnt many little things by watching the Kharkongor women at work. One of these was to fasten wooden clips on her washed clothes when she hung them out to dry on a windy day. As she watched the Khasi women busy at their work, Haima realized for the first time that even an apparently insignificant act such as drying clothes could actually be an art by itself. Again, it was from the neat and well-kept Khasi houses that Haima learnt to fix delicate lace curtains on the windows of her own house. Over and above all these small changes, it was her overall experience of Shillong which may be said to have brought some sort of a transformation in her very attitude towards life as a whole. Thus, whenever the unruly hill winds tried to rip off the roofs of their houses, Haimavati was filled with an urge to fly with the wind and to do something new. Her husband, sons and daughters were all busy with their own work. Both the sons, Borbaap and Sarubaap, now went to the Mawkhar high school. Bhabani and Gauri were admitted to the Assamese primary school in the neighbourhood. Panchatirtha had now finished his work with Arnold sahib and he had been entrusted with the task of arranging the official papers at the government's record room. But simultaneously he was also continuing with his research work in Sanskrit. He would read his books every morning and evening, making extensive notes in the margins. However, despite all his engagement with the religious and philosophical texts, no one had ever seen him performing any religious rituals at home. Yet, during the discussions on religion at the Asom Sangha he would impress everyone with his erudite comments.

A regular bus service was started between Shillong and Guwahati soon after the First World War. Taking advantage of this facility, Panchatirtha would frequently go to Guwahati to help his childhood friend Ramdutta Vidyavinod set up a Sanskrit Board in Assam. Both friends deeply felt how the absence of such a Board had adversely affected the level of Sanskrit teaching at the tols. Sometimes, the two friends would tour the villages of Kamrup and prepare a list of the Sanskrit manuscripts that lay scattered in different private collections. While returning from his Kamrup trips, Panchatirtha often carried some mementos home for Haimavati and the children. These included, for instance, a hand-fan with a deer-horn handle, a pair of wooden slippers or kharam with a silver toe-hold or a neatly moulded bell-metal baan-baati or bota. Although his neighbours crowded his house to have a look at these rather exotic items, Haimavati was more worried about what to do with all these useless things spread around the house. But one day, to her utter surprise, Panchatirtha landed up in Shillong with all the implements needed to set up a loom, neatly packed and stored on top of a bus. Then he got the frame of the loom made by a Khasi carpenter and, having set up the complete loom in the rear verandah of their house, he told his wife with a smile, 'Now your days will pass quickly to the staccato beat of the pedals and the battens of the loom.'

7

Both Haimavati's daughters studied in the primary school by the side of a mountain stream on the lower reaches of the hills. They went to school on their own. The school had some thirty students and two teachers. Padumi Das taught general knowledge and arithmetic. She had passed her middle vernacular examination from Nalbari, and had settled in Shillong with her husband who was a government employee. The short and stocky Padumi was always full of energy. Though she kept her students under strict control, she was always eager to teach them something new. She seemed especially fond of Bhabanipriya. When she made the children sit in a circle on the lawn by the bank of the stream to recite their multiplication tables, it was always Bhabanipriya who was asked to start the rounds. She would, in her soft voice, chant a line which was then repeated by the others, all swaying rhythmically to the chant. Sometimes, in her general knowledge class, Padumi 'baideu' took the students for a walk all the way up along the green banks of the stream to discover its source in the Riyad Laban hills. Once, she showed them how little droplets of water falling from the side of a cliff created small runnels which in turn joined together to take the shape of a stream. The children splashed their faces with the water streaming down from the cliffs and shouted in joy. And, much like a small girl,

Padumi baideu too joined in the fun and scooped up water to drink from the small streams. Her students were amazed to see this spontaneous, nature-friendly side of their teacher who was otherwise known to be a strict disciplinarian. And their regard for her increased tenfold. Sometimes, during school hours, there was a sudden hailstorm and the grass lawn in the front was covered with white hailstones. Once the rain stopped, Padumi baideu asked the students to collect the hailstones in a bucket and empty them on her table. Then she added different coloured ink on the mould and created a wonderful 'Land of Ice'. The children, ever eager to help her in this, ran around in excitement. However, there was no dearth of complaints from the guardians about Padumi baideu's unconventional methods of teaching. They often wrote to the secretary of the school that the children were being sent to school to study and not to waste their time on useless activities. When Haimavati came to know of these complaints, she simply dismissed them. For, as long as the girls were happy to go to school and were learning whatever was needed, she was quite satisfied.

But when Bhabani and Gauri finished with their primary school, they were faced with a problem. There being no high school in the Laban area, the girls had to go to a distant high school which had been recently set up at Jail Road near Police Bazaar. Most of the Assamese guardians were unwilling to send their wards so far. The easy way out was to keep the girls at home and prepare them for marriage once they completed primary school. But, since there was a dearth of eligible grooms in Shillong, most of the young girls were married off to grooms arranged by solicitous friends and relatives living in the plains. The parents of the girls seldom had the chance to go down to the plains to meet the prospective groom. Rather, they had to rely almost totally on the decisions taken by their relatives and well-wishers. Some of these girls who had grown up in the urban environment of Shillong often failed to adjust themselves with the rural surroundings in the plains while others fell sick and died early deaths. A few returned to their parents in Shillong after facing different forms of persecution at their marital homes.

Haimavati's reaction to these practices was to resolve never to marry her daughters in a hurry. She convinced Panchatirtha that their two girls should be given a chance to at least complete a few years at the high school. Several girls from Brahmopally studied in the Lady Keane Girls High School. Labanyaprabha, the headmistress of that school, happened to be a neighbour of Haimavati's. She had passed the entrance examination from Calcutta's Bethune College and her children were all well-educated. Labanyaprabha had appointed a Khasi woman whom everybody called Kong Laiziri, as the chowkidarni of her school and she was the one who picked up the girls from their homes in Laban and escorted them to school. Once school was over, she would drop each child back home. The Lady Keane school was situated on a hill which was quite a distance from Laban. The girls had to walk along a zigzag hill road from Laban. But neither rain nor sun could dampen the indomitable spirit of the group of girls. Kong Laiziri would line up the girls in twos and make them march to school. The girls would hum like bees in their low voices as they chatted incessantly the entire way. At first, Bhabani paired up with a girl named Sishirkana; but when Gauri joined the school group, the two sisters began to walk together. In the entire group, they were the only two girls who spoke in Assamese, though both of them were also quite fluent in Bengali. But when it came to sharing secrets meant only for themselves, the two girls chose to whisper in Assamese.

Even when walking to school during the rainy monsoon days of summer, the girls always found ways of adding to the fun. They would burst into shrieks of laughter as they tried to stall with their bare feet the rainwater that rushed down the road from the upper reaches. As each of them waded through the water streaming down the hill, slippers in one hand and umbrella in the another, Kong would try to restrain them. But occasionally, Kong too would be unable to resist the temptation of joining in the frolic.

During the long winter vacations from December to March, Haima's children had lots of other activities. As soon as they woke up to the cold mornings, they'd rush out to walk on the frost-covered lawn in front of their house, leaving their footmarks on the white frost. Then they would go for the plates of water which they had left overnight in the open. In each plate instead of the water there would be a round sheet of ice. Unmindful of the piercing cold, the children played different games with the pieces of ice. Sometimes, Haima placed orange juice instead of water on these plates. This was great fun for everyone as they started licking at the frozen juice as if it was ice-cream! In the soft sun of the winter afternoons, Haima sat down to knit or read. Occasionally, with the help of her kids, she'd prepare the thread for the loom. She wanted to keep them busy during the holidays. The boys would go up the hill to collect pine leaves and cones to light the chimney-fire in the evening. They collected the pine leaves with an improvised rake and then shoved them into a large bag. Bijoy had got himself

a small wooden contraption on which the boys could hurtle
down the slopes. This sort of 'vehicle' was a favourite of the
Khasi boys and Bijoy and his brother had got a friendly Khasi
carpenter to make one for them. He had to be coaxed but
eventually he took pity on them and nailed together four pieces
of wood, fixed a small wooden plank for a seat and attached
the small steel wheels which the boys had procured with great
difficulty from a garage. Thus when the precious vehicle was
ready, boys from the neighbourhood crowded around it eagerly,
taking turns to carry it up the hill and then noisily hurtle down
on it as if they were warriors seated on a chariot!

Quite often Haimavati sat with her children in the sun and
told them stories or even real tales that sounded like fiction. They
listened to her tales of childhood with the same rapt attention
as the story of *Pakhiraj Ghora* and *Champavati*. But the golden
afternoons of winter were quite short and momentary. By two
or three in the afternoon the sun hid itself behind the clouds
which soon covered the thick green hills all around. And, as
the sun set, necklaces of small fires appeared in the distant hills.
Who had set fire to the high hills? The children were mystified.
It was only later that they came to know that it was common
practice for the Khasi villagers to cut the undergrowth and
set it on fire to make the soil fertile for growing potatoes and
vegetables. As they looked at the hills covered in cloud and mist,
an unknown sense of fear and mystery filled the minds of the
children. It was as if these creatures of the night wearing beads
of fire round their necks were actually the symbols of some
primitive power that ruled the hills. As the evening drew to a
close and the children went inside to sit by the secure warmth
of the chimney-fire, the cicadas sang from the pine trees, just as
if someone were playing a loud string instrument. On certain

nights, when Panchatirtha came home late after a game of chess at the Asom Sangha, the children kept their ears pricked to catch the sound of his footsteps on the lonely road. The moment they heard their father step into the house with a fish tied with a thin bamboo strip dangling from the end of his walking stick, a deep sense of security filled their hearts.

8

The government school at Mawkhar was quite far from Laban. But Sarat, Bijoy and their friends had discovered a much shorter route, a narrow lane through the hills which helped them reach school in a shorter time. There were only a handful of Assamese students in the school. Though there were Assamese, Bengali, Nepali and Khasi students in all the classes, yet since most of the teachers were Bengali-speaking, lessons were often imparted in Bengali in the lower sections. However, if sometimes an Assamese teacher turned up, he would explain the lessons also in Assamese. But with most texts in Bengali, boys like Sarat experienced plenty of difficulties in the beginning because the schools in the plains from which they had come taught in Assamese. Nevertheless, both boys didn't take much time to gain some command over the Bengali language. However, from the sixth class onwards, the medium of teaching changed to English. There were several British and Anglo-Indian teachers who taught in the higher classes and they gave special emphasis on both spoken and written English. Saratchandra picked up his English quite fast and in his seventh class he secured the first prize for his recitation of Hamlet's soliloquy, 'To be or not to be...' at the school's annual day event. Panchatirtha, sitting in the audience, was filled with a sense of contentment. At least the hurt and humiliation which he had felt several years ago at Sivasagar seemed somewhat mitigated by his son's achievement.

One of Saratchandra's classmates at high school was Lakhan Singh Diengdoh. This handsome boy wasn't good at his studies but excelled in games and music. During the school's football matches, everyone vied to be in Lakhan's team because no other player could keep the ball under constant control and then carry it effortlessly through the goal-post. As Sarat was taller than the other boys, he was usually made the goal-keeper. Lakhan realised that Sarat was not too happy with this, and so he would often give him his place and act as the goal-keeper. For this, Sarat was deeply obliged to Lakhan and Lakhan too demanded his share of the friendship by copying the solved sums from the former's arithmetic book. Sarat was a bit more advanced than the others in mathematics and his classmates vied with one another to copy from his book.

Once, Lakhan requested Sarat to accompany him to Sohra, also known as Cherrapunji. His father owned a coal mine near Sohra and they also had an orange orchard. A happy and excited Sarat first broke the news to his mother. Haima saw how eager he was but she did not directly wish to say no to her son though she did not like the idea of him going that far with an unknown Khasi boy. So she left the decision to her husband. When Panchatirtha was told about it, he kept silent for a while and then said, 'Get me some information about Lakhan's father. I will think it over after that.'

The next day Sarat wrote down the name of his friend's father on the back cover of his school book and then showed it to Panchatirtha – Rabon Roy. Panchatirtha cried out in joy, 'I have no objection at all if it is Rabon Roy's son. I too will come with you to meet his father. He is a such a wise person, so well read and knows a lot about business. It is rare to come across such a gentleman here.'

Panchatirtha had met Rabon Roy only once or twice since his maiden journey to Shillong. Once Mr Arnold had asked him over to enquire about the monoliths that lay scattered in different parts of the Khasi and Jaintia Hills. Rabon Roy had given the Englishman detailed information about the society, religion and customs of the Khasi people and Arnold had made extensive notes. Then, next time he came to hand over to the sahib a few copies of the first Khasi monthly journal *U-Khasi Mynta* edited by U-Haramurari Diengdoh and printed at the Ri Khasi Press, Shillong as early as 1896. Later, Panchatirtha, with his limited knowledge of the Khasi language, struggled to read the articles in the journal. In one of his articles written in a clear and lively style, Haramurari had described how at an early age he was converted to Christianity and how, as his age and experience grew, he got increasingly drawn to his old Khasi religion. Now he was busy comparing the two religions to show how the ancient Khasi faith was free from some of the weak points which he had discovered in Christianity.

When he met Rabon Roy after all these days, Panchatirtha opened the conversation by discussing the *U-Khasi Mynta*. As both friends proceeded in Roy's horse cart along the winding road towards Sohra, Panchatirtha was totally captivated by the unmatched beauty of the hills and gorges on both sides of the road. The constant jingle of the horse bells mingling with the sound of hooves on the cobbled road created a sort of fairy-tale atmosphere as the carts made their way along rows of green and azure mountain ranges. In all, there were three horse-carts moving in a convoy along the narrow road to Sohra, with

Lakhan and Sarat in the first one, followed by Rabon and Panchatirtha in the next. The third cart was loaded with a variety of goods. The situation seemed ideal for some reflection and, all the while munching his areca nuts, Rabon Roy started speaking about the present and future of Khasi culture, 'It was because of the untiring efforts of people like Haramurari and Babu Jibon Roy that our old religious beliefs and customs have been saved. But will they really succeed? How long will it take for our indigenous traditions to be wiped away in the face of continuous attempts at conversion by the Christian missionaries supported as they are in full measure by the British government?'

'In our Assam too the Christian missionaries have been attempting this for several years now. But they have been able to convert only a small handful of Assamese people,' said Panchatirtha.

'The reason for this is that the base of the Hindu religion is quite strong. There are so many written texts in that religion that it would be impossible to read them all in one life. Today, with the coming of printing presses, common people too have gained access to some of these books. Hence, it is not easy for a foreign religion to make inroads. But our Khasi people do not have written texts. Christian religious texts have been translated into Khasi and printed by the missionaries and introduced in the schools. This has greatly influenced our young boys and girls. Babu Jibon Roy wrote a few religious books in the Khasi language and even translated and printed some Hindu moral tales. I have with me one of these. It is called *Saphang U Wei U Blei* and it is about our Khasi religion. In this book Babu Jibon Roy has explained that "niyam" and "dharma" are not the same thing. We keep ourselves busy with "niyam" which chiefly refers to our customs and folk practices. But we do not know much about the One who rules over everything from above. Had Babu Jibon Roy been alive today, he would perhaps have written so much more on that which affects us all,' said Rabon Roy with a sigh.

'Didn't respected individuals like Babu Jibon Roy think of setting up schools for Khasi children?' asked Panchatirtha as he rolled together some areca nuts and betel leaves and pushed them into his mouth.

'Not that they didn't. They did try. Some "Seng Khasi" schools run by the traditional Khasi organizations were started in the Sohra region and Babu Jibon Roy and Radhon Singh Berry between them wrote several Khasi textbooks. But the problem is that if the religious texts brought out by the Christian missionaries are not taught in these schools, then the government threatens to stop all aid.'

'That means these schools will have to eventually shut down,' said a worried Panchatirtha.

'Well, if the present policy of the government continues, it is inevitable that Christian religious texts will be taught in all the schools. This will bring about a major change in our society. Our children will come to forget our customs, our religion, our dances and songs and even our musical instruments and start aping those of the others,' observed Rabon Roy, despondently.

Just then, the Nepali driver of the third cart, which had in the meanwhile overtaken the others, steered it to the side of the road and pulled it to a halt. Immediately, the two other carts behind it also stopped, keeping as near as possible to the side of the hill. Panchatirtha and the boys alighted from their carriages and stood alongside. Soon, from the opposite direction a horse cart came hurtling down the road, its speed increasing every moment. The driver whistled at the stationary carts as if to assert his right. Rabon Roy looked at the speeding cart and laughed, 'It is a milk-cart. It carries milk bottles from the upper Shillong dairy farm for the sahibs and babus in town. That cart does not wait for anyone. Its speed on our roads is as unimpeded as that of the British sarkar!'

'Well, our people are getting a chance to drink some good milk because of the British sarkar,' commented Panchatirtha wryly.

9

It took two days for Panchatirtha and Sarat to return from Cherrapunji. Meanwhile an incident occurred in the family. A cousin of Haimavati's had come to Shillong in search of a job and was staying with them for about a month. Right from day one, Haima was not happy with the behaviour of this young man called Kandarpa. He never ever helped in the housework but always found fault with whatever Haimvavati was doing. Though young, he was much concerned with the concept of pollution. His main grudge against the Assamese people of Shillong was that they had become almost non-believers in the doctrine of pollution. Haimavati tried her best to keep Kandarpa happy although she was quite irritated with his habits. But slowly the young man seemed to change for the worse. Initially he was sufficiently intimidated by the unfamiliar surroundings of the place and would stay indoors after dark. But gradually he grew bold enough to stay out late and then he began to skip his dinner quite often. His excuse was that he had eaten with his friends. The day Panchatirtha and Sarat left for Cherrapunji, Haimavati served dinner to her children and, after putting them to sleep, waited till quite late for Kandarpa to return. Suddenly she heard a commotion outside and as she looked out through the curtains she saw two of her neighbours escorting an unsteady Kandarpa home. Quickly she opened the door and rushed outside. With contempt on his face, Indu babu said, 'Boudi, please go inside. This person is not in his senses. He has obviously drunk a lot and was lying on the road in front of our house. Luckily, someone recognized him as your guest and we managed to bring him here. Otherwise, the young men of the locality would surely have taught him a lesson.' Haimavati almost died of shame.

The next day, as soon as her husband arrived, Haimavati told him about the behaviour of their guest. Kandarpa was asked to leave Shillong immediately. But, even after he had left, Haimavati could not stop thinking about the entire episode. Lots of educated and half-educated young men from the plains had started coming to Shillong in search of jobs. But, if these young men became morally corrupt so soon, then surely everyone would be adversely affected. Meanwhile, the 'Brahmo Mahila Samaj', set up by the neighbouring women, held a discussion on the ill-effects of alcoholism on Bengali and Assamese youth. It was decided that an appeal would be made to the Governor's wife, known generally as the Lady Governor, to take immediate steps to close down the liquor outlets that had been set up in Laban during the years of the First World War to cater to the needs of the soldiers. The women insisted that the selling of alcohol in the area had done great harm to young people and needed to be stopped forthwith. Subarna-di, Labanya-di and Saradamoni put in their efforts to draft a memorandum which the members of the Samaj submitted to the Lady Governor at the Government House. The Lady Governor listened attentively to the women and soon the discussion extended to issues like the need for higher education in English and the appointment of lady doctors to attend to pre- and post-natal cases. Haimavati too was a part of the women's delegation, though she was initially quite uncertain about going to as important a place as the Governor's House. But it was the Brahmo women who finally convinced her to come along. They also persuaded two Khasi women of the Kharkongor family to accompany them so that the impression could be created that all three communities were represented. Yet, the conversation with the Lady Governor was carried out mainly by the educated Brahmo women. Although Haimavati sat quietly in a corner, dressed formally in her traditional Assamese silk riha-mekhala, the entire exercise added immensely to her self-confidence. Here, she saw that women too could actively work for the good of society. A few days after the discussion with the Lady Governor, the liquor outlet was moved from Laban and the women received a lot of praise from their menfolk. Apart from such activism, the women of Brahmopally were also quite advanced in several other matters. Newly-married Manjusree Dutta of Calcutta set up a Vidyasagar Pathaghar or library in a small room belonging to one of her neighbours. Subscriptions were raised from each family and books were bought for the library. Soon, the room was filled with books by Bankimchandra, Saratchandra, Rabindranath Tagore and a host of other new and old Bengali writers. Once the British officials came to know of the pathaghar, they also started donating their old books. It was a common practice on the part of English women to give away their entire collection of books along with the bookcases on the eve of their return to England, after their husbands had completed their tenure in Assam. By doing this, they earned a lot of goodwill from the locals while at the same time substantially reducing the bulk of their own luggage which had to be shipped home.

Haimavati visited the pathaghar quite regularly and brought home books to read. She paid the subscription from her own savings. Once, as she was looking for books in the library, a somewhat curious Manjusree asked her, 'Didi, don't you face problems while reading Bengali books? Aren't there printed books in your own Assami language?' Haimavati was somewhat taken aback and answered diffidently, 'Of course, we have quite a lot of printed books in Asamiya. The only problem is that here in Shillong they are not easily available. Moreover, I have been reading Bengali from a young age and find no difficulty in reading these books.'

That afternoon while on her way home, Haimavati's thoughts returned to Manjusree's comments. In the evening, as she was pouring tea for her husband, she raised the issue, 'Do tell me how many printed books there are in Asamiya. Don't we have any novels or storybooks?'

Panchatirtha mulled over the question and answered, 'Of course, there are many printed books in the Asamiya language. But the problem is that most of them are printed in Calcutta and it is quite difficult to get hold of them.'

'If we open a small library here, will we be able to bring Asamiya books from the plains?'

At this, Panchatirtha looked at his wife in amazement. Really, this ordinary woman was full of new ideas! He had all along felt an insatiable urge in her to do something new in life and it was this trait of hers that had always enthused him. But believing that a wife should never be openly praised, especially in her presence, Panchatirtha had always refrained from doing so. Nevertheless, he always tried to fulfil her wishes in some way or the other, because he had seen that, unlike most other women, Haima was never interested in expensive clothes and ornaments. Rather, she loved to wear mekhala-chadors that she had woven. herself and she also stitched her daughters' clothes. She didn't have a sewing machine of her own, so she often visited a neighbour to use theirs. Panchatirtha noticed this and one day he gifted her a Singer sewing machine.

Haimavati was always grateful to her husband for looking after her small needs. This time too, the moment Haima told Panchatirtha about her idea of setting up a library in Shillong, he looked quite interested. He had seen over the years that while some of the new Assamese residents of Shillong were quite interested in reading, they were not in the habit of buying books. Perhaps a library would be able to give some impetus to their reading. But who would take the responsibility of acquiring the books, especially since there was no bookstall for Assamese books in Shillong? When he tried to bring up the matter with his colleagues at the office, there wasn't much interest. But Tarabhusan Choudhury, who happened to be one of his co-travellers on his first journey to Shillong, showed great interest and discussed in detail the logistics of such a move – the number of Assamese people in Shillong, the size of the book-reading public and the estimated number of books that could be sold etc. He told Panchatirtha that his brother who lived in Calcutta was eager to set up a bookshop in Shillong and would be able to procure Assamese books. Accordingly, some months later, Tarabhusan's brother, Madhusudhan Chaudhury set up a bookshop named Bimala Agency in Shillong and, in due course, he became one of the leading publishers of Assamese books in the region.

Finally, the library which Haimavati had so eagerly wanted, was set up in the premises of the Asom Sangha. Initially,

Assamese books priced at four to six annas were brought from Samya Press, Navajivan Press, Bhudev Publishing House and Sri Kali Press, all situated at Calcutta's College Street. Gradually, books published from Guwahati, Dibrugarh and Jorhat also trickled in. Haimavati could now bring home a wide range of books covering titles like *Lahori, Manomati, Rahdair Ligiri, Nirmal Bhakat, Sarathi, Kendrasabha* to *Burhi Aiyar Xadhu, Panchatantra Xadhu* and *Isapar Xadhu*. When they saw how involved Haimavati was in setting up the small library, the Asom Sangha people entrusted her with the responsibility of running it. So, every Saturday, Haima would sit in the library from two to four in the afternoon, make a list of all the books and also write a number with her clear hand on the cover of each. This she had learnt from her visits to the nearby Vidyasagar Pathaghar. On Saturdays, Panchatirtha came back from office earlier than usual. On his way home, he would drop in at the Asom Sangha to have a look at how things were going. Watching Haima at work seated on a high chair, he was filled with a sense of pride. On her part Haimavati radiated a newfound confidence.

10

Gauripriya came to be called Sonamon by everyone at home. The name had stuck because Saradamoni mashima who lived nearby, had given this nick-name to her – she'd often cradle the child in her lap and call her Sonamon. Haima liked the name and accepted it for her daughter. Saradamoni's youngest daughter, Mita, was Sonamon's playmate. On holidays when Mita shuoted from the verandah of their house, 'Oi Sonamon, shall we play?' her mynah bird in the cage would also join in by screaming, 'Oi Mita, shall we play ?' The mynah could perfectly imitate the voices of the two girls. Sonamon would run outside and pretend to scold the bird, 'Oi Myna, please shut up!' At this, the happy mynah would shake her feathers and chant, 'Oi Mita, Oi Sonamon.' Everyone in the locality was amused at this shouting game between the bird and the girls. The other girls playing in front of the Kharkongor house, clapped their hands and laughed. Once, one of the little girls from the Kharkongor house who had been watching Sonamon and Mita at play, crossed the lane hesitantly and stood in front of Sonamon's house. Mita immediately waved to her to join. The girl cast her glances all around and then quickly stepped down the flight of steps into the sun-kissed courtyard where Mita and Sonamon were playing. For a while, both of them watched the girl who was dressed like a European child. Then Mita went up to her and said in broken Khasi, 'My name is Mita. She is Sonamon. What's your name?'

'Nancy', the girl replied, her voice barely audible. After repeating the unfamiliar name several times, Mita asked her, 'Will you play with us?' Nancy nodded. Her consent suddenly seemed to add new zest to their play. 'We are playing "house-house". This is my house and that is Sonamon's,' said Mita. The girls had set up house under two large black umbrellas. Sonamon rushed inside and got another umbrella. She opened it and handed it to Nancy, 'So, your house is now under this umbrella.' Mita and Sonamon then collected pebbles, empty bottles and discarded containers and placed them all below Nancy's umbrella so that her house could be complete. After this, all three of them went marketing. On the slope by the road, there were hundreds of small yellow and white wild flowers. The three of them started picking their imaginary vegetables. 'The white flowers are cauliflowers, the yellow ones are tomatoes,' said Mita as she picked up a whole bunch of flowers for herself.

'Of course not! The yellow ones should be bananas,' intervened Sonamon.

'The yellow flowers are called dandelions,' said Nancy. 'Wait, I will now show you some magic.' Nancy ran and carefully plucked a dandelion stem which sported a white cotton-like ball instead of a flower. Inside the ball there were countless small seed heads. Nancy pulled the pom-pom near her face and blew into the white feathery ball. In a moment bits of cotton started drifting upwards and the dandelion seeds were scattered far and wide while the three friends watched the spectacle, fascinated. After this, the three of them ran among the wild flowers and spent quite some time plucking the dandelion flower-heads and blowing into them so that the strong breeze would carry the soft cotton bits with their seeds all over the place. Once this dandelion game was over, the three girls held hands and walked back to Sonamon's courtyard. Meanwhile a strong gust of wind had played havoc with their umbrella-homes. The umbrellas had all been blown away and were lying one upon the other at a distance. 'These houses are no good. Let us build a new one where all three of us can stay,' said Mita, and straightaway their mothers' old saris and bedsheets were put to use to build a new house. Soon, the sun began playing hide and seek behind the clouds which quickly descended and covered the entire area, including their little play shelter. The girls, accepting defeat before the clouds, finally wrapped up their play.

11

The children of the Kharkongor family went to missionary schools. The school where Nancy's brother Frank studied was situated on the top of a scenic hill at Laitumkrah. As for Haimavati's sons, they had never seen that school. However, while walking along the road that skirted the school, they often caught a distant glimpse of its premises. Sarat and his brother had never had an occasion to talk to Frank. The boys of Brahmopally were naturally curious about this fair, handsome lad in his school uniform as he briskly walked to school by the road in front of their houses. But the young boy always kept to himself and didn't mix with the other boys of his neighbourhood. Even on holidays he didn't come to play. Nancy had told Mita and her other friends that her brother usually played his games and took his music lessons all at school. Nancy too went to an Anglo-Indian school on the top of a hillock covered with pine trees. She looked very smart in her warm navy-blue serge uniform and cap.

On the way to and from school, Sarat and Bijoy passed by Nancy's school. As they peered through the openings between rows of pine trees, they caught a glimpse of many other girls like Nancy playing in the school compound. Most of them were British and Anglo-Indian girls who stayed in the school's hostel while only a very few, like Nancy, were day-scholars who

walked to school every day. While going to school, Sarat and
Vijay often walked behind Nancy, trying to maintain a discreet
distance from her. Once, while they were walking along thus, a
sudden draught blew away Nancy's cap. Dumbfounded, the girl
stood helpless in the middle of the road. Then, all at once, Sarat
rushed down the hill-slope on the side of the road and retrieved
the cap from the bank of a stream below. As he handed it to her,
Nancy shyly thanked Sarat with a smile. His face radiated with
sheer happiness. Sarat was then a high school student who was
gradually becoming aware of his own self. Even though Nancy
was a small girl, he was filled with a feeling of self-importance at
being able to help her.

From quite an young age, Sarat loved to sing. He possessed
a sweet voice and had a good ear for tunes. In their Bengali
neighbourhood, music happened to be an integral part of
almost every household. Whenever Brahmo preachers arrived
from Calcutta on a visit to Shillong or Daccca, they would
stay as guests in one of the Bengali houses and, during those
special days, the entire nighbourhood would resound with
the tunes of Brahmo-songs. Along with his siblings, Sarat too
learnt these songs and sang them at home for their mother
who simply loved them. She found the songs to be much more
sober and contained as compared with the 'Bangali Gaan' of her
childhood at Jorhat. Panchatirtha, however, did not approve of
this for he believed that singing was not for boys. But Haima
refused to accept this view. She often argued that since women
had to give up music and dance after getting married, how
would new songs be in circulation if boys weren't allowed to
sing? In the face of such an argument, Panchatirtha was left
with little to say.

Sarat was learning the tabla from a neighbour. Sometimes he also played on the harmonium with his sisters. But it was the organ that attracted him the most. In the evenings, when the sombre tones of the organ floated out of Nancy's home, Sarat would stand in front of the house and listen, enthralled. Labanyaprava's son, Partha had learned to play the organ at his uncle's place in Calcutta and now, his father had bought him an old organ at a cheap price. In those days when English families left Shillong, they usually sold their pianos and organs to Indians or Eurasians at low prices. Sarat pleaded with his mother to get him an old organ. But with Panchatirtha's limited resources, Haimavati could never think of buying such a luxury item, however much she might have wanted to fulfil her son's desire. Experience had taught her that there were certain things that just could not be helped.

One day, Sarat came to know from a friend that one of his Anglo-Indian teachers was planning to sell his old piano for just fifty rupees. Only a single key of the piano was not working well. Sarat now insisted that his mother should somehow get together the fifty rupees for him. In this he was fully supported by his siblings who declared that they would forego their demand for new clothes for the sake of the piano. Left with no option, Haimavati hesitatingly raised the matter with her husband who immediately brushed it aside with an emphatic 'no'. While all this was going on, things suddenly brightened up for Sarat with the sudden visit of Haimavati's brother, Sivaprasad. After graduating from a college in Calcutta, Sivaprasad had joined as a manager in a tea estate in Upper Assam. He had come to Shillong to supervise the construction of a large bungalow which the owner of the tea estate was getting built as his summer resort, at the side of the Ward's Lake, After spending some time talking about their college days in Calcutta with his friend Banamali Panchatirtha, Sivaprasad took his nephews and nieces out to the Police Bazaar area for some shopping. There he first bought them foreign chocolates in the department store named Shillong Tailoring, a place which the children had often seen from the outside but had never entered. After this, they went to the Morello restaurant for tea and pastries. In all, it was a grand outing for the children. On their way back home, Sarat, after some hesitation, broached the topic of the piano with his uncle. Though Bhabani had tried to stop him from talking about it by pinching his hand secretly, Sarat paid her no heed and decided to go ahead. To their utter surprise, the children found that their uncle not only welcomed the idea but handed them fifty rupees to buy the piano. The very next day uncle and nephew went to Mawkhar and brought the piano home on a horse-cart. The coming of the piano changed the entire atmosphere of the house. While Sarat carefully fingered the keyboard to play a tune, his uncle practised some western dance steps. Everybody, including Panchatirtha, was simply enthralled by the sound of the piano.

The following day, several neighbours turned up at the residence of the Bhattas to have a look at the piano. Labanyaprava's son, Partha, started playing a Rabindra Sangeet with a western tune and Saradamoni joined in by humming the song. Suddenly the whole house seemed to be flooded with the sound of music. From then onwards Assamese, Bengali and sometimes strains from an English melody would mingle joyfully to create an atmosphere of celestial harmony in the Bhatta household on many a cold winter evening. Whenever Sarat tried to play a new song, he would seek seek his sister's help because he knew that Bhabani's sense of tune was much sharper than his. When brother and sister were busy in trying to perfect a tune, Haimavati would quietly sit near them with a piece of embroidery in hand. These were the moments when she felt a new sense of fulfilment permeating her life.

12

Preparations were afoot at the Asom Sangha to hold Durga Puja celebrations for the first time. All the Assamese residents of Shillong, old and new, decided that they would jointly hold the event. Meanwhile, with contributions from different sources, the Asom Sangha house was expanded, with a puja mandapa being built at one end. Young people enthusiastically prepared for the cultural events that would be held on each day of the pujas and in this they were guided by a person named Maheswar Goswami, a known expert in Kamrupia music and dance. Soon after his arrival in Shillong on government service, Goswami set up a small Kamrupi cultural centre to promote the traditional Assamese arts. Inspired by him, a number of young men took to learning dance and music, particularly the traditional instruments. Even though Maheswar Goswami was a staunch Vaishnavite, he had no problems with organizing cultural functions in the puja pandals. However, he never accepted *prasad* or *nirmalya* at the pujas. He was one who always stood firm on his own beliefs without ever hurting the religious sentiments of others. When he came to know that Sarat was a good singer, he instantly made him a part of his cultural troupe. Sarat and his companions were to perform *Borgeet* during the pujas while Goswami would accompany them on the khol. It was decided that on the evening of Ashtami

Puja, a play named 'Shonit Kunwari' portraying the romantic story of Usha and Aniruddha, would be staged where all the female roles would be performed by men. Bijoy, dressed in his mother's mekhala-chador, would have to play the role of Usha's friend, Chitralekha. The moment they heard of this, Bhabani and Sonamon were greatly amused and never stopped making fun of their brother who they feared would trip and fall while trying to manage his steps in a mekhala. At first no one had thought of including the girls in the cultural events associated with the pujas. But much to the amazement of all, Haimavati suggested one day that some of the girls should present a song. She pointed out that among the Brahmos, educated girls from respectable families recited poems and also sang songs. So, what was the harm in Assamese girls also doing the same? Although a few had their reservations about Haimavati's proposal, the young ones saw it through and she was given the responsibility of arranging things.

Haimavati began her work with plenty of enthusiasm. But as she moved from one Assamese house to another, she discovered how difficult it was to bring the girls out of their houses. Most of the Assamese girls were either married or were being prepared for marriage by the age of nine or ten. Dwaraka Nath and Ambika's daughter, Moini was the same age as Bhabani. But she had been married some two years ago to a Brahmin family of Mangoldoi. Though she hadn't yet gone to her husband's house, she was busy learning her family duties at her parents' place. Whenever she saw her, Haima was deeply saddened. Did she have any inkling of what her future held, Haima wondered. After repeated visits to every house, Haima failed to convince even a single family to allow their girls to sing in public. Utterly frustrated, she decided to give up. Just then, Maheswar Goswami came forward with a plan. Perhaps the item could still be put up if one could convince a few Bengali and Khasi girls to sing an Assamese song along with Bhabanipriya and Gauripriya. At this suggestion, Haimavati saw a new possibility open up and, to her pleasant surprise, it didn't take much time to convince Saradamoni's daughter, Sisirkona, to take part in the show. Saradamoni herself provided the clue to locate another girl. Lisimon, the Khasi girl who was Sisirkona's classmate at the Lady Keane School, could sing Bengali songs beautifully and had performed at several events arranged by the Brahmo Samaj.

Haimavati immediately remembered that this beautiful Khasi girl was Rabon Roy's youngest daughter. Sarat also knew Lisimon as his friend Lakhon's sister and had met her at their Mawkhar home. Lisimon was the youngest of three sisters. Both the older sisters were married and stayed with their husbands who were Christians. The husband of the eldest sister Helimon, was a pastor. Her other sister, Sitimon, had a large bakery where both she and her husband worked. Workers of the bakery carried huge baskets filled with bread and pastries for home delivery in different parts of the town. Sometimes Sarat would go over to Lakhon's place during lunch-break and fill himself up with slices of cake, jam tarts and muffins. He observed that Lakhon treated his younger sister, Lisimon, with great deference. As the youngest daughter of the house, she deserved all the respect, for in the future it was she who would have to shoulder the responsibility of managing the entire property of the Diengdoh family and also to ensure that all religious rituals were properly performed. In the beginning, Sarat found it somewhat difficult to understand all that Lakhon said. He didn't understand why a girl should be burdened with all the responsibility when there were two sons at home. Finally, one day he asked Lakhon, 'Your father's surname is Roy. Then why do you write Diengdoh?' Lakhon replied with his characteristic ease, 'Diengdoh is the surname of my mother's family.' Sarat was a bit confused and naturally took some time to understand these customs; but he soon came to accept them as belonging to a culture which was different from his own. Lisimon was the khadduh or the youngest daughter of the Diengdoh family and the entire responsibility of safeguarding the family tradition had fallen on her frail shoulders. So, from such an early age she was like a guardian of the entire family. Seeing this, Sarat's admiration for her increased several fold. It was quite a unique experience for him to learn to respect a girl who was much younger than him.

Haimavati decided to go over to Rabon Roy's house and request Lisimon's mother, Keliyan, to allow her daughter to sing at the Durga Puja cultural show. Keliyan Diengdoh was a busy woman. Apart from managing the accounts of her husband's business, she had to look after almost everything relating to her large family. No job was too small for her. Her belonging to an aristocratic family didn't prevent her from supervising the sale of oranges from their Cherrapunji orchard at the busy Bara Bazar. That day she talked of many things with Haimavati. Because she could converse in fluent Bengali, Haima didn't have any problems in talking to her. Although Keliyan had never before spoken to an Assamese woman, she had always been enamoured by their self-woven clothes. She minutely examined Haimavati's mekhala-chador, and then took out a muga jainsem and showed it to her. Her husband had brought it from the Ranee market. She had herself delicately embroidered the edges of the jainsem. Haimavati praised Keliyan's jainsem and promised to get for her daughters a few yards of some good muga silk from Guwahati. The two women chatted for some time and the Khasi lady promised to bring Lisimon over to Haimavati's house for the rehearsals. Haima left with a happy heart and a packet of areca nuts and oranges which Keliyan had packed for her with great care.

Practice sessions started at Haimavati's house soon after. Maheswar Goswami taught the girls to sing the popular song 'Asoma Nirupama Jananai' to the accompaniment of the harmonium and tabla. At the cultural event, Bhabanipriya, Sisirkona, Sonamon and Lisimon sang the song beautifully and with perfect co-ordination. Sarat accompanied them on the tabla. The audience responded enthusiastically with several rounds of applause and Haimavati's efforts were much appreciated. It wasn't an easy job to make two non-Assamese girls sing an Assamese song to such perfection. Dwarkanath Sarma, seated next to Panchatirtha, commented, 'Bhatta, it seems your household has become the cultural hub for this puja. Let's hope it will be possible to find girls again for next year's pujas.' Panchatirtha replied with a smile, 'Once some good work is initiated, one can hope that the people will keep it going'. Dwarkanath quickly moved to another subject, 'Bhatta, how long will you allow your girls to go on like this? Don't you want to think of getting them married?' Panchatirtha was somewhat taken aback and said, 'Well, I don't think they have reached marriageable age yet.' Dwarkanath munched his areca nut and said with a sly smile, 'Just because you say they haven't reached marriageable age, will people believe that? Today the entire audience saw that your Bhabanipriya has reached the marriageable age!' Panchatirtha was quite embarrassed at this. Really, that evening their Bhabani, dressed in her riha and mekhala, looked like a freshly blooming flower. Quietly he calculated her age. She had just completed twelve and had entered thirteen.

Later that evening Panchatirtha told Haimavati about what was being said about their daughters at the puja event. Haima's first reaction was of simple anger, 'The moment they saw the girl, the people had nothing else to say but her age! Ambika and the others too had only one topic on their lips – marriage. No one seemed to appreciate the effort that went into the song. Perhaps it appeared just like a marriage anthem to them!' Haima was upset and angry. Panchatirtha didn't say anything more. But some days later, when at the Asom Sangha Dwarkanath once again broached the topic of Bhabani's marriage in the presence of several other persons, Panchatirtha ventured to ask Haima with much hesitation, 'The people are saying that we are not concerned about Bhabani's future. Suppose we don't get a proper groom for her if we delay too much?'

Haimavati was silent. The same thought had been troubling her the past few days. How long would she be able to protect her daughters from the prying eyes of society? How long would she be able to shield Bhabani within the confines of a household which she had created with so much care? The mere thought of having to send her away to another house was unbearable to Haimavati. She was such a soft and pure girl. Would she be able to adjust to a completely new situation? She also didn't have much of idea about the intricacies of Assamese society. Haima herself had always tried to keep her daughters away from the narrow confines of the traditional Assamese society of Shillong. Assailed by such thoughts, she started spending sleepless nights.

Dwarkanath and his wife Ambika didn't give up on pestering Haimavati and Panchatirtha about Bhabani's marriage. They constantly reminded them how difficult it would be to find an eligible groom for Bhabani in Shillong. Even those young men who came from the plains to work in government offices were usually married. Some of them of course, indulged in the forbidden pleasures of the hill town before bringing over their families from the plains. Others had a legal family in the plains and another one in Shillong which they were unwilling to acknowledge. Ambika recounted all these gossipy tales before coming to her main point. She insisted that if the parents were serious about finding a groom for Bhabani, then their contacts in the plains would have to be kept informed. When he saw that Panchatirtha was slightly inclined, Dwarkanath wrote to a friend of theirs at Dergaon along with a copy of Bhabani's horoscope. After about two months, news finally arrived that a groom had been found. He was the elder son of a mauzadar and the family was a respectable one. The younger brother was studying at Cotton College in Guwahati. The mauzadar had agreed to accept Bhabani as a bride for his elder son but the wedding would have to be solemnized within two months in keeping with the boy's horoscope The moment Dwarkanath broke the news to Panchatirtha and his wife, Haimavati asked with some concern, 'The boy's younger brother is in college, but what about his own educational qualifications?'

Dwarkanath appeared a bit puzzled. Nonetheless, he answered, 'If all the sons go off to study, who will look after the vast land and property of the father? Doesn't the eldest son have a duty towards the family?' Haima felt that the second sentence was particularly aimed at Panchatirtha. It seemed Dwarkanath knew that in all these years Panchatirtha had kept no links with his parents. Haimavati and Panchatirtha didn't have any answer to Dwarkanath's question. Dwarkanath, aware of the couple's reservations, now fired his final salvo, couched in the softest of words but which completely floored the Bhatta couple, 'Even otherwise, there is always a prejudice that girls who grow up here in Shillong are very modern. And your girl is also quite old. You should thank your stars that the mauzadar has given his consent to the marriage without even wanting to look at her. If you continue to be choosy in these matters, let me assure you that you will end up keeping your daughter permanently at home.' Haimavati was dumbstruck. She had hoped for an educated young man with a modern outlook for her daughter, someone who would respect her qualities on an equal footing. Haima knew that several well educated young men of her Bengali neighbourhood had sent their wives to study in Calcutta and she too would have been happy had Bhabani and Sonamon got similar husbands. But, even if there were such young men in Assamese society, she hadn't come across any so far.

Haimavati had on several occasions tried to share her hopes about their daughters' future with her husband. But Panchatirtha seemed strangely indifferent. It appeared that he was bent on getting the girls married and be done with his responsibilities. Yet, strangely he loved them both a great deal. Haimavati was at a loss to understand why Panchatirtha saw the girls as a burden, while dreaming at the same time of giving higher education to his sons. The liberal atmosphere of Brahmopally had brought about a noticeable change in Haimavati's outlook. It was not that Banamali Panchatirtha was not aware of this. But he seemed to accept it as part of women's emotional response to new influences. As far as he was concerned, he was of quite a stubborn nature and did what he considered right. Whenever differences with Haima appeared to take a bitter turn, Panchatirtha tried to skirt the issue by adopting an indifferent and detached attitude. Thus, family peace was always maintained. But this left Haimavati with no chance of settling her many doubts and, at crucial moments of her life, she always felt that she was alone.

13

The wedding was fixed in such a hurry that it left Haimavati with no time at all to think deeply on anything. She didn't even consider it strange that no one from the mauzadar's family had come to see the girl. Once the marriage was finalised, Ambika and Dwarkanath virtually took over and the Bhattas allowed themselves to be completely guided by the Sarma couple. It was as if their own considerations were totally subsumed by the advice given by the Sarmas who now started visiting them almost every day. Neither Bhabani nor Sonamon had any liking for Ambika and they could always read signs of envy through the veil of her unending good humour and talkativeness. They had noticed that whenever Ambika saw Bhabani playing the piano, she would say with a sly smile, 'Well, this has indeed become a memsahib's household!'

Once when Ambika went outside and spat out her pan-juice in front of the house, Sonamon whispered in Bhabani's ears, 'Baideu, Ambika Mahi just spat pan-juice right inside our play-house.'

'Go and build another one at a different place.' Bhabani had said somewhat absentmindedly.

Once the date of the wedding was finalized, Panchatirtha and his wife went to his father-in-law's place at Jorhat, from where he decided to work out the details for the wedding.

Since the mauzadar refused to have the marriage at Shillong, it was decided to hold it at the bride's uncle's place and a happy Sivaprasad went about making all the arrangements. One day Sivaprasad drove Panchatirtha in his car to the mauzadar's house. At first sight Panchatirtha was quite pleased with what he saw. The mauzadar seemed to possess quite a lot of land and property and he noticed the two barn-houses full of paddy. In short, it was what one would usually term as a wealthy family of the village. A happy Panchatirtha was so engrossed in discussing the shastras with his new would-be relations, that he almost forgot to ask about the groom. Eventually, he did express his desire to have a word with the young man. The mauzadar went inside, but after a considerable length of time he came out and announced that his eldest son was not well and was unwilling to meet anyone. Only then did a fleeting sense of doubt cross Panchatirtha's mind. What would Haimavati say if he left without even seeing the groom? But the mauzadar's grave appearance deterred Panchatirtha from making any further request. Disappointed, both Sivaprasad and Panchatirtha returned home.

The moment she heard about the visit and the sickness of the groom, an unknown fear gripped Haimavati. What was she to do? Everything relating to the marriage was moving ahead at a mechanical pace but Haima seemed to have lost all interest. So tense was she that Bhabani and Sonamon became increasingly scared of going near her. They tried their best to keep up each other's spirits. Sarat and Bijoy occasionally came to give them company and strike up some conversation. The unbearable heat, the mosquito bites, sleeping under mosquito nets at night and being bitten by leeches whenever they went outside – all this was a totally new experience for them. The mere thought of having to leave behind Bhabani in the midst of all this, would make their hearts heavy.

The gloomy situation notwithstanding, the wedding ceremony went off without any significant hitch. They saw the groom for the first time when he came and stood under the ceremonial plantain tree. In appearance he was a fair, well-built handsome young man. When Panchatirtha welcomed the groom as the embodiment of Vishnu, he noticed that he looked somewhat strange. But the best man accompanying the groom quickly took him aside and seated him in front of the havan fire. And, as soon as the wedding rituals were over, the groom's party left in an unusually strange haste.

Then word came from the groom's place that on the *Khoba-Khoboni* day, or the third day after the wedding when the boy's family gave a party to welcome the girl, the bride should be sent to the groom's house along with her all her clothes, ornaments, furniture and utensils. Haimavati was once again shaken. She had hoped that the girl would be sent back to them after the formal 'house-entry' ceremony. She had also thought that she would keep Bhabani with her for at least two years before she attained enough maturity to go and manage things at her husband's. But the mauzadar's family insisted that since the girl had already attained puberty, they would like her to come over permanently. The very thought of a thirteen year old girl going to live with her husband upset Haimavati. She had never imagined that she would have to prepare Bhabani to face such a situation. It seemed as if some powerful dark force was propelling both her husband and Haima in some unknown direction. Otherwise, why would they accept all the demands of the groom's family and push their daughter into some imminent danger?

After some deliberation, it was decided that Haima's elder brother Sivaprasad and his wife Saraswati, her elder sister Kamala and Saratchandra would accompany the bride to her new home. They would all go in Sivaprasad's Ford car. All the gifts to be sent with Bhabani had already been loaded onto a bullock-cart and sent to the mauzadar's house in advance. Haima tried her best to keep calm as the moment of departure arrived. Bhabani was mechanically carrying out all the directions given by her aunt and uncles. But when it came to her taking leave of her parents, she started sobbing. It was as if the cocoon of protection and comfort which her parents had so long provided her was now being finally removed. Haima managed to control herself in the midst of Bhabani's sobs even as Panchatirtha placed his right hand on Bhabani's head and uttered the words of blessing, *kalyanamastu*. But the moment the car left, Haima rushed inside and broke down. When she saw her mother in such a state, Sonamon was shattered. She sat in a corner and sobbed away herself, convinced that the marriage was actually a mistake. For the first time in his wedded life, Banamali Panchatirtha too appeared quite helpless at the plight of his wife. He had never seen her break down in this way and wondered what had really gone wrong.

When the bride's party entered the groom's house, they immediately realised that the situation there wasn't quite normal. Although the groom's mother welcomed the bride according to custom, the festive atmosphere that should have been there was completely missing. The group of women who had come to see the bride, surrounded Bhabani and minutely observed her appearance, her clothes and her ornaments. Both Bhabani and Gauri had rosy cheeks which turned fullly pink when they came down from the hills to the heat of the plains.

Bhabani's bright complexion attracted everyone's attention and someone from the group sarcastically remarked, 'It seems there is no dearth of rouge, lipstick and other toiletries in Shillong. The bride's cheeks are proof enough.' As Bhabani lowered her face, aunt Saraswati rushed to her defence, 'Our girl's complexion is God-given. If anyone has any doubt, you can go and rub her cheeks and find out.' Instantly, a young girl went up to Bhabani and, pretending to pat the bride, started vigorously rubbing her cheeks with a handkerchief. When she couldn't find any trace of make-up on her hanky she looked embarrassed. Saraswati and Kamala smiled triumphantly.

The bride's party, having finished with the formalities, decided to leave early. Saraswati and Kamala gave the bride all the necessary instructions and were about to leave when Bhabani came up to them and sobbed into their anchals helplessly. Faced with a group of unknown people, an unfamiliar household and an uncertain future, Bhabani then sat still while her near and dear ones left. Sarat was already sitting inside the car, ready to depart. He had been stunned by his first meeting with his brother-in-law who, in response to his questions, had just stared at him stupidly before finally moving away. What had really happened? Sarat had no clue.

As the car negotiated the bumpy lane from the mauzadar's house and was about to hit the main road, a young man hailed it to a stop. When the car stopped, he came up to it and asked, 'Aren't you the bride's party returning from the mauzadar's house?' When a surprised Sivaprasad answered in the affirmative, the young man politely asked him to come out from the car for a few minutes. Irritated, Sivaprasad alighted and stood near him. The young man said, 'I am the younger son of the mauzadar and am a student at Cotton College in

Guwahati. The person to whom you have given your girl in marriage happens to be my brother. For quite a while now, he, my kakaideo, has been suffering from some mental illness. The village physician or bez had suggested that he would be cured if he got married. Before this marriage, they had married him to another girl. But unable to bear the suffering inflicted on her by my brother, the bride just fled to her parents' in a totally broken state. Now, rejecting all our pleas, my father has gone for a second marriage for my brother. God knows what will happen to the new bride. Because I opposed all this, I have been asked to leave the house. As for me, I have also decided never to step into that horrible house again. I didn't even come for the wedding. But I decided I had to warn you else I would not have been able to square it with my conscience. I beg you, please save the girl if you can.'

Stunned, Sivaprasad stood stock still. Then, turning sharply on the young man, 'Why should I believe you? No one else has hinted this to us.' The young man replied with a wry smile, 'Everyone around here knows me and also about the happenings in our house. But there are very few who would dare to come out with the truth. It seems that sacrificing a girl's life for treating a person's mental illness is no great deal for anyone. I have heard that your girl is educated and full of talent. In spoiling her life all of you will be committing a grave sin. Whatever has happened, has happened. The rest depends on you all. I have said what needed to be said. That's all.'

All this while Sarat had been listening to the conversation quietly. Ever since he'd met his brother-in-law an unknown fear about his sister had gripped him. How would the soft-natured Bhabani spend her life with such a weird person? Would her soulful and melodious voice be silenced for ever? His heart ached thinking of all this. Now that he heard what the young man had said, a sense of determination took hold of him, as if he had suddenly made a transition from adolescence to manhood. Holding his uncle's hand he said with newfound firmness, 'Let's go, uncle. We'll bring her back.' After this, it seemed that there was nothing left to be discussed. Sivaprasad turned the car towards the mauzadar's house and pressed the accelerator. Even as the car picked up speed on its reverse journey, Sarat noticed in the rear-view mirror that the good Samaritan was still standing by the roadside, his gaze fixed on their vehicle.

As the car stopped in front of the mauzadar's house, several persons strained their necks to have a look at it from the sitting room. Without uttering a word, Sivaprasad and Sarat just rushed inside, followed by Kamala and Saraswati. Having come face to face with the mauzadar, Sivaprasad almost screamed, 'Who gave you the right to cheat us like this?' Taken aback, the mauzadar replied, 'What are you talking about? Who says we have cheated anyone?' Clenching his teeth, Sivaprasad said, 'Don't you all feel ashamed at destroying the life of a young girl by getting her married to your insane son?' At this, the mauzadar said with a smile, 'The marriage is already over. What's the point in saying all this now? Whatever is written on the girl's forehead will obviously come to pass. Neither you nor I can do anything about it.'

'Why can't we? We will take her away from here and give her a new life.' Sarat almost choked as he said this. Sarat was not accustomed to raising his voice in front of elders, and was taken aback at the pitch of his own voice. At his outburst, one of the elderly gentlemen said, 'Look at this! Such haughty words from one so young! Take heed or else…' Sivaprasad garnered some additional strength, 'No one is going to stop us! We will take the girl with us right now – with all her things. Sarat, go and ask our cart driver to load her things on the bullock-cart.' The mauzadar accosted Sarat and tried to say something when Sivaprasad intervened and said with extra firmness, 'There is law in this country. If needed, we will approach the courts for justice.' However, Sivaprasad himself wasn't sure if the law could really intervene in such matters. The mauzadar too didn't have any knowledge about this and thought it best to keep mum. Meanwhile Saraswati and Kamala went inside and clutching her hand, led Bhabani outside. Without saying anything to anyone, they seated her inside the car. An immediate commotion followed and several women came out from inside the house. One of them whispered to Saraswati, 'You have really saved the girl! The boy had one of his fits today and rushed out with a machete to kill someone. Now he has been confined in his room.'

Sarat and Sivaprasad got into the car. Strangely, no one came forward to obstruct them. As the car moved forward on the village road, Sarat noticed the young man, the groom's brother, waiting at the end of the alley and asked for the car to be slowed down. When the youth approached them, Sarat held his hand and said, 'We will never be able to repay your debt.' The young man was a bit embarrassed and he replied, 'I have only done my duty. It is you who carried out the task so courageously. May God bless you. We'll surely meet someday.' The car picked up speed as it hit the highway and headed east.

14

It had been raining incessantly since Haimavati and the family came back to Shillong. The hill in front of their house was covered in clouds and the pine trees were bent under the full blast of the strong westerly wind. Haimavati couldn't sleep at night and all the while she was aware that her husband too wasn't asleep. The constant drumming of the rain on the roof and the whine and screech of the pines, made her feel all the more helpless. She knew from the sound of the rushing waters that the nearby stream was full to the brim. On earlier occasions, during such weather, Haimavati would always step out to take a look at the stream. She would be fascinated to see how the small and sleepy stream meandering through the pine forest would suddenly be transformed into a wild and unruly rivulet, its gushing waters turning frothy white as they broke upon the rocks. The very sight of the uncontrollable stream during the monsoon always inspired Haima with a strange sense of freedom. Yet, now that very sound of the fast flowing waters seemed to be assaulting her senses. She felt that the house she had set up with so much care was no longer secure and safe. What was the meaning of a house if it could not give security to its own children, she wondered. In the darkness of the night, Panchatirtha could sense the turmoil in his wife's mind and he tried to comfort her, 'Don't worry, after all there is God up there. He will give us some way out. Please try to get some sleep.' In the midst of nature's fury, Panchatirtha's calm words gave her some sort of assurance that, after all, the main pillar of her house was still quite firm.

The neighbours were unable to visit them because of the incessant rains. But as the weather gradually cleared up, the story of the Bhatta family's misfortune spread throughout Brahmopally. Saradamoni, Labanyaprabha, Indumohan Babu, Tarabhusan Babu and others dropped in to show their concern. Labanyaprabha assured Haimavati, 'Thank your stars that those days are gone when it was considered that a girl who doesn't go to her husband's house has no future. Make sure she gets an education and you will see what a bright future awaits her.' The women from Brahmopally referred to the newly enacted Sarada Act and told Haima: 'The country's law is now veering towards the rights of women and their marriage before the age of fourteen has been made illegal. There's also opposition to this law by well-known people who cite the sastras as evidence. But educated women have formed an all-India Mahila Samity and are trying to spread awareness of this new law. They are of the view that if girls are married at a young age, then the very purpose of women's education is subverted. We are also moving ahead to set up such a mahila samity in Shillong. You must come and join us, Haima. We must educate girls like Bhabani and make them stand on their own feet.' Such words greatly helped Haimavati regain her self-confidence and she made up her mind to prepare Bhabani for a new life. But she knew that for this, she would have to prepare herself first.

On her return to Shillong, Haimavati was filled with fear at the prospect of having to face the Assamese community. The very thought that she'd be at the receiving end of their pity was a serious blow to her self-esteem. But then, she decided that she wouldn't give anyone a chance to show pity towards them. Instead, she would build an unseen, impenetrable wall all around her family. One day, Ambika and a few other women turned up at her place to express their sympathies. But Haima was convinced that they had actually come only to take pleasure in her family's misfortune. So, the moment she saw the visitors at her doorstep, she told Bhabani, 'Go and play something on the piano.' Taken aback by her mother's unexpected order, Bhabani asked, 'Why, ma?' At this, Haima almost scolded Bhabani, 'Because I say so, that's reason enough.' Her mother had never been so harsh with her. In fact, ever since their return from Jorhat, she'd been unusually soft and caring. Surprised at her severity now, the poor girl lifted the piano cover and stared at the keys, wondering what to play. Then she heard her mother instruct her from the doorstep as she advanced to receive the guests, 'Play that Tagore song "*mono mor meghero sangi.*"'

Haimavati ushered the visitors into her sitting room with a smile. The conversation veered around the namghar and the Asom Sangha and then moved on to the library. Haima enquired about Mrs Hazarika and whether she'd faced any problems in running the library. Meanwhile, the notes from the piano floated in from the other room. Ambika asked in some surprise, 'Hasn't Sarat gone to school today?' Haima answered gravely, 'Yes, of course. It's Bhabani who's playing.' The women appeared a bit embarrassed at this and Ambika said, her voice heavy with regret, 'Poor girl! How will she spend her life now?'

'If one has a will, there is always plenty to do in life,' Haima calmly retorted.

Ambika couldn't control herself any longer. Unable to accept Haima's composure, she said aggressively, 'You didn't do the right thing by bringing her back. The boy sometimes behaves badly only because of a head injury he suffered as a child. They told us that once he got married and set up a family, the problem would disappear. But you've just destroyed her life without a thought for the consequences, you've finished everything for her by bringing her back.' Haimavati turned a steady gaze on Ambika. She swallowed the rage rising in her breast and said, coldly, 'So you knew all the time that something was wrong with him but you still chose to hide it from us? You knowingly tried to destroy the life of a young, innocent girl and now you've come to enjoy the fun? Well, let me inform you that we will not allow her life to be ruined. As long as we are alive we will make sure she has a new life. I will not allow you to ruin my family's happiness.' She was trembling with rage. She picked up the bota with tamul-paan on it with both hands, offered it to her guests and then quickly went inside. The women waited for a while and when Haima didn't emerge, they left hurriedly with a 'bye'. But the tune being played by Bhabani seemed to mockingly pursue them till the turn of the road.

One day, as she was walking home, Haima met Padumi Das who used to teach Bhabani in the local Assamese school. Padumi asked how the children were and then she said, 'Why do you keep Bhabani confined at home? A gem like her should not be neglected. Send her to Calcutta or Santiniketan. Education will bring a sense of completeness to her life. If she stays on here, the pettiness all around will totally stifle her. The distant hills appear high but they aren't insurmountable. Give her the strength to scale them.'

The words struck home. Gradually, Haimavati regained control of herself. As her mood changed, so did the atmosphere of the house. Sarat and Bijoy started regular school. Sarat would soon have to sit his matriculation exam and Bijoy's annual exams were also approaching. Kong Laiziri began to come round again to escort Sonamon to school. At the sight of a dejected Bhabani on the steps of the house, Kong Laiziri asked, 'Why aren't you going to school? Are you not well?' Bhabani shook her head and looked down. As Haima sat combing and plaiting her daughter's hair, Sonamon asked her mother, 'Ma, why can't married girls go to school?'

'Of course they can. But we don't plan to send Bhabani to school here anymore. We will send her to Santiniketan for her studies.' A surprised Sonamon said, 'Where is Santiniketan, Ma?'

'It's quite far from here. But Labanyaprava Didi knows people there. They'll make all the arrangements. We have heard that it is a very beautiful place. Just like an ashram. Kabiguru has set it up and he also stays there.'

'Wow, you'll be staying at Kabiguru's ashram, Baideo! You'll be able to learn so many new songs and dances!' Sonamon spoke to Bhabani who was still sitting quietly on the steps. Bhabani didn't respond. This was the first time she was hearing the new plans for her future. Earlier too her marriage had been planned in a similar manner – suddenly and without any warning. Then too no one had thought it necessary to ask for her opinion; and things were no different now. Bhabani quietly tried to turn things over in her head. But Santiniketan, Rabindra sangeet and such things seemed to her to belong to an entirely different world. After the terrible experience she had had after leaving the sanctuary of her home, Bhabani had ruled out all thoughts of ever leaving home again.

Haimavati's plans were, however, different. She no longer believed in leaving decisions relating to their children's future to her husband. After what had happened to Bhabani,

Panchatirtha too wasn't as sure of himself as he had been earlier. He had now begun to slowly accept his wife's decisions. So, when Haimavati asked for his view on sending Bhabani to Santiniketan, Panchatirtha raised only a feeble objection and asked whether it would be proper to send the girl so far away. But Haimavati reacted sharply, 'When we decided to get her married we never for once thought that we were pushing her into hell. Why should we be scared now of sending her to a sacred place like Santiniketan? And what's more, we don't need to consider what the Assamese community will think about this. It would do her good if we distance her from such a society.' After this, Panchatirtha was left with no reason to disapprove. As advised by his wife, he took the help of his neighbours at Brahmopally to finalise all arrangements for getting Bhabani admitted to school at Santiniketan. He decided that he would accompany her there. They would take the steamer to Calcutta from Guwahati and then proceed to Bolpur by train. Bhabani packed her belongings and once again prepared to leave home. The day she left on her new journey, she felt that her heart had really broken into two. One part of it she left behind in the green, memory-filled house of hers nestled among the clouds; the other part she held on to as she ventured out to a completely unknown world and an uncertain future.

15

Ever since his first visit to Shillong, Panchatirtha had wanted a house of his own in the hill town. Some friends from the Asom Sangha suggested he buy an old house in the Assamese locality of Laban. But after so many years in Brahmopally he'd become so used to the place that he had no wish to move. Haimavati and the children too had made the house their own. But news arrived one day that the owner of the house had retired and was returning from Dacca to take up permanent residence in Shillong. This meant that the family would have to move. Panchatirtha was in a real dilemma. Sarat's matriculation examination was just round the corner and it would take some time to find some another place to rent. He began searching but did not find a single house that suited his needs. One day, during a trip to Bara Bazaar he happened to meet Rabon Roy and told him about his predicament. Rabon reassured him and told him that there was a vacant plot of land near his wife's house and if Panchatirtha bought it, he'd be able to provide all possible help to get the house built quickly. Panchatirtha was greatly relieved. He felt that this co-traveller from his first trip to Shillong must have been someone really close to him in an earlier life. Full of gratitude, he gave Rabon a big hug, carefully placed a tamul-paan in his mouth, and took his leave with a free and unburdened mind.

Panchatirtha then took a government loan which he used to buy the plot of land and build a house. Soon the construction of the house began. Haimavati and Panchatirtha did not have the slightest idea of how a good, liveable house could be built within such a short time. A few pine trees felled from the adjacent forest, some stones, two truckloads of sand collected from the nearby river bed, mountain reeds, crushed limestone and some corrugated iron sheets were all that was required to build the house. There was no need for cement and bricks. Banamali Panchatirtha was simply captivated by the expertise of the Khasi carpenters in splitting the pine trunks and sawing long planks out of them. The men provided by Rabon Roy took just about a month and a half to complete the house as they happily whistled their way through their work. The polished wooden floors of the house plus the smooth walls plastered with lime and sand resembled any sahib's bungalow. The lower part of the walls of the front rooms were slightly rounded with polished wooden planks to give the feel of a wainscot design. Those days such houses, which were quite common in Scotland, were being increasingly built in Shillong.

Panchatirtha's house was built on the slope of a small pine forest, the ground of which had been cleared without cutting down too many trees. A marked feature of the place was that the southern wind constantly blew through the swaying pines and created quite a sound. Panchatirtha's constant worry was that someday a tree uprooted by the strong winds might fall on his house. Rabon Roy reassured him, 'There are so many trees here. But it is very seldom that a pine tree gets uprooted. These are new trees and their roots are deeply entrenched in the stones below. Well, I have thought of an appropriate name for your house, High Wind. It's an English name, but sounds quite nice.'

The idea of giving a name to his house had never occurred to Panchatirtha. But he gave in to Rabon's enthusiasm, and when a small wooden board, with the words 'High Wind' inscribed on it was finally hung on the wicker gate, the wind seemed to blow across the house with a renewed zeal. When accompanied by the soulful music of the cicadas, the music of the wind was heart-rending and deeply touched the soul.

When the house was finally ready, Panchatirtha consulted the almanac for an auspicious moment and then arranged for a naam-kirtan, a naming ceremony, to be held. The young persons from the Asom Sangha came and performed the naam. Following this, Haimavati cooked khichidi for the guests. Rabon Roy came, along with his family. On that special day he wore a short front-open endi silk shirt, a turban made of exquisite golden muga silk and a spotlessly white dhoti. His wife Keliyan, and daughter Lisimon, wore muga jainsems. After the naam-kirtan was over, Rabon Roy told Panchatirtha, 'We also call our religion "niam". The meaning is the same as yours – remembering God and following certain rituals and customs.'

As the Bhatta family prepared to leave Brahmopally, almost every neighbour invited them for a farewell tea or dinner. Each member of the family was quite sad to leave the neighbourhood which had become so much their own. Both Mita and Nancy shed tears when they came to say good-bye to Sonamon as the horse-cart loaded with household goods was about to leave. Sonamon also started sobbing. Both Sarat and Bijoy were quite upset. But for them it had become common practice to walk the distance from Mawkhar to Laban every day and they didn't think that their moving to the new house would break their links with Brahmopally or Laban. As she walked behind the horse cart, Haimavati seemed somewhat dejected. But the prospect of setting up a house of her own gave her new hope. After she had sent Bhabani to Santiniketan, she had felt that the second phase of her life at Laban was finally coming to a close. But after moving to Mawkhar, she had wanted to give up her work at the Asom Sangha library, but the group of young men at the Sangha entreated her, 'Mahideu, How can you leave us like this? How far is Mawkhar from Laban really? For our sakes, please do take the trouble to come here and look after the library. If you are late while getting back some days, one of us will escort you back home. You're an inspiration to us, your presence encourages us to work for the community.' These words brought back some of Haima's lost enthusiasm. She could see new possibilities among the younger generation. Very likely their minds were much more open than those of the older generation. Maybe, they too would realise the significance of Tagore's words, '*dibe ar nibe, milabe, milibi, jabena phire*'. It was with this belief that Haimavati decided to continue her links with the Asom Sangha.

As soon as he settled in his new house, Panchatirtha applied to a civil society organisation called Shillong Station for a water connection. Initially set up to provide tap water to the white residents of the European Ward, Shillong Station had already given water connections to areas like Laban and Mawkhar. So High Wind was also given a connection. Everyone was happy with the new house and its surroundings. There were a few Khasi families living nearby. The hill on which the house stood was thickly covered with pine trees and here too Sonamon's favourite dandelions were in full bloom, growing wild everywhere. The only difference was that Mita and Nancy weren't there to give her company. But she had already made friends with Wanli, Nina and Queenie whose families had recently converted to Christianity. Unlike Rabon Roy, the menfolk no longer wore dhotis but were clad in trousers and shirts, although they still retained their turbans. The numbers of such newly clad people were on the rise in the streets of Shillong. Rabon Roy, however, had not given up his traditional attire and it seemed that he was one of those who would stand alone against the winds of change.

Once he was done with his entrance examinations, Sarat, and several other young people in the Asom Sangha became increasingly involved in the organisation's cultural activities. In those days a person from Manipur named Lokendrajit Singh had come to Shillong to work in one of its many government offices. He was accomplished in Manipuri dance and the art of playing the khol. Maheswar Goswami lost no time in making him a member of his troupe. Soon after this, preparations began to stage an *Ankia-Naat* of Sankaradeva in Shillong. It was decided that the play would be staged not at the naam-ghar, as was the usual practice, but at the Asom Sangha where the dance sequences would be directed jointly by Lokendrajit Singh and Maheswar Goswami. Though there were some objections to this in the beginning, yet the graceful dance postures and the rhythmic movements finally won everyone over. For young men like Sarat there was no end to their zeal. It had become almost a rule for him to walk up to the Asom Sangha every evening, take part in the rehearsals and then come back home at night. Sometimes, his father also accompanied him. Panchatirtha would spend his time playing chess with the members of the Sangha and also watch the rehearsals of the play 'Parijata Harana'. One such evening Sarat came home earlier than usual. As he walked down the small lane through the pine forest leading to their house, he was surprised to hear the clear notes of a piano streaming out of their house. He had given up playing the piano ever since Bhabani left for Santiniketan, because each time he touched the piano, he was reminded of his sister's sad face. She was the one passionately in love with the instrument and it was she who had inspired him all along in his tryst with music. Sarat tried to listen to the tune that was being played. It was a totally unfamiliar one, similar to something that he had heard long ago on the organ at Nancy's house. Sarat knew that it couldn't be Sonamon as she had never been interested in playing the piano. She was someone who liked to run around and have fun in the hills. Bijoy usually spent his leisure hours in painting. Who could it be then?

As he walked into the house, Sarat was greeted by an unexpected sight. Lakhon's sister Lisimon was playing the piano and seated on a chair beside her, Haimavati was listening with concentration to the music. When she saw Sarat at the doorstep, Lisimon stopped playing and quickly tried to put the piano lid down. Sarat stopped her and said, 'You play so well! Please don't stop, please play that tune again.' Hesitantly, Lisimon started playing again. Standing by her side, Sarat watched the concentration on her face and her fingers flying over the keys with a lightness of touch, with admiration and some deference. He had met Lisimon on several occasions, she'd often visited their house at Brahmopally to practise singing for Durga Puja with Bhabani and Sisirkana. After they moved to High Wind, the two families would meet often and Sarat had come to regard Lakhan's sister as one of his own. But now, suddenly Lisimon seemed so different. With her neatly braided soft hair, her rounded face seemed much more attractive, the pink chequered jainsem on her shoulder adding a further shade to her already rosy complexion. In his mother's presence Sarat became a bit self-conscious and moved away from the piano. Lisimon stood up to leave. Haimavati felt that she should say something to deal with the situation and commented, 'The piano was lying idle and the house has been so empty ever since Bhabani left. You also have no time. So I asked Lisimon to come over and play. Her sister's children are learning on their piano and she does not get much chance to play there.'

'This tune sounds quite familiar. Where did you learn it?' Sarat asked.

'From my brother-in-law who is a pastor. It's a hymn played at church, a type of spiritual music like the ones sung by the Brahmos,' explained Lisimon.

Sarat escorted Lisimon to the door. 'These days I am seldom at home to play the piano. Please come and play whenever you wish.'

Once Lisimon left, Sarat had a sudden urge to go back to the piano which he hadn't touched in over a month since the entrance examinations. Now, he sat quietly on the piano stool for a few moments and then, slowly began to play Tagore's '*madhabilata dole*'. He felt a strange sensation as his fingers slid over the keys Lisimon's fingers had touched. Maybe it was that feeling which added a new sweetness to his music that evening. He played for quite a while with full concentration and once again the house was immersed in music. Haimavati listened as she worked, and felt that she had once again discovered a new rhythm in her life.

16

There was a festive atmosphere in the Bhatta household the day the entrance examination results were announced. Sarat had secured a first division. Padumi Baideu, Mahesh Goswami and several other well wishers came from Laban to congratulate the young man. Panchatirtha brought sandesh and chanar khurma from Morello's to entertain the guests. The mashimas and kakimas from Brahmopally came with their home-made sweets and Haimavati was overwhelmed by all the love and affection. She felt that these were the people who were really close to her heart and were her actual well-wishers. Without their support she would never have been able to overcome her sorrow and pull out Bhabani from such a disaster. Even as the celebrations were going on, Rabon Roy came and invited them over to his house to share his happiness – Lakhon had also cleared the exams with a second division. It was a special event for Keliyan Diengdoh's family because Lakhon was the first to clear the entrance examination.

The following evening the Bhatta family visited Keliyan's home. In the neat and tidy sitting room, polished wooden furniture had been tastefully arranged and there were white lace curtains on the windows. Several members of the Diengdoh family were gathered there, everyone enthused at Lakhon's success. Lisimon served the guests with cakes, pastries and doughnuts which she had brought from her sister's bakery. Everyone ate their fill and there was much praise for the food. As she picked up a sandwich, Haimavati was reminded of an old incident. With a smile, she told the story. 'When we were children, bread, cakes and biscuits were never allowed into a Brahmin house. Families which indulged in such things were derided as "sahib's family" and their girls usually faced problems in getting married. My father, who worked in Shillong, was fond of these delicacies but my mother never allowed them inside the house. Once, when father was taking us by steamer from Guwahati to Jorhat, he offered us slices of bread with butter. That was the first time that we tasted bread. At our Jorhat home when I tried to relate the incident about the pieces that were sliced and given to us on the steamer, mother would wink at me to keep quiet and I realised that what we had done was not really acceptable. But even after I grew up, the memory of that incident has stayed with me. In Shillong, my husband brought a loaf of bread home for the first time, I remember saying excitedly, "This is exactly the one which was cut into pieces and given to us on the steamer!"' All the guests were greatly amused. Panchatirtha joined in the laughter and added, 'If people from our village see us now, they would certainly say that the dark kali-yug is here.'

Keliyan nodded, 'Our people have newly learnt to eat cakes and biscuits. There was a time when rice was our main food, and with it went some vegetables and fish. But now our people have taken to the things eaten by the 'phareng' sahibs. We've also eagerly accepted their clothes, religion and language. I don't know whether this change is good or bad.' Keliyan looked at her grandchildren. The families of both her daughters had become Christian and she was aware of the tension between tradition and modern practices within her own larger family. She seemed to have a feel for the eventual outcome of all this. As the Khadduh or youngest daughter of her family, she knew that certain things were now out of her control and she had given up thinking about the possible changes that could affect the life of her youngest daughter, Lisimon. It was as if the wheel of time, after moving slowly for all these years, had suddenly picked up great speed. All this while, Kong Keliyan continued to cut her betel-nuts, keeping a loving eye on Lisimon who was busy serving the guests.

Panchatirtha wanted to send Sarat to Cotton College at Guwahati, but his son was not at all eager to go there. A college section had been recently added to the missionary institution at Lumawrie Hill and both Sarat and Lakhan had gained admission to the Intermediate class there. Most of the teachers in the college were Irish missionaries, though there were also a few Indians in the faculty. Sarat was quite happy with the environment of the college. The neatly kept green college compound also had enough scope for games and sports. The Irish brothers taught their pupils with great earnestness and paid special attention to the personality growth of their students. Of all the teachers in the college, it was Brother McBryde that Sarat liked best. This young missionary with blue eyes and golden hair was deeply involved in all matters relating to the college. He taught English literature and history in the Intermediate class. On the days he took history lessons, he would come to the classroom much before his students and draw a detailed map of the period of study on the blackboard. In the school division Brother McBryde taught geography and there too the students would often try to copy his maps in their notebooks. Sarat especially liked Brother McBryde's English literature classes. When he taught Shakespeare, he would get the students to enact roles and would also join in himself, picking out a character to play. He was easily at his best when he read out the dialogue of a particular character and got so carried away by it, that his students felt that he was that character personified! He had by heart most of the scenes of the play which he taught in class and kept a sharp eye on the expressions and pronunciation of his students. If someone's mode of expression was stiff, he would knot his fingers together and say, 'Your language is like these knotted fingers of mine. Please open up your fingers and your language will start flowing.' His students found this very amusing and they all tried to follow his instructions.

When he came to know of Sarat's interest in music, Brother McBryde took him into the college's cultural group. He himself was quite good at playing the violin. Once, during a cultural event at the college an English chorus was being presented, with most of the singers being British or Anglo-Indians. There were one or two Khasi boys as well. Brother McBryde accompanied the group on the violin and Sarat was on the piano. Following this, Sarat spent many evenings with Brother McBryde in the music room of the school. He soon learnt to play western classical music on his piano and also to read from the music book. It was during this period in his college days that Sarat became acquainted with the compositions of masters like Beethovan, Mozart, Chopin and Vivaldi.

On certain evenings Brother McBryde would go for walks with his huge Alsation and Sarat would accompany him. During their long walk from Laitumkrah to Mawkhar, they would discuss many things and, as they neared High Wind, Sarat would invite him to spend a few minutes in their house. But Brother McBryde always said goodbye with a smile because he seldom visited anyone. On one of these walks, Sarat asked him, 'Sir, what is the difference between the freedom struggle going on in your country and ours?' McBryde appeared a bit taken aback and said, 'Why do you ask?' Sarat didn't pay much attention to the somewhat quizzical tone of the response and continued casually, 'No real reason. I merely wanted to know if there is any similarity between the movement being led by Mahatma Gandhi in our country and that being led by De Valera in yours.' McBryde was quiet for a while. Then, gravely, he said, 'Both leaders are talking of a non-violent struggle. But if the opposing side tries to suppress the movement in a violent manner, it remains to be seen how far non-violence can be successful. Everyone knows how the British brutally killed our freedom fighters during the Easter 1916 rebellion. The same thing happened at Jallianwalla Bagh. You can see the reaction to it. Fires of revolt have sprung up everywhere.' Sarat noticed that McBryde's blue eyes were suddenly alight with the fire of revolt but, as he waited expectantly to hear something more from him, the missionary suddenly fell silent. Sarat realised that Brother McBryde was no longer interested to extending the conversation. The nation's political situation was passing through a difficult phase and the missionaries always avoided discussing political issues with their students in college. The students simply had no idea of the inner world of these men committed totally to the mission of education and Sarat was naturally a bit surprised at Brother McBryde's political outburst that evening. It was only a few months later that Sarat came across a rather strange piece of news.

One evening as Banamali Panchatirtha was talking to his wife about something he had heard in his office, Sarat found himself listening intently from the adjacent room.

'Today I heard from Kalita who works at the IGP's office that the revolutionary leader from Ireland De Valera was recently in Shillong. The Irish brothers of Sarat's college had invited him over and also arranged for a felicitation programme. The students, however, were kept out of it.'

'Why did the Irish revolutionary come here?' Haima always wanted to understand everything fully.

'He came to India to meet Mahatma Gandhi. I don't know why he came to Shillong. Perhaps he was invited by his countrymen here.'

Sarat now understood why Brother McBryde was so taken aback by his question. But he found it quite thrilling that, unknown to all of them, De Valera had visited their college.

It appeared that the freedom movement being led by Mahatma Gandhi had not had much effect on the students of Shillong. Most students at Sarat's college came from an affluent background and were quite indifferent towards political agitations and revolutionary activities. A small number of Assamese, Bengali and Khasi students, however, discussed the national movement among themselves and they were much enthused when Subhas Chandra Bose, staying at Ashley Hall by the Ward's Lake, addressed several meetings in the town. And when, to everyone's surprise, Brother O'Leary invited Bose to his college, there was palpable excitement among the students and the faculty. Sarat and several other students welcomed Subhas Bose at the college gate with a garland of blue forget-me-not flowers and that evening, the students were greatly stirred by Bose's speech. He told them how the British had dubbed him a terrorist and sent him to Mandalay jail where his health broke down; how, following his release, he was treated back to health in Shillong by Dr Bidhan Chandra Roy.

Four months in Shillong's beautiful natural surroundings had restored him, he said. Towards the end of his speech he jokingly asked the students, 'Do I really look like a dreaded terrorist?' Bose thanked the Irish Brothers and told the audience, which consisted not only of the teachers and students but of several leading personalities of the town, that the Irish revolutionary De Valera was a friend of his and of how the Indian freedom movement had been inspired by the Irish struggle.

The immediate effect of Subhas Chandra Bose's magnetic personality and his speeches in Shillong was the birth of several small radical groups among the Bengali population of the town. But their radicalism was confined solely to heated discussions held within the confines of home and they never took to the streets to make a point. Sarat, Lakhon and many other young men were proud to have a leader like Subhas Bose and they felt that he alone could provide true leadership to the country. For them, the other Congress leaders lacked the courage and determination needed to snatch freedom from the British and guide the country's future; it was in Bose alone that they discovered the qualities needed for true leadership of a nation like India.

The discussions at Brahmopally, the revolutionary poems and songs, the contact with underground activists hiding in different houses and the play of new ideologies, all created a turmoil in Sarat's mind. New ideas about freedom, justice, equality and the nation's resurgence were beginning to take on romantic hues and, inspired by Tagore's *Chandalika* and the Ashok Kumar-Devika Rani starrer *Achyut Kanya*, Sarat too imagined for himself a role in the greater struggle to establish a society free of untouchability and caste. He had a vague idea in his mind that if every conscious individual protested against injustice, a more equal and just society would come into being; that revolutionary change would automatically follow if every citizen vehemently protested social wrongs. In line with Shelley's *Prometheus Unbound*, Sarat seemed to believe that in the long run evil would destroy itself and the edifice of social prejudice would finally collapse. The world would become a beautiful place once people were ready to welcome the new and accept change. Idealistic young men like Sarat were yet to realise that a different sort of organisational preparedness was needed to bring about revolutionary change and perhaps because of this, they were not attracted to the movement led by Gandhi. In any case, most of the hill areas of the northeastern region, Shillong included, were virtually untouched by the freedom struggle. Assam's capital city wore a quiet look even during the height of Gandhi's non-violent struggle. Its government employees kept themselves scrupulously away from any anti-government talk, although in a few Bengali houses belonging to small businessmen, young men and women who shared the Congress or Communist ideologies would gather in secret to debate on the means to be adopted to throw the British out of the country. When at Brahmopally, Sarat and Bijoy would sometimes quietly listen to the heated political arguments of certain guest-relatives of Labanyaprava and Saradamoni. However, because they were so young, they were kept out of these discussions and they too, on their part, were happy not to be involved, preferring their role as listeners.

It was only after he joined college that Sarat became acquainted with terms like 'freedom', 'liberty' 'equality' and 'fraternity' and was quite excited at understanding them. But when Brother McBryde discussed the French Revolution in class, Sarat couldn't really link these new ideas to the freedom struggle that was going on in his own country. For him, these abstract ideas of his imagination seemed to have little relevance to the actual state of affairs in his homeland. He was quite worried when he first heard of Gandhi's non-violent resistance to British law. Wouldn't such violation of the laws of the land lead to chaos and instability? But, the Irish revolt led by De Valera did not give rise to such apprehensions in his mind. On the contrary, the revolutionary call from a distant land inspired him. Though Sarat was fond of singing revolutionary songs, yet when it came to the immediate situation surrounding him, he somehow always avoided the company of activists and revolutionaries.

17

The same year in which Sarat and Lakhon passed their Intermediate examination, Lisimon secured a first division in her Matriculation Examination from the Lady Keane School. Both the results were announced within a few days. Streams of people started visiting Kong Keliyan's house to congratulate Lisimon on her success and once again packets of cakes and pastries began pouring in from Helimon's bakery. Even as these celebrations were going on, news came of Sarat and Lakhon's success in the exams. Both of them had been placed in the first division. The two families were now full of happiness and in a celebratory mood. Lots of Assamese visitors from Laban, Rilbong and Laitumkrah turned up at Panchatirtha's house. Almost everyone had the same suggestion to offer – there were plenty of vacancies in the government offices where Sarat could be absorbed. One day, after all the excitement had died down and the number of visitors petered off, a despondent Sarat was sitting in his friend Lakhon's house. Lakhon wasn't at home and Keliyan, seated on a stool by the fireplace, was busy knitting. Sarat seemed to be quite sad and worried, Keliyan asked him, 'Why, what's the matter? Are you upset over something? Any news of Bhabani?' Sarat promptly answered, 'Yes, she's fine Amoi.' Haima had taught her children to address Keliyan as their Amoi. Lisimon and Lakhon too called Haima Amoi and

addressed the fathers as Tawoi, these being the Assamese forms
of address meant for the friends of one's parents. 'Next year
Bhabani will also take the Matric Examination. She now plays
the sitar quite well and also sings,' said Sarat with a tinge of
pride in his voice. 'That's really fine. It is good for the family
if the girls sing and dance and are happy. Darkness descends
on a house if they are sad and dejected', said Keliyan as she
placed the knitting needles and ball of wool on her lap and
poked the fire with a chimney rod. Instantly, the flames leapt
up and brightened the room. Lisimon arrived with three cups
of tea on a tray and offered a cup to Sarat. Then she pulled up
a murha and sat down beside her mother. Sarat noticed that
the light from the fire added an extra glow to her rosy cheeks.
He regarded Lisimon for a while, then said rather abruptly,
'God knows what Bhabani will do when she returns home after
her exams.' Mother and daughter looked at him in surprise.
Then, her mouth full of tamul-paan, Keliyan laughed out loud
and said, 'Once the girl comes back, the entire feel of the
house will change. She will have to take full responsibility of
everything along with Haima and Sonamon. And, when your
parents grow old, it is she who will be their companion, just
like our Lisimon.' Sarat didn't say anything He quietly sipped
his tea and then stood up to leave. Lisimon escorted him to
the gate and then announced softly, 'Sarat, I am going to work
from tomorrow.'

'Work? What work?' Sarat looked at her in astonishment.

Lisimon looked him in the eye, gave him a gentle smile
and replied, 'It's a job I'd love to do. I will be working at the
Ri Khasi Press which was set up by Babu Jibon Roy. Babu
Jibon Roy's daughter also works there. It was from that printing
press that Jibon Roy brought out the first Khasi newspaper

U Khasi Minta. Now his son, Sibcharan Roy is bringing out another paper. I will be looking after that.'

Sarat tried to take her words seriously and said, 'The Khasi people have only just started reading newspapers, right? But will they accept the news published in these papers?'

'You are right. They may be new to reading. But for generations they have been accustomed to carrying the spoken word from place to place.' Suddenly Lisimon plucked a small fragrant flower from a nearby bush and waved it under Sarat's nose. 'Do you know the name of this flower?' When Sarat shook his head in surprise, she laughed and said, 'Even this little flower spreads the news of its fragrance among the people. That's why it's called Pathai Khubor, which means the sender of news!'

'What a beautiful name! Just like an Assamese or Bengali name, Khabar Pathai or sender of news,' Sarat responded enthusiastically. He wanted to know more about this from Lisimon and asked, 'Babu Jibon Roy was a very progressive person, wasn't he? How many persons are there in Assam who, like him, really think about employment for women?'

'One can go on and on about all that Babu Jibon Roy did. It's quite baffling how one person can do so many things in a single lifespan,' replied Lisimon, who was now sitting on a roadside slab of stone. That evening she told Sarat about the many aspects of the life of Jibon Roy and the social movement he had initiated. Sarat had heard some of this from his Khasi friends. He also knew that the Government High School where he and Lakhon studied had been founded by Babu Jibon Roy. But listening to Lisimon's account on that bright moonlit evening carried a different kind of joy. Lisimon continued to speak about how Jibon Roy, who was born at Sohra, had tried so hard to bring about economic and social changes among the Khasi people. 'It's amazing that this man studied Sanskrit, Bengali and English books and translated quite a few into Khasi and had them published. He also wrote several books in Khasi to help lay readers understand their culture and religion. We still have two of these and our mother reads passages from these to us sometimes. When the British decided to move the capital from Sohra to Shillong, it was Babu Jibon Roy who was their principal advisor in setting up this beautiful town. On his own initiative, Jibon Roy had started coal mining at Sohra but he faced a lot of resistance from a 'ferang' named Henri Inglish who tried all sorts of intrigues to take down his business. But incidentally during the great earthquake of 1897 all the mines belonging to Inglish Company were destroyed while Jibon Roy's mines remained intact. This resulted in Jibon Roy securing near monopoly over the coal trade and he made massive gains from this. Strange are the ways of God, aren't they?' asked Lisimon as she looked up at the clear blue sky.

'But I believe that if a person does not put in his own effort, then God really can't be of much help,' Sarat responded in his usual rational manner.

'Maybe you are right after all. It wasn't in Babu Jibon Roy's nature to sit idle in the hope that someone else would help. I have heard my father say that after the 1897 earthquake when all the brick and mortar houses in Shillong were instantly reduced to rubble, a British official went to visit Babu Jibon Roy. He found him sitting in the midst of the ruins of his house holding a piece of paper on which was written, 'Try once again'.

'He certainly was a Renaissance man in the true sense of the word. But the Assamese people know so little about this man who belonged to their own province,' said Sarat in a tone of regret.

'What is the Renaissance?' asked Lisimon.

'I'll tell you about it some other day,' said Sarat. Idly, he picked up a pine cone from the ground and threw it far away. 'Your society is so good. A person can do whatever one wishes. But in societies like ours, our choice is so restricted! Either you take up a government job or become a teacher.'

Lisimon placed her hand on his shoulder and affectionately asked him, 'What would you really like to do?' Sarat did not reply. Her very touch made him forget everything. In the distant hills, rows of fires had been lit by some peasants preparing for jhum cultivation. Placing his hand momentarily on Lisimon's, Sarat looked at her face. The play of the evening light and shadow seemed to add an air of mystery to her. She appeared so ethereal to him. Embarrassed, Sarat quickly removed his hand and said, 'Well, one day I will tell you about my dreams. Bye for now.' He left quickly, but the memory of her touch continued to linger.

Sarat was so engrossed in thought that he didn't even notice that instead of taking the road home, he'd turned in the opposite direction and was now walking towards Burra Bazaar. The traders had already shut shop and were returning home. Sarat walked down a flight of stairs by the side of the now silent bazaar and then turned right to take a narrow winding lane upwards. He joined a stream of Khasi men and women with their conical bamboo baskets called thapas full of fish and vegetables, moving up the narrow, winding road through the pine wood towards Laban. Sarat could recognize some of them. These traders would set up shop at Laban's small triangular 'batti bazaar' from where office-goers returning from work in the evening would buy their fish and vegetables. Finally, Sarat too reached Laban. Not sure why he had taken this path, he now suddenly started climbing the uphill road towards Brahmopally. He felt like spending some time at Subarna mashi's place, which was always filled with guests. Whether it was a jalsa, a kirtan session or a political discussion, something or the other was always going on in that house. As he stepped onto the wooden verandah of the house, Sarat could hear a large number of voices inside. When he pushed open the door he could see several persons of the locality seated there in front of a new radio-set, listening to the news and talking animatedly. The moment she saw Sarat, Subarna mashi warmly welcomed him and then, pointing to the radio, said, 'Haven't you heard the news? The Second World War has begun.' Sarat noticed that the news of the war had agitated the entire audience. Would the British be able to win this war? What would be the position of the Congress leaders? A few of those present boldly asserted that they were privy to news that the Congress would take advantage of the situation and fan a revolt within the army so as to drive the British out of the country. Netaji's supporters vehemently opposed this, saying that no one but Netaji could really achieve such a feat. Instantly the discussion veered round to Subhas Bose's valour and leadership. Meanwhile, someone commented, 'This is really dangerous news,' and at once everyone started speculating on the terrible consequences of what had happened. In the midst of all this, Subarna mashi's voice could be heard lamenting the sudden disappearance of sugar, flour and cooking oil from the market. 'What will happen to us now?' With this, the conversation changed course and people started discussing the different ways in which essential foodstuff could be stored for the future. A Bengali babu sitting next to Sarat chipped in, 'One shouldn't be concerned only about the horrible consequences of such a war. Let's not forget that there is also another side to it. The government will now need lots of contractors to supply food for the army. There will also be plenty of new jobs because the army will recruit a lot of young men as officers through the short service commission. We should take advantage of all this. Else, others will grab the opportunity.'

As he walked home, Sarat's head was full of the events of the evening. He wondered what he should do in such a situation. The idea of being a contractor did not appeal to him at all and he dismissed it right away. But that of joining the short service commission and becoming an officer in the army seemed to somewhat excite him. Till then he hadn't thought at all about the terrible ordeals of the war front. But the image of the British army officers in the streets of Shillong, their smart uniforms and self-confident looks suddenly seemed to inject a new alertness to his steps. Unaffected by the cold breeze biting into him, Sarat almost ran down the slope of the Laban hill. And, as he raced down, he noticed that the crescent moon accompanied by the evening star was shining brightly in the western horizon. Venus looked so big and bright that he wondered if the planet, which seemed heavy with so much light, would really be able to continue hanging in the sky and not plunge into the hills. Then, all of a sudden, Lisimon's face lit up before him and he could feel once again the thrilling sensation of the very special evening that he had spent with her.

18

Banamali Panchatirtha's job tenure was finally drawing to a close. His main worry these days was how the family would manage on his paltry pension, especially since prices of all essential commodities had shot up because of the War. Meanwhile Bhabani had returned home after finishing her Matriculation at Shantiniketan. Her younger sister, Gauripriya, would be taking her Matric examination from the Jail Road School in two years' time and Bijoy had just joined the Intermediate class at college. It was Panchatirtha's wish that both the boys take up jobs to help the family. He had full confidence that Sarat would do well in his BA and take upon himself the responsibility of the house. He had wanted to send him to Cotton College at Guwahati for his graduation. But Sarat was adamant about not leaving Shillong. He argued that going to Guwahati wouldn't really help his studies, especially since the freedom movement was in full swing and plenty of school and college students were getting involved in it. Quite a few of them had even left college to join in the satyagraha and had been sent to prison. He told his father that in such a situation he would never be able to complete his studies in Guwahati. Panchatirtha pondered over his son's arguments. He too would be retiring within a year or two and all of them would be in a fix if Sarat was unable to complete his graduation by then. Hence, it was decided that Sarat would do his BA from the same missionary college where he studied for his Intermediate. However, it was about his younger son that Panchatirtha was starting to have some doubts and he wasn't too happy with him. He had observed the change that was taking place in this handsome young man who always happened to take the lead in everything. Earlier, he was enthusiastically involved in the activities of the Asom Sangha and had been a leading member of the cultural troupe organized by Maheswar Goswami. He had excelled as a satriya dancer and had won accolades for his acting skills. But now he preferred to keep to himself, spending most of his time in a corner in his room, reading. And, if someone entered, he would instantly try to hide what he was reading. Some days he came back home really late and always gave the excuse that he has busy with 'some urgent work'. Panchatirtha's mind was filled with worry and he kept wondering whether his son was going astray.

One evening, on his return from office Panchatirtha saw that none of his children was home. He asked his wife in some irritation, 'Well, it seems the children have stopped coming home in time. Have you been keeping track of where they've gone?' Haimavati folded up her work at the loom and quickly made some tea for her husband. She poured a cup for herself as well and came and sat beside him. 'Everyone is busy with their own work. Sonamon has a dance performance at the school's annual function and Bhabani has been guiding the group. She will sing a Tagore song for that dance and they've both gone to rehearse. They should be back soon. As for Sarat, he has gone out to talk to one of the Brothers.

'But where has Sarubaapu gone?' Panchatirtha asked with some anxiety. Haimavati was silent for a while and then said in a measured tone: 'He 's gone to a meeting, he said he would be late.'

'What meeting? Has he joined the freedom movement?' Panchatirtha sounded quite worried.

'I don't think so. I think he is with some other party. They are not with the Congress. They have joined a new party called the Communists,' Haimavati calmly replied.

'He told you all this? Why doesn't he talk to me? Had I known, I would have prevented this. Do you know what the Communists really are?'

There was despair and anguish in Panchatirtha's words. But Haimavati could see that this was not really anger but the claim of a father to a son and his doings. All these years, Pachatirtha had kept himself busy with his studies and his official work, leaving the entire responsibility of running the house and looking after the children's education to Haimavati. He considered his duties were fulfilled once his daughter had been married and his sons' upanayan had taken place. Now, especially after the failure of Bhabani's marriage, he had increasingly left it to his wife to decide on almost everything. It was as if that evening he suddenly realized that it would be wrong to let his sons go astray. Yet, he was a bit reassured by what Haima had said – after all they hadn't gone out of their mother's control. Meanwhile Haima continued calmly, 'I'm sure that Sarubaapu will not do anything wrong. They are just thinking for the good of the poor and the impoverished, for people whose lives revolve around the sickle and the sheaves of grain. They feel that once the nation achieves independence, these people must get their rights. It seems there is no divide between the rich and the poor in Russia where everyone has equal rights.'

Panchatirtha looked at his wife in sheer astonishment. Was it possible that this quiet and composed lady dressed in a muga riha-mekhala had also turned Communist? He had heard about the Communist ideology but had never deeply thought about it. Now that these ideas had finally entered his own home, he was forced to confront them. He observed Haima's composure and said, 'Since he has confided in you, it is you who should keep an eye on him – where he goes, what he does, who his friends are.'

'I don't know much about all this. But I know that a young person called Hemango Biswas has formed a people's cultural group whose aim is to spread revolutionary ideas among the masses through dance, music and plays, they go from one end of Assam to the other. These days the songs that Sarubaapu sings are about revolution, the rights of the proletariat and so on. Listening to them, one gets really affected,' Haima said, with some enthusiasm.

'Oh, okay now I know! The other day a Bengali babu in our office told me that a relative of his named Hemango Biswas is in Shillong because he has some kind of illness and is being treated by the well-known physician from Calcutta, Bidhan Chandra Roy at his bungalow at Kench's Trace. Since he is under Bidhan Roy's care, he is sure to recover,' said Panchatirtha, sounding a bit worried. Haimavati tried to change the course of the conversation and said, 'It seems all the great personalities of Calcutta are making a beeline for Shillong. Kabiguru Rabindranath has also been here several times. Whenever I pass Brookside, the house in Rilbong, I think of the poet. I wonder which poems he composed while staying in that beautiful place?'

'Many well-known people come here to spend the summer. Netaji, Swami Vivekananda, Sir Asutosh Mukherjee, all of them have been to Shillong to rest and recuperate. Asutosh Babu stayed for a few days at Norex, that house just behind the Pine Mount School built by Babu Jibon Roy. I remember going there to meet him,' Panchatirtha became thoughtful as he recounted the past.

Meanwhile, evening was advancing and Bhabani and Gauri, who had just returned from their rehearsal, switched on the newly fitted electric lights. A little while later Bhabani ran her fingers over the keyboard and played a tune as she started singing the Tagore number about the wild winds that stir the mind – *Pagla hawa, badal dine//Pagal amar mon neche uthe.* Outside, the clouds were racing madly across the sky and the swaying branches of the pines were creating their own music.

19

Haimavati had finished reading almost all the books in the library of the Asom Sangha. As it was, Assamese books were very short and she could easily finish a book while sitting in the library on Saturdays when the afternoons were quiet. But Bengali books, whether short or long, needed more time and attention. So, she brought these home and read them at leisure. One day while she was cleaning her son's room, she found a book tucked under Bijoy's pillow. It was in Bengali and was called *The Mother*. Glancing at the cover, she noticed an unknown name, Maxim Gorky. Must be some foreign author, she thought. Haimvati had read a few translations of books by foreign authors and found that many of the stories had plenty of similarity with happenings in her own country. That's why she picked up the book, apparently attracted by its title. Seated on a murha beside the azalea bush with its deep pink blossoms in the corner of their wide green lawn, she started reading the novel. In no time she was totally immersed in the story and for the next two days she searched for every opportunity to sit down with the book. The moment the others left the house, she would pick it up. Once, Bijoy returned from college earlier than usual and found his mother fully engrossed in reading. He smiled and quietly tip-toed up to her and then, placing his hand on her shoulder, whispered 'Mother'. Sarat and Bijoy normally addressed their mother as 'Bouti', although Bhabani and Sonamon called her 'Maa'. When Haimavati looked up, surprised, Bijoy laughed and said, 'It wasn't you. I was only calling out to Pavel's mother!' Haimavati gave an embarrassed smile and said with a tinge of hurt pride, 'It seems she is your real mother now. Who cares for a worthless one like me?' Bijoy warmly embraced his mother and said with a lot of emotion, 'Bouti, since you are enjoying reading Maxim Gorky's *The Mother*, you will now have to inspire all of us by being our true mother.'

'First of all, you must prove yourselves by doing some good work. Only then will we be able go forward with you.' This time, Haimavati asked her son about something that had been troubling her for a long time. 'Tell me, is it true that the Communists are supporting the great war and are siding with the British against Gandhiji? Why aren't you with the Congress volunteers who are following the path shown by Gandhiji to liberate our country?'

Bijoy was silent. Then he said, his tone soft. 'Many people have asked us the same question. At first, I didn't know much about the issue. Now I understand. The other day these things were discussed in one of our meetings. We have now decided to support the British in their war efforts because Germany's has attacked Russia, which means it is an attack by fascist forces on a Communist nation. Hence, all the Communists of the world will support the Allied Powers. Otherwise, fascism will crush all of us.'

'I don't understand all this,' said Haimavati. 'But don't you want to drive out the British and make our country free?'

'Why shouldn't we? Of course we want to drive out the British. But if Independence means the transfer of power from a set of imperialists to a set of capitalists, then there will be no freedom for the proletarian masses of the country. Independence and freedom have very wide connotations for us, Bouti. Just have a look at the leaders of the Congress ministry which is holding power under the British. All of them are zamindars or rich landholders and tea planters from the plains. These new capitalists are sitting here and dreaming of becoming kings in the future. They're not worried about either the working people of the plains, or the poor Khasi villagers here.' Bijoy's voice rose in excitement. Haimvati stood up and said, gently, 'That will do for now. Come and have your tea.'

She went to the kitchen and busied herself with the tea. She lit the flame and put the kettle to boil and watching the leaping flames, she became thoughtful for a moment. The other day her husband had talked of his retirement and asked her to keep an eye on the future of their children. Haimavati knew that her husband had unflinching faith in her ability to correctly guide their children. But her heart was full of doubt. Did she really have all that power? She was fully aware that as they grew up, each one of her children has developed his or her own personality. Would they really follow her advice? And, how much experience did she really have to understand their hopes and aspirations? Even then, Haima quietly resolved to tell Sarat about his father's apprehensions and ask him to be ready to shoulder the responsibility of the family.

20

The customs and rituals of the ancient Khasi faith were scrupulously practised in Kong Keliyan's house before the family accepted Christianity. Gradually, these traditional practices came to be replaced by Christian festivals with Christmas being observed with great fanfare in the houses of both Keliyan's daughters. Every Sunday, dressed in their finest, they went to church with their families. However, in deference to her parents' wishes, Lisimon still continued to adhere to the old practices. Being the youngest daughter or Khadduh of the family, it fell on her to observe the family rituals. It was Kong Keliyan's wish that Lisimon should at least once represent her family at the annual Nongkrem dance festival. This, she felt, would greatly add to the family's prestige. Lisimon did not oppose her mother and prepared herself mentally to take part in the annual dance which was held with full religious fervour at a place called Smit.

The date of the Nongkrem festival was fixed every year by the Syiem or raja of Khyriem and the Syiem's messengers would announce it by distributing ringlets made of cane. Once the news reached the Diengdoh family, there was much commotion. Old gold and silver ornaments and the necklace made of large red payla beads were taken out and polished. Running her fingers over the beads, Keliyan fondly recollected her virgin days when she too had worn those beads to the dance. One by one she took out the valuable ornaments and clothes from a large wooden box and carefully placed them on the bed. The red blouse with a lace border around the neck now looked as if it would not fit Lisimon. The yellow jingpin too would have to be lengthened a bit while the jainsem made of muga silk which looked a bit old would have to be replaced by a new one. All the women of the Keliyan household now took upon themselves the responsibility to turn Lisimon into the most beautiful dancer of the world! Lisimon, who had never learnt such dances, was taught the steps by her mother. Keliyan told her daughter that this dance was an integral part of their religious tradition and had to be performed with a lot of devotion. Soon, Lisimon mastered the art of moving her feet according to the rhythm of the drums without ever lifting them from the ground.

The residents of High Wind caught the excitement in the Diengdoh family. Bhabani and Sonamon made it a point to visit their Amoi's house almost every day to check how the preparations were progressing. The borders of the dhara that Lisimon would wear would have to be done up in delicate fringe knots or dahis and the jainsem on her shoulders would have to match the length of the dhara. Haimavati took upon herself the job of preparing the dhara and she started doing the dahi bata during one of her visits to Keliyan. As the day of the festival drew close, the two families discussed how they would go to Smit. The boys decided that they would take the shorter route through the woods, while Panchatirtha, Rabon Roy and the women would go in two motor cars.

The Nongkrem festival was being held at Smit for three days. On the first day the Syiem of Khyriem, and his sister worshipped the goddess Ka Blei Synsha and after a goat was sacrificed, he and the priest and all his ministers, took part in the dance festival. On that day, homage was also paid to the ancestors. Throughout the following day, virgin girls and boys danced in groups and this continued till the evening. Although Sarat, Bijoy, Lakhon and their friends had started walking at daybreak, they reached the dance site at Smit just as the dance was about to begin. They could hear the sound of drums and the clanging of cymbals and the occasional shout of 'Ho-Kiyu' as they panted up the last hillock. When they reached the green clearing surrounded by small hills they saw several young maidens dancing to the rhythm of drums and the sound of pipes. The boys in their dhotis, coloured jackets and canvas shoes were each carrying a yak-tail whisk and dancing around the girls. At first glance, Sarat didn't even recognise Lisimon among the many decked up dancers and it was Lakhon who pointed her out to him. The muga dhara, the long-sleeved green coloured blouse, the gold and silver ornaments and the beads gleaming in the sun had added an almost ethereal air to her. She was wearing a small tiara on her head. Her shiny black hair was tied in a knot, with the loose silky ends hanging down to her shoulders. As her hair swayed to the rhythm of the dance, Sarat watched her, entranced. He had hoped that she would at least look up at them once as she passed the spot where they were seated. But she never raised her eyes even once, almost as if she feared some disaster would strike if she didn't stubbornly hold on to the ground with her feet and her eyes. Sensing Sarat's mood, Lakhon whispered into his ear 'Actually this dance is meant to invoke blessings for the earth. That's why the girls are praying with their eyes and the delicate movement of their feet is meant for the earth's fertility.' Sarat was silent. But he felt that in the midst of all the girls swaying and dancing to the rhythm of the drums, Lisimon herself was the Earth Goddess.

He wondered if he would ever again be able to talk to her with his earlier ease.

As the dance continued, a patch of dark cloud appeared as if from nowhere and released a shower of rain. Everyone opened their umbrellas and the family members rushed to protect the dancers from the rain. But the dance continued uninterrupted, as if the presence of the rain god in this worship of the earth was an anticipated event.

21

A few days after the Nongkrem dance festival, Lisimon joined the Intermediate Arts class at Lady Keane Girls' College. This was what her mother Keliyan wanted. Ever since she had learnt that two of Babu Jibon Roy's granddaughters had graduated from Lady Keane College, she'd decided that one of her girls too must pass the Bachelor of Arts examination from the same college. She was convinced that Lisimon would be able to bring laurels to the family. And it was out of question that anyone in the family would oppose Kong Keliyan's decision. However, Lisimon didn't like the idea of walking all that distance to college. The Lady Keane College was situated at the top of an isolated hillock in the cantonment area of the town and the road to the college was quite a lonely stretch from Police Bazar. LIsimon thought it would be good to have a friend for company on this walk and so she decided to convince Bhabani to join alongside her.

Haimavati was happy with Lisimon's proposal. She felt that if she could put Bhabani in college, it would take a big load off her mind. Panchatirtha too didn't express any reservations. Since his daughter's return from Santiniketan, he'd been worried about her future. Yet, at no time did he give serious thought to working out something for her. Now, it looked as if her life was about to take a different turn. Panchatirtha thought that if Bhabani was able to get a job as a teacher, all his worries would end. No one even tried to find out if Bhabani had some dreams of her own and everyone seemed glad that she would now be going to college with Lisimon.

There were very few girls in the college, and most of them belonged to the Bengali families of Brahmopally. Bhabani seemed to know almost everyone. When she met her onetime neighbour, Nancy, Bhabani was struck by the change in her appearance. Unlike most Khasi girls, she was now quite tall and slim and her skin too had turned more fair and rosy. Her soft chestnut brown hair was trimmed short in a style resembling that of the Englishwomen around and although, like all Khasi girls, she was wearing a jainsem and a tamakhli, yet she looked like a foreigner. Lisimon explained this to Bhabani, 'Nancy's father was an Englishman. He returned to his country when both Nancy and her brother were quite small.' Bhabani replied, her tone tinged with pity, 'One feels so sad about them. Why didn't their father take them along with him?' LIsimon replied with some irritation, 'Why should they go and leave their mother behind? They've not had any problems living here with her. They are well off people. Their father also left quite a bit of money for them.' Bhabani quickly realized that it was best to avoid such a conversation with Lisimon because her view seemed quite different. But she planned to discuss it later with her mother.

One evening, while sitting by the chimney-side and knitting along with her mother, Bhabani broached the subject of Nancy. She told her mother what Lisimon had said. Haimavati was silent for a while and then stirring the coal fire with the iron poker said, as if to herself, 'Here there are plenty of children like Nancy. Some have English fathers while others have fathers who are Assamese, Bengali or from other plains communities. But irrespective of who the father is, the mother's family takes great care of the children and brings them up with love. All the women come together to do this. Had this happened in our own community, the wife and the children would have had a hard time.' Bhabani pondered over her mother's words and then said, 'In that sense, Khasi society is a really good one. But is it right for the men to go away and leave the entire responsibility of the family to the women?' Bhabani's question made her mother realize that her daughter's state of mind had undergone a major change. She had developed the power to think for herself. It was as if Haima had finally found in her daughter someone with whom she could now share her thoughts. The many questions in Bhabani's mind had brought the mother and daughter much closer. Looking at her daughter's face, radiant in the firelight, Haima said, 'Well, this seems to be the way of the world. It is the women who have to carry the burden of the family. But it is the outsiders who have created all these problems in Khasi society. I think their own menfolk are not like that.' Haima was thinking of Keliyan's family where all the work was shared equally by both men and women. Still, it was a sad fact that the burden was always so much heavier for the women.

Haimavati also discussed these matters with her husband. Things which she could not speak freely about with Bhabani, she confided in Panchatirtha. In turn, Panchatirtha would often astound her with his stories of how several well respected seniors of the Assamese community had relations with Khasi women, had fathered children with them and had set up families in Shillong, all on the sly. Subsequently they had given up their Khasi wives and were happily married to Assamese women. But even after this, the Khasi women seldom made claims on these men. Sometimes though, if a Khasi child recognized their father on the street and called out to him, 'U pa', these heartless men would quickly move away. It was possible that these men often helped their Khasi families with money but they never accepted the offspring as their own. When she heard these stories, Haimavati forgot her usual self-restraint and often spoke out. 'One gets really disgusted with one's own people. Were our men not ashamed of cheating like this? It is the strength of Khasi society that it can so easily accept those we consider illegitimate. But one day when these children will grow up and come to know the identity of their fathers, won't their minds be filled with hatred and bitterness towards our people?'

Panchatirtha listened to Haimavati's outburst with his head bowed and said, in agreement with her, 'The Assamese here haven't given serious thought to all this. This is one of our greatest weaknesses. We seldom think about the future. Just see, so many people have come from the plains to work here. Yet the unparalleled beauty of this place has made no impression on their minds. Nature has with an open heart poured out all her bounties here and our people have taken full advantage of it. Yet, they have not given back anything in return. Rather, we have failed to give due respect to the original inhabitants of this place.'

Haima now spoke of the Bengali community. She had noticed that the men and women of Brahmopally spoke Khasi fluently, while the Assamese residents of Laban restricted themselves to using just a few Khasi words in the marketplace. However, not knowing even these few words would not have been a problem for them because the Khasi shopkeepers had, for their own convenience, created a language which was a mix of Assamese, Bengali and Hindi and transactions were easily carried out in this.

'The Bengali Brahmos have been done a lot of social work in the Khasi Hills. Apart from Shillong and Cherrapunji, they've worked hard in the interior areas to spread education and make medical treatment available to the villagers. That was how they gained some mastery over the Khasi language. From a much earlier time, the Brahmos have been involved in much the same work that the Christian missionaries are doing now with the support of the government. But the Brahmos never got any help from of the government, nor will they in the future,' said Panchatirtha.

'But even if the work of the Brahmos has now come to a stop, institutions like the Ramkrishna Mission will continue with their welfare activities, won't they?' Haima asked.

'You are right. The effect of Swami Vivekananda's lecture at Quinton Hall here can still be seen among the Khasis. A lot of people were attracted to his ideas and work when they read the editor Haramurari Diengdoh's write-up in *U Khasi Mynta*.'

Haimavati thought for a while and then, as if speaking to herself, said, 'If the Bengali Brahmos could draw so close to the Khasis, why haven't we? The other day Kong Keliyan told me that at the Brahmo mandir near our house at Mawkhar, the services were once conducted by a Khasi gentleman. I wonder why our own religious institutions haven't been able to do any good work among the Khasis?'

This time there was a note of despair in Panchatirtha's voice, as if he was remembering some of the bitter experiences of his life. 'Actually, our Assamese people are hesitant to share their ideas among other people. They lack the missionary zeal of the Bengalis or the Christian missionaries. If any one of us attempts something new, he faces a lot of ridicule and is prevented from going ahead. But in the case of the Bengalis, if one thinks differently and tries to chart out a separate path, scores of others will join in. One always encourages the other to embark on something new and out of the ordinary. This is not to say that there is no sense of rivalry amongst them. But it is not as dangerous and self-defeating as ours.'

22

There weren't many students in Sarat's BA class and, barring a few, he happened to know most of his teachers. There were several Bengali professors and most of them were highly qualified, with degrees from Calcutta or Dacca. The college campus stood adjacent to its school section which was run by the same missionary organisation. Although Sarat never had the chance to read in that elite school, every time he walked through its pine-covered grounds on his way to college, he felt a sense of excitement. In the distance, he'd often see schoolboys playing cricket or at their drills, with a priest in a spotless white habit instructing them. Sarat's only link with the school was Brother McBryde. He was the one who had introduced him to the piano teacher of the school, Mr Pinto. McBryde taught history in the BA class and that was why Sarat had chosen to do an Honours degree in that subject. After classes, Sarat would often go to the school's music room and listen to Mr Pinto on the piano. At times, Mr Pinto would take note of the young man sitting patiently beside him and ask him to play a piece from the music book while he played a different octave. These were really precious moments for Sarat. On some days, he would take a sheaf of music sheets home with him and try the notes on his own piano.

One evening Sarat was fully engrossed in playing a western tune which he had recently leant, when Lisimon entered the room. She stood behind him, silent, listening. When he finished, Sarat got up to close the lid of the piano when Lisimon softly said, 'What wonderful music! Whose composition is it?' Sarat handed the music sheet to her, 'Beethovan's sixth symphony in F major. It is also called the "Pastoral". I am trying to play just the first movement. There are four movements in all and you need a symphony orchestra to play it in full. Nowadays one can listen to such symphony orchestras on gramophone records.'

Lisimon was lost in the world of music. 'This is divine music! All of nature – the plants and trees, clouds and hills – seems to be dancing to its melody. Perhaps, it was after listening to such music that Robi Thakur wrote his song *anandadhara bahise bhubane* – the stream of happiness is flowing through the whole universe.'

'Will you sing that song?' Sarat entreated.

'No, no. These days I hesitate to sing Rabindra sangeet because I can't pronounce the words correctly. Only when I listen to Bhabani singing, do I realize my mistakes. She is the best singer in the college and even the Bengali girls can't match her.'

Bhabani, Sonamon and Bijoy came into the room. Bhabani was already humming the *anandadhara* song and she coerced Lisimon to sing, with Sonamon also joining in. All three then sang that song of happiness and Haimavati, who was in her room stitching something, listened to it spellbound. Bhabani's deep voice seemed to have emerged from the very depths of the ocean while Lisimon's resembled that of a rippling, playful stream. Yet, both the voices perfectly merged into one unified whole, the cadence rising and falling with equal and wondrous ease.

The moment the song was over, Bijoy applauded. 'Excellent! You all will have to sing this song at our cultural evening which will be held at the Opera Hall. Saratda will play the harmonium and we'll ask Parthada to accompany him on the tabla.' In an instant, Bijoy finalized his plans. The People's Theatre Association was having a programme in Shillong where some leading singers from the plains would participate. Several boys and girls belonging to the Shillong Progressive Youth Club would also join the event which would be dedicated to the memory of the great Khasi martyr, U Tirot Singh.

The following days were taken up with Bijoy's endless enthusiasm and the joyful participation of High Wind's residents who loved music. Bhabani and Lisimon rehearsed the *anandadhara* song several times till it was perfect. Sonamon and two other girls kept themselves busy with the dance item called mukti which was being taught by Labanyaprava at her Brahmopally house. There was an infectious energy among the young boys and girls. The members of the People's Theatre group were engaged day and night in rehearsing, making posters and finalizing arrangements to receive the guests from the plains. The job of drawing the posters fell on Bijoy as his skills were already known among his peers. He captured the scenic beauty of Shillong on large sheets of art-paper, and added the date and venue of the programme in his neat handwriting. These were displayed in key places in the town. The arresting visuals attracted large numbers of people.

On the day of the programme there was quite a crowd at the Opera Hall in Police Bazaar. Assamese, Bengali, Khasi and other communities came together to enjoy that melodious evening. The artistes who had come from the plains happened to be friends of Hemango Biswas. The most talented among them was Prashanta Hazarika. This young man had won the hearts of the audience with his own compositions which he put to music. That evening, as Bhabani and Lisimon were presenting *anandadhara*, Prashanta was outside the hall, smoking and talking with some of his friends. The moment he heard the song, he snuffed out his cigarette and stood still. Then he pushed his way into the hall through the crowded entrance and stood where he could see the singers. He saw Sarat was next to him. 'Who is that girl with the bass voice? I haven't heard such a striking voice in a long time.' Bijoy replied with some pride, 'She's my sister, Bhabanipriya. She has learnt music from Kabiguru Robi Thakur at Santiniketan.' Prashanta continued to listen to the song, entranced. On the floodlit stage, Bhabani in her golden muga riha mekhala and Lisimon in her muga jainsem looked stunningly beautiful.

The song ended and the hall resounded with several rounds of applause. Prashanta Hazarika was heard saying loudly, 'This is true music indeed! How well they have spread the strains of happiness and inspired everyone!' He put an arm around Bijoy and said, 'Let's go to the green room and congratulate the singers.' But Bijoy demurred, 'Not now, maybe later,' and he quickly moved away. Perhaps he thought Prashanta was being over enthusiastic.

23

Once the cultural evening was over, everyone who'd been involved in organizing it decided to go on a picnic. In Shillong any time of the year, barring the rainy season, could be picnic time and whenever guests from the plains turned up in Assamese and Bengali households, a picnic would invariably be arranged. Moreover, people didn't have to go far to seek out a picnic spot, there were many clean and beautiful places, full of trees, streams and lush green grass, within walking distance of most homes. Today though, the group decided to go to a slightly distant place in Upper Shillong and a bus was hired from Jamatullah, a businessman from Police Bazaar, to take the six families to their picnic spot. The residents of High Wind, Kong Keliyan, Lisimon and Lakhon from the Diengdoh family, Saradamoni, Labanyaprova and Suvarnaprova and their families from Laban's Brahmopally and Asom Sangha's Maheswar Goswami family all set out for Upper Shillong on a bright Sunday morning. When Prashanta Hazarika learnt that Bijoy, Sarat, Lakhon and Partha were busy preparing for the picnic, he joked, 'So you are all going on a picnic without me? But just wait, I'll turn up and embarrass all of you.' Ultimately, Prashanta Hazarika too was invited to join the group. After the Opera Hall event, Prashanta had stayed on in Shillong for a fortnight and was busy planning the awareness programmes the theatre group would conduct in the Brahmaputra and Surma valleys. During this time, he also composed and set to music several new songs.

A small bus from the Jamatullah Company collected the picnickers from different spots and then began its journey to Upper Shillong. It was a slow ride up the winding road lined with pine trees and since there weren't enough seats in the bus, the young boys congregated in the aisle. The bus was a redesigned version of an Albion vehicle from the time of the First World War. Its almost incessant rattle as it moved on its hard pneumatic rubber tyres only added to the fun of the picnickers. Those who were standing proved to be the most boisterous of the lot as they fell upon each other every time the bus swerved while taking sharp turns. Saradamoni and Labanyaprova's jokes and witty comments added to everyone's mirth.

The group finally alighted at a patch of green grassland near the upper Shillong Diary Farm. A rippling stream ran by its side and it was on its bank that preparations for the picnic began. Kong Keliyan and Haimavati stepped into the stream to wash the large fish they had brought from Bara Bazaar. As they pulled the fish out, they shouted, 'Look at the fish we've caught!' Instantly, everyone joined in the excitement and came forward to help in cleaning the fish. The women from Brahmopally had come prepared with home-made spicy condiments and soon they set about preparing a range of mouth-watering dishes.

Short walks in the nearby bridle-paths, improvised games and a late lunch took up most of the day which ended much sooner than expected. As the sun was about to go down, Prashanta started strumming a tune on his guitar. Lisimon exclaimed, 'Hey! That's a Khasi folk-tune. Where did you learn it?'

Prashanta replied with a smile, 'Well, I learnt it from the hill streams, the wild wind and the restless clouds.' Lisimon started humming the tune, and everyone asked her to sing. She smiled, and looked at her mother and said, 'My mother sings it much better.' At this Sarat pleaded, 'In that case, both Amoi and you sing it together. It will be so much better!' Kong Keliyan fixed her eyes on the distant hills and started to sing and Lisimon joined in with her soft voice, swaying to the rhythm: *Syntiew ka Ri Ri*. Prashanta's guitar suddenly took life and he started playing, totally engrossed in himself. Then, to the amazement of all, he followed this up with an Assamese song which he had composed and set to the same folk tune. Everyone was spellbound by the heart-touching melody and lyrics of the song. Bhabani found herself looking at Prashanta in wonder and admiration; he asked her to join him, 'Come, sing along with me!' For a moment Bhabani blushed in embarrassment. But by then Mita, Partha, Bijoy and all the others had already joined in the singing. Bhabani now responded to the irresistible pull of the folk song 'in full throated ease', as Keats would have said.

24

When High Wind was being built, Banamali Panchatirtha wanted that each room should be bright and airy. So he had the house fitted with many windows. These beautifully designed windows with glass panes were made by Khasi carpenters who excelled in timber work. Though they gave the house an attractive face, Haimavati sometimes complained that it was quite a job to open and shut so many windows every day. Panchatirtha responded to her complaints with a smile, 'In the Sivasagar house there were just one or two wooden windows and during the rains when these were shut, it would be dark inside even at midday. In this house, once you open the windows, the rooms are flooded with air and light and even the clouds float in occasionally. With this, the mind also opens up. And, because of the glass panes, one can look into the outside world even when the windows are shut. Then, why do you complain?' Haima knew that her husband was right. She shared his view that a windowless house really cast a pall of gloom upon the mind. Some of the houses in Laban were like that, with just a few wooden windows. Those who stayed in them often argued that too much circulation of air within the house made things uncomfortable. Yet, whenever Haima visited those houses, she would always feel suffocated. Maybe, she thought, it was only a reflection of her mind, for she would often have a feeling of suffocation even while listening to the conversations that took place in these houses. She had always been in favour of an inclusive society where everyone would live in peace and harmony. But the people who had come from the plains of Assam had disrupted the social equations which existed earlier. Most of these newcomers had cocooned themselves within their caste prejudices and the superstitions they had brought along with them from their home towns or villages. Haima often wondered if her vision of an ideal society wasn't actually an illusion floating in the clouds.

Over a period of time things happened that made Haima quite bitter. By now, it was quite well known among the Assamese and Bengali communities of the town that Bhabani was a good singer. Prashanta Hazarika's praise had contributed to this. But all this had not affected Bhabani's amiable nature and whenever someone tried to praise her too much, she was always embarrassed, 'I was just an ordinary singer at Santiniketan. I still have a lot to learn.' Once Bhabani had been invited to sing at an event in the Asom Sangha. After discussing things with her brother, she decided to sing a number written and set to music by Prashanta. When she had finished rendering the song almost perfectly, a woman called Mrs Mahanta who was sitting near Haima commented: 'She has indeed sung very well. But some people always see only the faults. They insist that Bhabani's Assamese pronunciation has a Bengali touch – for instance, she pronounces the word "bis-sa" as "bishwa" with an extra stress. This, they say, doesn't sound right.' Then, lowering her voice, Mrs Mahanta whispered into Haima's ear, 'People are gossiping that Bhabani has been seen with Bengali boys these days. Such nasty people! They see only the dark side of everything!' Haima flushed in anger. She controlled herself and said, 'The person who has written this song insisted on that pronunciation. Prashanta Hazarika seems to be an Assamese.'

That evening, while walking with her family from Laban to Mawkhar, Haima was unusually silent. Her mind was filled with worrisome thoughts even as she felt the fervour in the voices of Sonamon and Bhabani. Would they be able to save themselves from all this dirty gossip, she wondered. Or would they be eventually finished while fighting the many crocodiles that teemed in the river of life?

25

Two years passed by. Sarat graduated and left college, Bijoy
passed his IA examination, and began teaching in a Middle
English school at Mawkhar. He had no wish to do his BA and
wanted to do something else. But he had no idea of what it was
and how he would do it. For the time being, however, he was
content to be a part of the cultural centre run by Maheswar
Goswami. That kept him quite busy. He also liked to paint
and was drawn to the work of an artist from Brahmopally who
spent hours alone in lonely spots in and around Shillong trying
to capture with brush and paint the beauty of the place. He
painted life-like portraits of people and reproduced nature on
his canvas, and the locals began to call him the 'creator'. Bijoy
sometimes visited the artist's makeshift studio in a small room
and was captivated by the beauty of his canvases. The artist too
encouraged Bijoy and explained to him the different techniques
of painting and the method of working with oils and water
colours. He also taught him how to prepare a canvas and said,
'One cannot become an artist merely by gaining mastery over
technique. Painting a picture and writing poetry is the same – a
complete painting is the result of the maturity of one's ideas.'
Bijoy listened intently to what he said and tried to understand
every word. One day he came across his artist friend at the
Shillong-Guwahati bus station. He was carrying a small suitcase

and on his shoulder was slung the familiar bag with his painting material. He told Bijoy, 'I am leaving for Calcutta. There is no inspiration left for me to paint. There are very few people here who can appreciate or understand art and most refer to my paintings as photos! And my family wants me to take up a job and earn a regular income.'

'But is there anyone in Calcutta who can help you?'

'No, there isn't anyone there who can take care of my daily needs. I will have struggle to survive. But it is through struggle that an artist finally arrives. At least there I will get a wide world where my paintings will be appreciated.'

They said goodbye. Bijoy now began to think of his own future. Would he ever be able to take such a step towards a life of struggle? Would he ever be able to leave behind the enchanting surroundings of Shillong, the security of his home and everything else?.

And then one day, in a most unexpected manner, the idea of leaving home for a distant place cropped up for the most timid and quiet member of the family. Bhabani received an invitation from a gramophone company in Calcutta for a recording of a song to be included in an album of Assamese songs. Along with it there was another proposal. The Calcutta centre of the All India Radio had, in a separate communication, asked her to come for a voice audition. Obviously, it was Prashanta Hazarika who was behind both these moves. He had already got a job in the Calcutta radio centre and had set up house in that city. There was a third letter and it was from Prashanta. Together, these three letters threatened to upset the peaceful course of her life just as Bhabani, having cleared her exam, was settling into perfecting her singing skills. Prashanta's letter was directly addressed to Bhabani; he requested her not to decline the offers made by the gramophone company and the radio centre and assured her that he would make all arrangements for her stay in Calcutta. He added that she could ask Sarat or Bijoy to accompany her. It was a brief letter written in formal language but Bhabani's bewilderment while reading it did not escape Haima's notice. Everyone in the family read the three letters and they were happy for Bhabani. But it was Bijoy who knew that behind these proposals something else lay hidden. He remembered Prashanta telling him in a lighter vein after listening to Bhabani for the first time, 'I have fallen in love with your sister's voice.' He had not like that comment at all and had replied gravely, 'Prashantada, your love is a precious thing. So please do not bestow it just on a voice.' A surprised Prashanta had then replied, 'Why? Do you think that my love is not befitting for Bhabani? It certainly doesn't become a progressive youth like you to think on such caste lines.' This had instantly provoked Bijoy to speak at length on all the traumatic events in Bhabani's life. A shocked and surprised Prashanta had kept quiet for a while and then had said, 'It's just not possible to let a precious life like Bhabani's wither away like this. Let me see what I can do.'

Prashanta Hazarika would drop in at High Wind each time he visited Shillong and his presence, coupled with songs and music, added to the warm and friendly atmosphere of the house. He was greatly attracted by the openness of the family. Each person had a distinct personality and independent views which they aired easily. Beginning with Panchatirtha everyone including the youngest, Sonamon, actively participated in the political discussions and never hesitated to voice their opinions. Haimavati too was articulate about social transformation, women's rights and the many injustices women were subjected to. Prashanta often discovered shades of Rabindranath, Saratchandra or Tolstoy in Haimavati's statements and listened to her with wonder. She would wrap up her arguments in a few words and then move on to her housework. But Prashanta clearly felt that this woman had the capacity of gauging the minds of each of the persons present in the house.

Haimavati had learnt to see through a lot of things. She could sense Bhabani's attraction for Prashanta by how self-conscious she was while reading his letter. Seized by an unknown anxiety, she felt that she would never be able to forgive herself as a mother if she now pushed Bhabani towards another hazard, after having saved her from one. When she told her husband about her fears, Panchatirtha in his usual detached manner said, 'Don't you worry. Dharmaprabhu will always protect her.' Though she had often heard her husband refer to Dharmaprabhu, she had never asked him who he really meant by this. Yet she had observed that her husband, who never performed any religious rituals or took part in the worship of any deity, always spoke of Dharmaprabhu with great reverence.

Finally, the time arrived for a decision on Bhabani's trip to Calcutta. Sarat, who had always wanted to visit Calcutta, at once agreed to accompany her. But Haimavati, after some reflection, announced her verdict. She said that her husband would go with Bhabani to Calcutta because he had several friends and acquaintances in that city. Their stay could be arranged in one of their houses. Noticing Sarat's disappointment, she added, 'Barbapu can go some other time. Maybe we could fix for him to study for his MA in Calcutta.' In the end, everyone agreed with Haimavati's suggestion. But Haima continued to feel a bit disturbed and, as she packed Bhabani's things, she wondered whether she wasn't actually preparing once again to send her daughter away for good. In sending Bhabani to Santiniketan she had never thought like that. Haima steeled her mind and blessed Bhabani as she prepared to leave.

With good wishes from all, Bhabani and her father finally left for that city of dreams which had always beckoned multitudes of hopefuls. Some hopes were fulfilled, others aborted. Yet, everyone seemed to believe that once there, something positive was sure to happen.

26

A few days after Bhabani and her father had left for Calcutta, news came from Kong Keliyan's home that Rabon Roy had suddenly taken ill in his mother's place near Cherrapunji and was being attended to by doctors from the Ramakrishna Mission. His condition was not good, so Kong Keliyan, Lakhon and Lisimon hired a car and left immediately for Cherrapunji. It was after two days of anxious waiting that Haimavati and the family received the shocking news that despite all efforts by the doctors, Rabon Roy had passed away in his mother's home. A pall of gloom fell over High Wind as everyone felt helpless at the unexpected departure of a father-figure they had so loved and respected. No one could believe that such a sturdy and active person who was engaged in a variety of business and other activities and who had also spent a lot of time in reading and reflection, could leave this world so suddenly.

The cremation was followed by four days of ritual mourning and finally the bones and ashes of Rabon Roy were deposited in the mow-bah or ancestral burial place of his maternal clan. A few days later, the Keliyan family returned to their Shillong home where friends and relatives gathered to offer their condolences. The large number of people who came to share in the family's grief during those days bore testimony to the wide popularity of Rabon Roy among all the communities living in the town.

Haima and her family did all they could to take care of the stream of visitors to Kong Keliyan's house. Everyone missed the presence of Panchatirtha and he was informed about the tragic incident by telegram. But Haima was a bit surprised when no reply came from the other end and she consoled herself by thinking that perhaps the telegram hadn't reached its Calcutta address in time.

Then, one day a strange wire came from Panchatirtha. Haima was sitting on the sunny stairs in front of the house and reading a half-finished book when the postman came and gave her the telegram. She could read the English letters and also understand a bit of the written language. After reading her husband's name, she repeatedly tried to understand the text of the message. Whatever little she understood was enough to upset her. Holding the copy of the telegram in her hand, she slowly went inside and slumped into a chair. Endless worries raised a storm in her mind and she wondered who she should speak to or whose advice she should seek.

Just then Sarat and Lisimon entered the room. Haima was still sitting dazed, clutching the telegram. Sarat glanced at his mother and immediately read the contents of the telegram: 'Prashanta and Bhabani married yesterday. Details will follow.' Bewildered, Sarat sat down at his mother's feet and Lisimon looked on in amazement at both mother and son. After a long silence, Sarat said with disbelief, 'Why did father have to give such important news in this manner?' To this, Haima replied, 'I've not understood your father to this day. He will always do what he considers right. He will never listen to any one. And what is the worth of a girl anyway? She can be dismissed with a mere telegram! The last time she was handed over to that family without a second thought, and now...' Haima was too distraught with grief to finish her sentence. Sarat was deeply upset when he saw his mother break down in this way. He was suddenly very angry with his father. How could he possibly have done this without even asking his mother? Lisimon, who was listening, intervened in her low voice, 'Maybe Tawoi was helpless? What would he really do if Bhabani and Prashanta decided this themselves? He will surely give us all the details when he returns. It is no use being so upset now. Prashanta is a nice person and I know that Bhabani likes him. They'll both be happy.' Lisimon's simple reasoning helped to normalise things a bit. Haima got up from the chair and went inside. It seemed as if she had suddenly aged.

About a week after the telegram, Banamali Panchatirtha alighted from a taxi in front of his house. Sarat and Bijoy ran up to him and collected his belongings while Sonamon rushed inside to inform her mother. Haima didn't react and kept herself busy in the kitchen. After a wash, Panchatirtha sat down in his favourite chair and Sonamon brought him tea and snacks. Sipping his tea, Panchatirtha said gravely, 'Go, call your mother.' Haima finally came and sat down on a murha. Noticing that all the three children were looking at him, Banamali was a bit embarrassed and tried to smile. After this, he addressed Haima, 'What could I do? I had no way out. Such was the wish of Dharmaprabhu.' Sipping his tea he then narrated in a totally detached manner how Prashanta took them to the gramophone company's office where all the formalities of signing the papers were completed, of how Bhabani's song recording went off perfectly and how Prashanta had bought a gramophone from the New Market and gifted it to him so that they could all listen to Bhabani's songs on the record. At the mention of the gramophone, Sonamon cried out eagerly, 'Where is it?' and instantly went in to check her father's luggage. Meanwhile, Panchatirtha continued with his account of how Bhabani had been selected at the audition of the radio centre. She had been allotted particular dates to record her programmes. All this, he added, necessitated her stay in Calcutta. 'That's why you so skilfully found a solution to the problem!' Haimavati interjected at last, her tone filled with sarcasm and anger. As she listened to her husband who seemed to be narrating not his own story but that of someone else, Haima had already lost all patience. Detachment too had its limits. This time Banamali appeared a bit taken aback by her voice and tried to explain. 'Actually things are a bit more complicated than you think. In Calcutta we put up at Dhiren Lahiri's house and he took great care of us. One day, Dhiren Babu proposed that Bhabani be given in marriage to his eldest son. I too liked the offer because the young man was quite handsome and also had a good job. But when I sounded Bhabani about this, she was furious and straightaway told me that if ever she had to marry again, then it would be Prashanta and nobody else. Only then did I understand the matter. When I called Prashanta over and asked him if what I had heard from Bhabani was true, he replied in the most firm manner that he would like to marry Bhabani and give her the opportunity to become a well-known artiste. I seriously thought about it and then decided that it would be best for both sides if the marriage took place in Calcutta. Then came up the question of how the marriage should be performed. I decided against the traditional havan because that would not be possible. So it was decided to have a temple marriage where garlands would be exchanged and a registration would follow. I went to the temple and everything went off well. I am sure that Dharmaprabhu will keep them both happy.' Panchatirtha smiled contentedly.

'Well, is that all? Didn't you ever think about caste and what people would say?' Haimavati asked, her voice choking with emotion.'

'What's the point in thinking about all that? I have always believed that he who sticks to the right path is the real Brahmin. You have read Rabindranath. Don't you remember what Rishi Gautam said to Satyakam in Tagore's poem, *abrahman nohe tumi tato, tumi dwijuttam, tumi satyakulajata* – he who tells the truth is better than a Brahmin. One needn't be afraid of gossip, as long as one sticks to the right path.' Panchatirtha said this almost as if he was speaking to himself, and then he went off to the other room. All this while Sarat and Bijoy were listening to their father in amazement. This was the first time they had heard him stating his beliefs. Their respect for this strange, detached person suddenly increased.

In the days that followed, Haima confined herself to her home and tried to make sense of what her husband had said. It seemed that a sudden gust had blown off all those beliefs which, over the years, she had held on to as precious tradition, without ever giving much thought to them. She now tried to view the problem of caste from an entirely new angle and asked herself whether caste wasn't just confined to externals like food habits and rituals related to ideas of purity and defilement. Then a new thought came to her mind – what really was her own caste? Was she a Brahmin just because she was a Brahmin's daughter or wife? If such was the case, then why was she deprived of acquiring those qualities that are supposed to be the mark of a Brahmin? She asked herself why, despite being a sharp student, she had not been allowed to finish school, when several of her classmates belonging to other castes passed the Matriculation examination because in their case child-marriage was never a must? Why were Brahmin girls and women like her forbidden to practise the Vedic rituals? Why wasn't she allowed to witness her son's upanayan or listen to the Gayatri mantra? She remembered how she wasn't even allowed to see her daughter's wedding ceremony in front of the holy fire nor was she allowed to offer *tarpan* in memory of her own parents. If all this was true, then she wondered whether she was really a Brahmin. And her two daughters? They too didn't seem to have any caste. Slowly, her mind acquired a new firmness. She resolved that her children should receive recognition just as human beings, not as members of any caste. She felt that, after all, her husband was actually right.

A few days later there was a long letter from Bhabani. It was addressed to her mother. Though there was some measure of sadness at having to leave home, it was evident from the letter that she was very happy with her new life. She wrote that her first programme of songs was to be broadcast soon from the Calcutta radio station and she wanted the entire family to go and listen to it on the radio set at Amoi Keliyan's place. The letter helped clear some of the doubts in Haima's mind and she felt much lighter. After all these days of self confinement in the house, she decided to go out and she was soon walking towards Kong Keliyan's place.

Just as she was about to open the gate of Kong Keliyan's house, Lakhon hurriedly came out He wished her and quickly took her leave. These days Lakhon was busy managing his father's business. He had bought two old buses from the Ghulam Haidar Company and was thinking of plying them on the Shillong-Cherrapunji route. Minor repairs were being carried out at the new motor-garage set up by Haji Kasimuddin where the first electric dynamo of Shillong had been installed.

Thus, much before Dr Bidhan Chandra Roy set up the Shillong Hydro Electric Company there were electric lights at Kasimmuddin's house and this was in the first decade of the twentieth century.

27

The newspaper that carried news of Sarat's success in the BA examination had many other stories as well. The Quit India movement was at its height: thousands of freedom fighters were in prison, and large numbers of their colleagues had fallen to police bullets. Netaji's Azad Hind army, supported by the Japanese, stood facing the British on the Kohima-Imphal road. The army hospital at Shillong was filling up with wounded soldiers. When Sarat went to his college to collect his mark-sheet, he saw that a temporary hospital had been set up in a corner of the college compound. It was here that the wounded white soldiers belonging to the Royal Scots, the Queen's Own Cameron, Highlanders and other regiments were being kept. When Sarat approached the temporary hospital in search of Brother McBryde, the missionary came out to meet him. He was wearing an apron and was busy tending to the wounded soldiers. He congratulated Sarat on his success and advised him to go to Calcutta for further studies.

Wounded soldiers had been housed in several rented places in the town. There was an air of uncertainty all around. But despite that, the overall atmosphere was quite peaceful. It seemed as if the political storm in the plains had not stirred even a single leaf in this town. Government employees continued to carry out their duties, businessmen and contractors took full advantage of the war situation and made a quick buck. Whatever might have been the actual state of mind of the British rulers, they never betrayed any sign of their inner tumult as they carried on with their day-to-day activities in the most normal manner. They continued with their evening walks along Camel's Back Road which skirted Ward's Lake and the Government House, they went to the weekly horse races in the Polo Grounds, played golf at the picturesque Golf Links, rode their horses on the winding paths of the Long Round and got together at the Shillong Club in the balmy evenings for drinks and intimate conversations.

Meanwhile, another set of rulers arrived in Shillong and got busy establishing themselves. These were the newly elected Indian members of the Assam Legislative Assembly – they brought a new dimension of power politics to the town, though this had little actual influence on the lives of ordinary citizens. Interestingly, each political group moved along its own orbit, but occasionally their internal struggles caught the eye of the interested observers, creating minor ripples. The moment Germany attacked the Soviet Union, the Communist Party of India reversed its earlier anti-war stand and now began to support Great Britain by declaring the war to be an anti-fascist people's war. Following this, the ban on the party was lifted by the British and communist prisoners held in different jails in Sylhet, Bengal and Assam were released. Many started frequenting their old haunts in Shillong. Revolutionary politics once again created a turmoil amongst the members of the Bengali community. The cultural centre with which Bijoy was associated also suddenly buoyed up its activities.

Apart from some Assamese political activists from the plains, there were also some body builders who came and took shelter in a room adjacent to the kitchen at High Wind. They were apparently onetime members of the Guwahati Byayam Sangha and had later joined the Communist party in order to add to their muscle-power. Bijoy spent most of his time with these people – after finishing his Intermediate Arts, he had dropped all plans of going to college. He would leave home early in the morning, sometimes making himself a quick breakfast of a cup of tea and two slices of bread, being careful not to disturb his mother. He'd return for lunch and spend some time at home, and then he'd be off again in the afternoon. However, in the evenings he usually returned in time because there were strict instructions from Haima that everyone should be back home by nightfall. Panchatirtha generally maintained a studied silence about Bijoy's activities. But Haima sometimes asked him, 'Do you plan to do only this? Have you ever thought of your future?' Every time he was asked this, Bijoy just smiled and started singing a verse from a Bengali revolutionary song, *bharater grame grame muktira sangrame, lakha lakha kisan eshesche, cheye dekho aaj* – can't you see the peasants coming in such large numbers in search of liberation? Haima asked, 'Where will you find peasants from the villages in this place? If you are really intent on doing something, then go to the villages in the plains. Start your real revolution there by facing all the hardships of the village and going through all the mud and slush.' Bijoy never responded; he just walked away with a twinkle in his eye. He often discussed the revolution with his friends, and they planned their moves with Bijonbehari who had taken shelter in Shyamcharan Babu's house at Brahmopally. Here they sang revolutionary songs and made attractive posters. But despite all their efforts, they had not been able to recruit a single person from the Khasi villages for their cause. However, this did not deter them and they believed that if they continued with their efforts, one day success would be theirs.

Sarat was not particularly interested in his brother's political activities. He participated occasionally in the programmes of the People's Theatre Group at the Opera Hall and sang a revolutionary song or two or accompanied someone on the tabla. But he never went beyond this and Bijoy too did not insist. On this, there seemed to be an unspoken agreement between the two brothers and they never interfered in each other's work. Yet, whenever necessary, they were always ready to help each other. As for Sarat, he had been seized by an awful sense of uncertainty ever since his BA results were announced. The date of his father's retirement from service was drawing near and one day Panchatirtha told him in all seriousness that he should join the Shillong Government High School. He mentioned that the headmaster of the school was eager to have him. But Sarat was not keen. Brother McBryde had repeatedly asked him to go to Calcutta to do his Master's and this interested him too. Yet, whenever he thought of his father's financial situation, he felt it wrong to nourish such hopes.

One evening, engrossed in these thoughts, he was walking towards Police Bazaar. A little ahead of Khan Motor Works. a narrow lane up a hill led towards Lady Keane College. It was a lonely walk up this road flanked by rows of pines that spread across to the bungalows of army officers. Sarat always loved this stretch. He kicked a pine-cone down the slope and was surprised to hear laughter ring out from behind him. He hadn't seen Lisimon who had been following him all this while. 'Well, you kicked it with so much anger! Do you have plans to join a football team?' this with mischief in her eyes. Sarat's spirits immediately lifted. After Bhabani's departure to Calcutta his visits to Lisimon's house had become less frequent. But she would always come over to listen to the gramophone at High Wind. She also played some new tunes on the piano whenever she came. Lisimon was now taking the examinations in music conducted by London's Royal Academy of Music and it required a lot of practice to get through the final round of tests. For that, she was taking piano lessons from Patsy Graham of the Pine Mount School. Every day after school, she had to go to the music room where, along with some other senior girls, she was learning the piano from Miss Graham.

As the two started their slow climb up the road, Sarat tried to explain his predicament to Lisimon. Lisimon listened quietly for a while. Then, impulsively holding his hand, she said with great tenderness, 'Your mind is like those clouds. You want to fly off somewhere, don't you? No one can really keep you tied to one place. I know that very well.' As she said the last words, her voice quivered a little. Sarat looked at her and suddenly understood something. The touch of her hand and the look in her eyes gave him a strange sensation. All these days he had easily accepted the warmth and intimacy of her friendship but now something seemed to have changed. He held her hand in a firm grip and said, self consciously, 'I would never leave this place for good. It is very close to my heart, very much my own. You know that I don't have a home anywhere else. Even if I go for my studies, there is no doubt in my mind that I will come back to you.' His voice shook with emotion. Lisimon continued to walk silently for some time. A wild breeze that suddenly blew across the pines ruffled her smooth hair. Letting go of Sarat's hand and pushing back her hair from her face, she said in a steady and composed voice, 'Get prepared to go to Calcutta.

Ask for help from one of your rich uncles who works in the tea gardens. Moreover, what is there to worry since Bhabani and Prashanta are already there in Calcutta? As for me, I will wait for you here.' She choked slightly as she said this and then took her leave and crossed the road towards Pine Mount. Sarat stood by the side of the road for a long time watching her retreat into the distance, the soft golden rays of the evening sun adding a mystical hue to the surroundings.

28

After that evening's walk with Lisimon, Sarat was filled with a new energy to chart out a path for himself. That very day he wrote a letter to his uncle Sivaprasad, asking for financial help to study in Kolkata. His uncle was quick to reply. He was pleased with Sarat's performance and asked him to begin his preparations to leave for Calcutta. He promised to pay his course fees, but Sarat would have to arrange for his own board and lodging. After this, Panchatirtha and Haimavati could not object to his decision to leave. It seemed that this couple had reached an unwritten understanding never to interfere in the wishes of their children. Perhaps it was the shock they received at Bhabani's first marriage that helped to strengthen this resolve. Panchatirtha arranged everything for his son's trip to Calcutta and because he had done so well in his BA examination, he was able to easily get admission to the MA classes at the university. Arrangement for his stay was also made at a students' mess where the expenses would be within Panchatirtha's means.

Finally, the day arrived for Sarat to seek his parents' blessings and leave for Calcutta. On the eve of his departure he went to take leave of Keliyan Amoi. Lakhon warmly embraced his friend and wished him all success. He was already quite prosperous in his business. With two of his buses plying on the Shillong-Cherrapunji road, Lakhon was now planning to introduce his buses on the Shillong-Guwahati sector as well. He had always wished to set up a shop at Police Bazaar. But most of the space in and around Police Bazaar had already been occupied by Ghulam Haidar, Jamatullah, Bannerjee, De and Company and other major business firms from Bengal. These firms had made the entire area a part of their business empire, and many of the big establishments belonged to them or their relatives. Since this left no space for the local traders, Lakhon decided to open his shop in the Burra Bazaar area and stack it with cakes and pastries and stationery goods generally used by the Khasis. Over and above this, Lakhon had improved and extended his father's coal trade at Sohra and had also developed some orange farms. He made it a point to always be at Sohra during the orange plucking season. While some of his produce was dispatched to Shillong, the rest went by ropeway to Bholaganj in Sylhet. The sight of the baskets, full of oranges, merrily dancing down the ropeway to their destination filled his heart with happiness. Meanwhile he had also acquired a sweetheart in Sohra whose face was as bright as the Cherra oranges. This naturally reduced his presence at the Mawkhar home considerably. But on that particular day he was home to say good-bye to Sarat. He offered to drop Sarat at the Police Bazaar bus stand in one of his buses and everyone happily approved of his decision.

The next day, all the members of the Panchatirtha family, along with Kong Keliyan, Lisimon and Lakhon boarded the bus for the station amidst much mirth and banter. Sarat booked his luggage in the goods van and then went to board the Planter Company's bus for Guwahati. Finally, the moment of farewells had come. Sonamon hugged her brother and started sobbing. Sarat gave her a kiss and asked her to prepare well for her Matric Examinations. Sonamon wept, 'Tell Bhabani baideu about me. Why hasn't she written to me all these days? I miss her so much! Tell her that I am hurt.' Kong Keliyan thrust a small leaf-wrapped packet into Sarat's hands and said, 'This is lemon, ginger and salt. Take it when you feel sick on the way.' Sarat looked down at the group crowding below his window and felt that each one of them was so very dear to him. Yet, it was Lisimon, standing slightly apart and looking at him with moist eyes, who seemed the closest of all. The evening before, the two of them had gone for a long walk by the side of the Bishop-Beadon Falls. They had quietly walked hand-in-hand listening to the roar of the rushing waters below while the cold wind swept through the deep pine forest. The plaintive notes of the cicadas rang out from the trees and the two-fold call of the mysterious cuckoo floated in from a distance. Sitting down on a large stone by the side of the stream, both were overcome by their feelings. Resting her head on Sarat's shoulders, Lisimon had asked in a voice filled with emotion: 'Will the two of us be able to set up house when you return after two years?' Caressing her soft hair, Sarat had replied confidently, 'Yes, of course. No one can stop us.' At this, Lisimon was somewhat reassured and the doubts and premonitions which had burdened her evaporated all at once. Her mind suddenly lighting up like the clear evening sky, she gazed at the cascading waters and said, confidently, 'There is a well known story among our people. A young fisherman called Reno fell in love with a mermaid and went off with her to set up home. Before he left to join his sweetheart, he told his loving mother that as long as the river flowed in gusto, full of sound and fury, she would always hear his voice coming through the waters. But if the river fell silent, then she should know that he was no more. What a splendid tale about the relationship between man and nature!'

29

After Sarat's departure, the atmosphere at High Wind became noticeably quieter. Neither Bijoy nor Sonamon were particularly interested in playing the piano and after fiddling with the keys for a while, they would move off. They did not share the persistence of Sarat or Bhabani when it came to music. As for Haimavati, once she was done with her work in the kitchen, she loved to spend most of her time at the loom. Panchatirtha would sometimes tease her, 'For whom are you weaving all these clothes? Maybe you will be able to earn something from them after my retirement!' Haima's reply was the same, 'There is never any record of all a woman does. No one ever remembers the cooking, cleaning, swabbing and the washing of clothes and dishes. That's why I like doing something that will leave a mark. The designs that I make on my loom and the pullovers or cardigans that I knit with so much effort will surely survive for some time.' At this, Panchatirtha would nod his approval. Sometimes, he thought that if this woman had ever had the chance to study, she would probably have done something remarkable.

One evening, on his return from office, Panchatirtha had some news for Haima. A well-known woman leader of the Congress, Chandraprava Saikiani, was coming to Shillong to form a branch of the Mahila Samity and the women of Laban

had got together to welcome her. He asked his wife to go
to the meeting. Haima had almost stopped going to Laban
after Bhabani's marriage because she felt that one unpleasant
comment made by some acquaintance could upset her for
several days at a stretch. But now, with the rise of nationalistic
sentiments amongst Assamese women, the times were changing
a little and they no longer seemed solely occupied with petty
matters. Moreover, news from the plains about the freedom
movement had started reaching the hills much faster. Both the
Congress and Muslim League leaders were busy trying to take
over the reins of power and form a government of their own.
Their immediate aim was to secure power through whatever
means possible and establish their political control in Shillong.
As a result, the hot political winds from the plains had wrought
a change in the usually cool atmosphere of the hills.

Haimavati went to attend the meeting at Laban at the
newly built conference hall of the Assam Club. In a fiery
speech Chandraprava Saikiani exhorted the women to form
their own organization and stay united. She asked them to
organize themselves and fight for their social and political rights
because unless they did so, even Independence wouldn't be
able to ensure their legitimate place in society. Haimavati and
all the other women were enthused by the powerful words of
this graceful woman and they were especially impressed that a
woman was addressing them from a public platform, something
that had thus far seemed unimaginable. The meeting resulted
in the formation of the Assamese Mahila Sangha. Haimavati
was made the treasurer because she was known to be good with
accounts and paperwork. With this new responsibility, Haima's
visits to Laban became more frequent. The city had a new bus

service, which included two of Lakhon's buses. One of these, the Mawkhar-Laban line brought Haima free of charge up to Laban's Batti Bazaar. This three-cornered small market was so called because every evening it would function under the light of kerosene lamps and torches. Adjacent to this bazaar was the Assam Club. Sometimes while returning home from the club, Haima dropped in at the bazaar to buy some fish from Kong Bi, the beautiful Khasi girl. During the day, Kong Bi worked at a government office and in the evenings she joined her brother in selling fish in the market. Her tidy clothes and polished shoes never failed to impress Haima. Sitting on a bamboo murha, Bi cleaned the fish and carefully wrapped the freshly cut pieces in a plantain leaf before handing it over to the customer. Haima held her in high esteem because of her expertise and grace.

One day the secretary of the Mahila Sangha, Padmavati Baideu, informed the members that the new general elections to the Legislative Assembly were to be held soon and candidates had been nominated in Assam by different political parties. For the women's reserved constituency, the Assam Congress had nominated the well-known woman activist of Shillong, Bonelly Khongmen and now it was the turn of the women of the town to work untiringly to get her elected. Meanwhile, for the reserved seat from the hills, a member of Shillong's Khasi elite, J.J.M. Nichols-Roy had been nominated and it was almost certain that he would win uncontested.

Assamese and Bengali women from areas like Laban and Rilbong, where they constituted a majority, went from house to house seeking votes for Kong Bonelly Khongmen. Members of the Assamese Mahila Sangha, however, were hesitant to go to Khasi localities like Mawkhar and Burra Bazaar and since

Haimavati knew quite a few people there, she was given that task of campaigning amongst the Khasi families. Haima was dependent on Kong Keliyan's help to get the support of the Khasis. But the moment she talked to Kong Keliyan, she knew that she was up against a hurdle. The first thing that Kong Keliyan asked her was which Khasi group Khongmen belonged to. Haima tried to convince Keliyan that though Khongmen was a Mikir woman, she had made Shillong her home and was married to a Khasi. So even if she did not belong to any of the Khasi clans, she was a tribal woman and belonged to Shillong. Keliyan's second question was more direct: what was the purpose in sending this woman to the Assembly? Weren't there enough men there to speak for the women and the tribals? All the while chewing her areca nut and betel leaf, Kong Keliyan then told Haimavati in a tone of finality. 'The norms of our Khasi society are a bit different. "The hen never crows", this is what we believe.'

Haimavati was astounded at Kong Keliyan's words. She could not understand how such thoughts could flourish in a society where women's position was so much higher than among the Assamese and the Bengalis. Among Khasis, there were absolutely no restrictions on women's movements, the family name came from women, women engaged freely in trade and business, they took up government jobs. She was at a loss to find some suitable argument to convince Keliyan. How would Chandraprava Saikiani have dealt with such a situation, she wondered. In Kong Keliyan's presence, Haima felt utterly confused. She ttied to put forward her point of view. 'No less a person than Jawaharlal Nehru will be coming to Shillong shortly to introduce Bonelly Khongmen to the people of Assam. There will be a meeting at the Assam Club.' At this, Kong Keliyan smiled and said, 'Okay, we will go to see this Nehru. Isn't he the one who will one day become the king of the country?'

All this while, Lisimon was sitting by Kong Keliyan's side and listening to the conversation. She was accustomed not to interrupt while her mother was speaking. But just as Haima was about to leave, she came out and said gently, 'Well, it seems that it has not always been a mark of our tradition that Khasi women never speak in men's assemblies. There was a time when, during moments of crisis facing the Khasi states, the women of the Syiem's family also took part in the deliberations and expressed their views. When the British tried to build a road from Cherrapunji to Sylhet through the Khasi hills, the then Raja of the Nankhlow kingdom, U Tirot Singh, had called an assembly of the neighbouring Khasi states and in this the women of his clan also took part. The cunning English sent large quantities of foreign liquor to the Darbar hoping to create confusion amongst the people. But, to the surprise of the British administrators, the liquor was promptly returned with the warning that no member would drink till the proceedings of the Darbar were over. Interestingly, it was the women present at the meeting who took that decision. I read about this in some of the papers that are available at the Ri Khasi Press. So, if we really have such a tradition, then where is the harm in women going to the Assembly and expressing their opinion? Amoi, in this election, I will help you in whatever manner I can.'

Haima was deeply moved by Lisimon's wise words. Gently patting her cheek, she asked Lisimon to accompany her to some of the Khasi households in Jaiaw, Mawprem and Mawkhar. Lisimon readily agreed. Haima's involvement in the electioneering infused new life into the High Wind and everyone, from Sonamon to Panchatirtha, took part in animated discussions about the prospects of the different candidates in the elections. At his mother's request, Bijoy made some posters. Their revolutionary organization did not oppose the elections this time. The 1942 decision of the Communists to support the British war efforts had alienated them from the nationalists and keeping this in mind, they had avoided adopting an anti-election stance. Rather, they stood with the Congress in its decision to oppose the Grouping Plan of the Cabinet Mission and had joined in the statewide protests. Bijoy excitedly told his mother how Hemango Biswas had urged the youth to join the Indian People's Theatre Movement. 'Hemangoda has set up a Surma Valley Cultural Squad in Shillong and now they are planning to take their songs to the villages of Assam. Prashantada will come from Calcutta to join them and he has already written several new revolutionary songs.' Bijoy burst into song as he said this. At moments like these, Haimavati would simply gaze lovingly at Bijoy, her dear Sarubaapu, and ask herself whether this lively and vivacious son of hers would ever get the recognition he deserved from society; whether those who were full of praise for him and were encouraging him in his political and cultural activities, would continue to be fond of him in the future?

The day Jawaharlal Nehru came to the Assam Club to address an election meeting, there was much excitement among the Assamese and Bengali women's organizations of Shillong, The Congress volunteers saw to it that the meeting passed off peacefully and well. The Asom Sangha had decided to welcome Nehru with an Assamese phulam gamosa and Haimavati was asked to weave it. When Padmavati Baideo finally welcomed Nehru by draping the gamosa around his neck, Haima thought it to be the most precious moment of her life. And when Nehru, along with Bonelly Khongmen and other Congress leaders seated on the dais, listened intently to the inaugural song 'Jaya Jaya Bharata Janani' presented by the students of the Assamese Girls' High School, Haima just couldn't hold back her tears of happiness.

30

The soft morning sun played hide-and-seek on the lush green lawn in front of High Wind and the azalea bushes were in full bloom, every bit covered with bright purplish pink flowers. It was many days since Bijoy had woken up to such a bright and beautiful morning. Election fever was subsiding and the pealing of victory-bells signalling Independence could be heard in the distance. Alongside, threatening dark clouds of communal strife loomed over the country. The People's Theatre Group, to which Bijoy belonged, was preparing to go to the towns and villages to spread the message of communal harmony. There were in all some seven to eight young persons in the group which included the younger daughter of Subarnamashi, Khukumoni. Haima had noticed that of late Khukumoni had begun spending a lot of time with Bijoy. Though she thought the girl to be somewhat fickle-minded, she refrained from saying anything to Bijoy.

Stretching himself upon the green lawn in front of the house, Bijoy was enraptured, watching the white wisps of cloud drifting away in the deep azure sky. As he looked, the clouds constantly changed shape and formed ever new patterns. This play of the clouds had inspired him once to create several of his watercolours. But of late he had not been able to devote much time to painting. The morning sky, the sun, the breeze, the clouds and the sweet two-fold call of the cuckoo drifting in from the distant hills, all this now enthused him afresh to pick up his colours and paintbrush. Just as Bijoy got up to fetch his sketch-book, he noticed Lakhon walk in through the wooden gate. It was unusual to see his busy friend at this hour. 'Good morning,' Bijoy called out, 'How come you are here at this hour? Any news?' Lakhon came and sat down beside him on the grass. He asked after Sarat and Bhabani and then said, 'There is a bit of a mess in our work here. I'm thinking of moving to Sohra.' Bijoy smiled, 'Is it because someone is dying for you to come there?' Lakhon returned his smile, and then became grave again, 'I want to tell you something else. Recently the Minister for Public Works, Nichols Roy, had given me a government contract for building a hostel near the Assembly building for the newly elected members. This decision was taken jointly by Bardoloi, Medhi, Nichols Roy and other ministers. I got the contract for the job and started the work by transporting sand, stones and other building material to the appointed place. And now, without any warning, the Assamese Speaker of the Assembly has opposed the move and he is being supported by several other Assamese ministers. They are saying that the moment the country becomes free, the capital will be shifted from here to the plains. That will put an end to the local people doing such business. And the problem will be further compounded if Sylhet becomes a part of Pakistan because all our trade routes will be cut. I am really worried and wondering what to do now.'

Bijoy thought for a while and said, 'If the hostel is not built, where will the hundred odd MLAs stay?'

'Some of them will be at the Earle Sanatorium while others are busy buying houses and land in Shillong. The beautiful bungalows of the European Ward are already being acquired by the politicians, MLAs and senior bureaucrats and after the white ferangs leave, the Assamese and Bengali babus from the plains will take over those houses. Besides, the most scenic hillocks of Shillong have already been bought by the Rajas of Tripura, Bijni, Sidli, Mayurbhanj and by tea planters from Assam as well as rich businessmen from Calcutta. They have already built their beautiful mansions there. Whenever I think of the fate of our Khasi people, I get very worried.' The feeling of resentment was writ large on Lakhon's face as he said all this and Bijoy had nothing to offer him by way of reassurance. It suddenly occurred to him that all those people from different communities who were living in this small town, had never actually considered the verdant green hills all around as their home. If they had really believed it was, then they would have certainly shared the hopes and sorrows of the local people and made them a part of their lives. Bijoy wondered why everyone from the plains always described their 'real home' as being somewhere down in the plains. He recalled how, when he studied at the Assamese Lower Primary school at Laban, people often asked him where his 'real home' was, and how they laughed when he replied that it was in Laban, Shillong. 'The real home is the one in the plains where you go to during your winter vacation,' his friends explained. Bijoy recalled how he was often at a loss when this happened because unlike with the other boys, his family had never been to the plains for any long period, they had only made brief visits to his grandparents who lived in Jorhat. And, after their deaths, the only person they visited sometimes was their uncle who worked in a tea-garden. How could he think of his uncle's home as his 'real home', Bijoy asked himself. High Wind was their only home and wherever they went it was this place that always beckoned them back.

When Bijoy raised his head, his eyes met Lakhon's and he knew that he must say something, 'We are all proud of the cosmopolitan character of this city. The atmosphere is much freer than in many other places. But if others try to extend their dominance over the indigenous people here, then it is certain that the social environment will be badly affected. And, why is there all this talk about shifting the capital to the plains? Isn't this place a part of the province of Assam? The only difference is that of the plains and the hills!' Lakhon responded quite emotionally, 'It would be great if all the Assamese people thought like you, Bijoy! Our Khasi leaders still introduce themselves as Assamese. The other day, when Nichols-Roy was addressing the Assembly, I heard him using the expression "We the Assamese" several times. But the Assamese leaders do not consider us as their own. Otherwise why should they object to the capital being in Shillong? We have heard that they will also not allow the setting up of Assam's first university here.'

Bijoy's mood became quite gloomy after Lakhon left. Even the golden sun and the blue skies could not brighten his spirits. He went into his room and shut the door behind him; he then pulled out a drawing-board and the palette to mix his oils. He could see through the window a lone pine tree standing outside. Its leaves were swaying slightly in the breeze. But the actual picture that emerged on the board was quite different – it was that of a storm-lashed unruly dark tree. Yet, through it all one could see a glow in the distant horizon which seemed to signify that despite the storm, the hope of a new life still flickered in the distance.

31

When Sarat was preparing to take his final MA examination, the city of Calcutta was virtually on the brink of widespread communal violence. The results of the General Election had been announced just before the examinations and after the spectacular success of the Muslim League, Huseyn Shaheed Suhrawardy was sworn in as the Premier of Bengal. This created much chagrin and anxiety amongst the Hindus of that city. The atmosphere was tense and almost every day new rumours made their rounds in Sarat's mess. Inflammatory pamphlets and leaflets warning of a bloodbath on the 16th of August were being regularly distributed in the buses and trams of Calcutta. Students who were not local to Calcutta began to prepare to rush back to their hometowns as soon as the exams were done. But Sarat was determined not to leave Bhabani behind. As for Prashanta, he was already about to leave for Assam with his People's Theatre group. So, along with Bhabani and her baby girl, Sarat and Prashanta left Calcutta by train. They spent a night at Prashanta's house in Guwahati, and then Sarat left for Shillong. When the bus he was travelling in reached Jorabat, the gate there was yet to open; for only after the buses from Shillong arrived, would their vehicle be allowed to go up towards Shillong. The system of gates at Jorabat, Burnihaat, Nongpoh and Mawlai had been introduced when vehicles started to ply regularly on the Guwahati-Shillong road.

Now, passengers stood by the side of the road waiting for the gates to open. Sarat saw quite a few known faces among the group, mostly Assamese and Bengalis who worked in government offices at Shillong. There were also a few businessmen. Sarat noticed one of them looking at him and realised he had met him before. The person approached him, 'Aren't you Banamali Panchatirtha's son ?' When Sarat replied in the affirmative, he introduced himself and said, 'It's been quite a while but I remember meeting you near our house at Dergaon. I am Hariprasad Kataky, the youngest son of the mauzadar. My elder brother was married to your sister.' A flummoxed Sarat looked at him wordlessly. The young man continued, 'My brother died about two years ago. His mental illness had become worse and one day he set fire to himself in his room.' Instinctively, Sarat uttered '*Ish Ram*'. The young man now hesitantly asked, 'How is your sister?' Sarat told him that she was now in Calcutta with her new family. 'Great! May she always be happy.' Sarat felt a deep sense of gratitude for this young man. Had he not accosted them and told them the truth about his brother on that fateful day, who knows what would have happened to Bhabani? Then extending his hand towards the young man, he asked, 'What are you doing at present?' Still holding his hand, Kataky replied, 'I graduated from Cotton College and then went to the Calcutta Medical College from where I got my degree. Now I am working in the Berry White Medical School at Dibrugarh. But since Assam does not have a single medical college, there are very few doctors here. During the war, it was almost impossible to get doctors and nurses

to work in the makeshift hospitals. Some of us plan to send a
memorandum to the Premier of Assam with a suggestion that
the temporary hospital set up at Dibrugarh for the treatment
and nursing of American soldiers be turned into a full-fledged
medical college. This is what I have come to Shillong for – to
hand over the memorandum. Will you help me in this? Of
course, only if your parents do not object. I do understand
the problem.' Sarat's immediate response was positive and he
replied that he would certainly try to help.

The very next day, Hariprasad Kataky, accompanied by
Sarat, went and met Premier Gopinath Bardoloi. Bardoloi
assured him that Dr Bubaneswar Barooah had already met him
regarding the matter and that they had been discussing it for
some time. He said that very shortly his government would try
to set up a medical college at Dibrugarh. But they would have
to wait till the country gained its independence.

After Kataky left Shillong, Sarat told his parents about
his encounter with the young doctor and also gave them the
news of the death of the mauzadar's son. Both Haima and
Panchatirtha were stunned into silence. After a few moments
Panchatirtha said in his usual detached tone, 'Dharmaprabhu,
may your wishes be fulfilled.' Haima didn't say anything. But
Sarat noticed that her eyes were filled with tears. He, however,
didn't care to find out whether these were tears of relief or of
gratitude to an unknown power. Soon, she fetched him a cup
of tea and sat beside him. 'If a medical college comes up in
Dibrugarh will our boys get a chance to study there with some
help from the government?' Unable to catch the meaning of his
mother's words, Sarat glanced at his father's face. Panchatirtha,
however, could understand the sense of his wife's query and
said, 'Your mother is thinking about our Sarubaapu. The boy

has totally given up studies and has become a drifter. But I am about to retire in a few months. Medical studies are quite expensive, my pension money will not be enough to cover that.' Sarat reassured his mother and said, 'As soon as my results are out I'll get a job. Don't worry, I will meet his expenses. Please try to reason things out with him when he returns from the plains this time. Tell him that one can also serve society by becoming a doctor.'

As the day of Panchatirtha's retirement drew near, the issue started to be discussed frequently in the house. Haima was already planning to somehow reduce the household expenses. But there seemed to be very little that she could do. In any case, she had never been extravagant but now she would have to be extra careful. As for Panchatirtha, he had immense faith in his wife's capacity to somehow manage the household. More than the financial situation, he was worried about how he would spend his time after his superannuation. He had long planned to write a book on the administrative pattern of ancient Kamrup, based on the work that he had done with Mr Arnold. Arnold had already published a book on those lines. But Panchatirtha had collected a lot of material which did not figure in that book and he had also garnered additional information about copper plates and stone inscriptions during the sessions of the Sanskrit Board which he had attended so regularly. And he now began to look forward to a post-retirement life where he could focus on his academic work.

Meanwhile, worried about the impending financial crisis at home, Sarat decided to go and meet Brother McBryde. He went over to his old college and met his missionary teacher who seemed to have aged somewhat. Both of them talked at length about the situation in India as well as in the world. McBryde told

Sarat that unless India attained economic self-reliance after independence, colonialism was bound to continue in a different form even after India won political freedom. When McBryde was talking about the struggle for Irish independence, Sarat intervened at one point and asked, 'A storm is approaching your homeland. Won't you go home to experience that storm?' In answer, McBryde just smiled and said, 'For me my workplace is my homeland. The place where I am right now can never be an alien land for me.'

'What if the people of this land see you as a foreigner and an outsider?'

'If that were so, then I would consider it my failure because it would prove that I have not been able to integrate my work with the needs of the local people here,' McBryde replied in his usual tone of quiet conviction. On his way back home across the Lumaurie hill, Sarat thought about what McBryde had said. Meeting him was always so reassuring. When he heard about Sarat's financial worries, McBryde asked him to join his old college at once as a Lecturer in History, without waiting for his results. At this, Sarat felt so much lighter. It had started drizzling slightly as he was coming down the hill, but he was enjoying the droplets of rain on his face and head. Then, suddenly a gust of wind from the south was followed by a heavy downpour and Sarat was totally drenched by the time he reached home. When he opened the gate of High Wind and ran inside, he saw a smiling Lisimon standing on the verandah. He greeted her happily and shouted, 'Go get me a hot cup of tea please. Else I will freeze in the cold!'

32

Independence, Partition, communal strife, all this left the plural society of Shillong quite shaken. But the town's endlessly creative spirit and capacity to rejuvenate itself, successfully weathered all these storms. The disastrous Referendum in Sylhet just before Independence brought thousands of Hindu Bengali refugees. who left behind their hearths and homes, to seek shelter in Shillong. There was a time when the rich zamindars of East Bengal had acquired large estates in Shillong where they came to spend the summer. After Partition, most of them bought land and property and shifted to West Bengal while only a few such families stayed behind in Shillong in their large houses. But the Bengali refugees who settled in the congested localities which came to be known as Sylheti paras at Jail Road, Rilbong and Laban, belonged mainly to the lower-middle class. According to the policy of the new Indian government, most of these refugees were given government jobs, while a section of them took loans from the government and started their own businesses.

Within a very short time the entire scenario of this small town changed beyond recognition. The once lonely roads where people usually moved only during office hours or the small crowds which gathered during bazaar days were now replaced by hundreds of unknown faces. It was as if the old Khasi inhabitants of the town were almost lost in the midst of all these newcomers. When Bijoy and Sarat were small boys, they would always rush into the house in fear whenever they saw a certain slightly tipsy Khasi man on the road in front of High Wind, returning home in the evening after his drink of *ka kyiad.* They would peep out through the curtains at the gentleman in coat and trousers with a white pugree on his head, till he finally disappeared from view. But such characters had almost vanished from the roads of Shillong. Instead, they had been replaced by babus from the different districts of Assam and East Bengal trudging back home from their offices in the evening with bags full of fish and vegetabled from Batti Bazaar, talking loudly among themselves and disturbing the evening calm. The local Khasi people whom they crossed on the way, would maintain a strange silence, as if their voices had been stifled by all this noise.

Sometimes when Sarat and Lisimon went for a walk together, they would be embarrassed by the inquisitive glances from these strangers. For them it seemed improper that the two of them were walking together. Lisimon would then pull her *tapmoh khlieh* tightly over her head and try to walk as fast as possible with her high heels. These days, both of them walked together up to the Barik traffic point and from there Lisimon went off towards Pine Mount School while Sarat walked the rest of the way to his college. On the way Lisimon told Sarat many juicy stories about her new job. The old music teacher of Pine Mount, Patsy Graham, had left for England soon after Independence and Lisimon had joined in her place. In the mornings, she played the 'marching tunes' on her piano at the school assembly as the girls marched into the hall in single file. Then she accomanied the girls while they sang some Christain hymns. 'These days there aren't many Christian girls in our school. Most of them happen to be Hindus or Muslims. But all of them sing the hymns,' she told Sarat one day. Sarat looked at her in surprise. 'Your school is not run by Christian missionaries. Then why are Christian prayers sung there?' Lisimon laughed. 'Maybe the girls feel that the religion of the school is Christian and they don't find any reason to object to it.' Then she added more seriously, 'I am however very fond of Negro Spirituals and I have introduced such a song in the school opera this time. I will play it for you some day at home.'

Thinking all the while about Lisimon, Sarat would continue his part of the walk up to the college. These days there was a certain sense of cheerfulness in him which was reflected in the spring in his steps. His job had been made permanent after his results were declared and his parents too were happy. He felt that there were no more barriers for him to keep his promise to Lisimon and he was confident that his parents would not object to making her their daughter-in-law. Besides, Lisimon's family was also very fond of him. Sarat quietly resolved that once Bijoy left for Dibrugarh, he would tell his mother about his decision.

Once the medical college started functioning in Dibrugarh, Sarat wrote a letter to Hariprasad Kataky. Kataky was now a doctor in the Assam Medical College and with his help both a seat and a scholarship were arranged for Bijoy. But even after all this, Bijoy seemed reluctant to leave Shillong and go to Dibrugarh. Sarat tried his best to reason with his brother and told him about the selfless service to humanity rendered by doctors during the great revolutions. He talked at length about the invaluable contribution of the Indian physician Dr Kotnis during the Chinese revolution. But Bijoy seemed undecided about his future and preferred to stay on with his progressive group in Shillong rather than take a decisive step that would change the course of his life.

Meanwhile the debate about the Communist Party's role in independent India was gathering momentum and a lot of contrary views were being aired. In the beginning, the Communists thought of working within the democratic framework to raise the level of the anti-imperialist and anti-feudal struggle in independent India to a full-fledged people's revolution. Then, under the leadership of Ranadive, the party opted for an armed revolution to be achieved through guerilla struggle. This resulted in an immediate ban on the party by the Indian government and the Communist Party members were rounded up by the police throughout the country. Just before the ban was announced, the members of the Communist Party in Shillong gathered in a secret conclave. But strangely Bijoy and a few others were not invited to it. The main reason for this was that those who did not support the Ranadive line were not trusted by the other party activists and they had heard Bijoy expressing his reservations about it on some occasions. The contradictions within the party left Bijoy highly confused and unhappy. Yet, he put his heart and soul into the making of Hemango Biswas's shadow play based on the life of the Khasi freedom fighter U Tirot Singh. Sometimes, during the preparations, he became absent minded. He realised that within their organization there had emerged an inner circle from which he had been excluded for some unknown reason. Even Khukumoni, who always preferred his company to others, had lately started to avoid him. That was why he was now no longer privy to most party decisions. Then, all of a sudden the members started going underground, there were arrests and imprisonment and Khukumoni and several others just disappeared from Shillong. It was only much later that Bijoy would come to know that Khukumoni had married someone in Calcutta. However, he thought it prudent not to discuss all this with anyone at home and kept a low profile for a few days. Then, quite unexpectedly he announced at home that he was prepared to go to Dibrugarh and would leave within a few days. Haima thanked her stars, prayed to God and then started her preparations to send Sarubaapu to Dibrugarh.

The day Bijoy left, both Sarat and Lisimon accompanied him to the motor station at Police Bazaar. After they returned home, Lisimon went over to High Wind and asked Haimvati, 'Amoi, do you remember the girl from the Kharkongar family, called Nancy? She did her BA from our college and she too left for Dibrugarh by the same bus to do her medical studies there.'

33

Both Bhabani and Prashanta moved to Guwahati as soon as the new radio centre was set up there. Their songs were now being regularly broadcast from Guwahati. The duets sung by them gained popularity throughout the state within a short span of time. Songs full of promise of revolutionary change written and set to music by Prashanta ushered in a new wave, especially among the new generation. Bhabani now frequently visited Shillong and during their stay at High Wind there was much fun and joy. Lisimon too would come often and join in the song sessions. Prashanta and Bhabani made her agree to take part in some of the programmes broadcast from the Shillong centre of All India Radio. The Shillong centre occasionally broadcast Assamese plays but there was always a dearth of female artistes. Hence, Lisimon would often get calls to participate in some of these. One evening the entire family of Panchatirtha sat around their new radio-set to listen to a play where Lisimon had played a role. The weather was terrible that day and consequently the radio reception was very bad. The dialogue frequently became inaudible. Despite this, everyone listened to the play with a lot of attention.

When the play ended, Panchatirtha praised Lisimon generously. 'This girl, Lisimon, has such a sweet voice! Her pronunciation too is perfect. There are very few girls with so much talent in our Assamese society here.' When Sarat saw Haima nod in approval, his heart was filled with pride and happiness and his hopes soared high. Considering it the right time to speak his mind to his parents, Sarat asked Sonamon to go to the other room. Then, in a voice full of trust and confidence but quivering slightly with emotion, he told them that he wished to marry Lisimon and that she too was willing to become his wife. For a moment, both Banamali Panchatirtha and Haimavati sat still in their chairs and didn't utter a word. Sarat looked at them expectantly. At last, Panchatirtha spoke in a measured tone, 'We know that she is a good girl. We too love her a lot. But marriage is a different matter. I am not worried much about their religion since both Kong Keliyan and Lisimon are still not Christians and have kept to their traditional faith. But they aren't Hindus. Yet, if religion teaches us to lead a moral life and follow the rules set by the Creator, then there is little difference between the Khasi and Hindu religions. This is all I have learnt from the books written by Babu Jibon Roy and Radhon Singh Berry. But, as per the tradition followed by people like Kong Keliyan, theirs is a matrilineal society where the women are the main pillars of the family. Because of this, the girl does not move to the groom's house after marriage. Rather, it is the son-in-law who goes over and stays with the bride's family. We are totally against such a practice.'

Haima had been silent when her husband spoke. Now she said, 'Since both the families live near each other, there should not be any difficulty in Lisimon's coming over to our house.' Sarat looked at his mother gratefully. He had always respected her balanced views and on this occasion too he believed that his mother would not let him down. But Banamali Panchatirtha quickly changed the course of the conversation. 'Things aren't that simple. Lisimon is the youngest daughter of the Keliyan family, their khadduh. It is she who will have to perform all the pujas and rituals in memory of their forefathers. But as the eldest son, after my death Barbapu would have to carry out all the rites and rituals on behalf of our family. What is even more important is that even if this marriage takes place, their children will not belong to our family, they won't be ours. They will use the Diengdoh surname and not ours. I am sorry but I can't agree to such a marriage. It goes against our tradition.' Panchatirtha laid special stress on the last few words. Haima was quite taken aback at the firmness with which he spoke. Panchatirtha too seemed a bit uncomfortable at his own words and he quickly left the room. Haima saw that Sarat was looking at her helplessly. She tired to comfort her son. 'Such decisions cannot be taken in a hurry, my son. Let me have a word with Keliyan. She will certainly suggest a way out.'

A few anxious days passed. Then one afternoon Sarat was returning home from college when he saw Lisimon at the Barik traffic point. The moment he saw her sad face, he guessed the imminent bad news. Both walked towards Ward's lake and sat down under their favourite Himalayan pine tree by the side of the lake. The tall tree was almost covered by a bougainvillea which was in full bloom with its deep purple flowers. Earlier, that sight had always delighted them. But on that particular afternoon the flowers stood mute witness to their gloom. Then, slowly Lisimon started telling him all that had been happening at their place ever since the family had got to know about their decision to get married. 'When Amoi came and broached the topic of our marriage with my mother, she said that although she had no reservations about it, but because I was a khadduh, she would have to consult all the seniors of her family before coming to a decision. Yesterday, my uncles and aunts, sisters and brothers all gathered and discussed the matter for a long time. Finally, they decided that I would not be allowed to leave my ancestral home after marriage, because the responsibility of showing honour to our ancestors lies on me as the khadduh. When my mother told Amoi this morning, your mother replied that if I couldn't go as a bride to your house, then the marriage is virtually off. What should we do now?' As she asked this question, Lisimon broke into tears. Sarat replied in anger and frustration. 'Have we come to this world just to offer oblations to our forefathers? Don't we have any space of our own?'

The two sat for a long time on the grassy slope beneath the Himalayan pine. Gradually, the sun went down behind the clouds and darkness began to descend. With it, a light mist enveloped the trees and a cold breeze made them shiver. It was as if two helpless souls were getting lost in the gloom. Eventually, they got up and started walking towards home. When Lisimon was about to take her leave as they approached High Wind, Sarat held her hand and said, 'Please marry someone else and start a family. Try to forget me.' Lisimon replied with heartbreak in her voice. 'If you can do that, I'll also try. But I will always remain yours.' Her words caught in her throat as she suppressed a sob. Then she quickly walked home, crying all the way.

34

After her exchange with Kong Keliyan, there was a tumult in Haima's mind. She feared that just as her husband Panchatirtha had gone against his parents' wishes in the matter of his marriage and had totally snapped his ties with his family, her son might also do the same. The very next moment she told herself that her Barbapu would never do anything that would hurt their feelings. She believed that he was of a sober and balanced bent of mind, unlike his brother who was quite unpredictable. Besides, Haima had unshakeable faith in her children. Each one of them had a distinct personality and she had always tried to understand and accommodate their needs. But the tempest that had now hit Sarat's life, seemed to have struck her as well. Her son was no longer as open as he used to be and he had started spending most of his time reading alone in his room. He had also given up playing the piano. Sonamon too had realized that something was amiss and her usual warm and boisterous behaviour towards her brother had changed. She had given up her music and dance while preparing for the Matriculation Examinations and had never stepped on the stage after her memorable performance as Sutradhar in the *Ramavijaya-nata* at the Asom Sangha.

Haima had always hoped that her husband would eventually shed his rigid stance towards Sarat and Lisimon and give his consent to the marriage. It was her knowledge of her husband through all these years that had strengthened this feeling. He, who had decided all by himself to give his daughter in marriage to a young man from another caste would, she believed, ultimately relent for the happiness of his son. But she soon realized that after his retirement, Panchatirtha had changed a great deal. She had observed that once the discipline of his job was gone, his life had become increasingly rudderless. However much Haima pushed him to devote himself to his studies, Panchatirtha seemed to be shackled to his earlier routine of leaving home in the morning for some destination of his choice. Every morning around ten, he would get ready and leave home with a purpose, only to end up in some Assamese locality in Laban or La Chumiere where he would spend time chatting with other retired men. He was almost always late for lunch. Then there were occasional Brahma-bhojans to attend. There was always a shortage of Brahmins for the Brahma-bhojans during religious ceremonies held in the homes of the Assamese ministers and bureaucrats of the town. Though there was quite a sprinkling of Brahmins among lower grade government employees, yet it hurt the prestige of the highly placed officers and ministers to give them the status of respected guests in their households. Panchatirtha's case was different. He was a Sanskrit pundit of repute and his scholarship had also been recognized by the British rulers. Hence, they were gratified when Panchatirtha accepted their invitations.

In the beginning, Banamali Panchatirtha was somewhat hesitant about his new social role. But gradually he got used to it. Panchatirtha, who had never indulged in superstition of any kind and would instantly dismiss practices like palm-reading by saying, 'This is all bunkum! Even monkey-palms have lines', now started discussing the evil influence of planets on human beings, while sipping tea in the posh drawing rooms of high officials. Haimavati was bewildered at this strange transformation in her husband and the more Panchtirtha immersed himself in all this, the more her worries increased. Soon the entire schedule of his daily activities underwent a change and he often fell ill after a session of Brahma-bhojan at someone's place. Haima was very unhappy over all this but she didn't have the courage to displease the gentlemen from the elite circle who came with invitations for her husband. Finding no way out, she discussed the matter with Sarat, only to realize that her son had developed a sense of apathy towards his father. Whenever she mentioned anything about him, Sarat would just try to avoid the subject and move away. This change in the environment of her family was deeply upsetting for Haima. But she had always stood like a straight and tall pine tree against all storms, bending at times but righting herself soon.

On winter mornings, it was Panchatirtha's habit to get up a bit late. From his bed he kept track of how Haima lit up some firesticks and heated the frosted water pipes so as to make the water flow. A little later, she plucked an orange or two from the tree which stood in the midst of the white, frost-covered lawn and her footsteps would leave their marks on the frost. Unmindful of the biting cold, she went about her daily chores as usual. As Panchatirtha, lying on his bed, followed his wife's busy schedule, his mind was filled with tender feelings towards her – the woman had so many qualities and yet she had never demanded anything in life.

Panchatirtha sat up on his bed as Haima came in with a cup of tea. And, then he suddenly felt a piercing pain in his left leg. He tried to reassure Haima that this was perhaps because of his bad posture in bed, or it could also be the cold. He assured her that once he had had his tea and taken a few steps, the pain would disappear. But when it did not subside even after two hours or so, Haima heated some mustard oil and garlic pods on a charcoal burner and brought the concoction in a small brass bowl. As she was massaging her husband's leg, Sarat came in and took the bowl from his mother's hand, continuing to massage his father's foot. The heat from the burning charcoal on the small iron chula and the hot oil massage spread a feeling of relaxation throughout Panchatirtha's body and the touch of his son's hands seemed to bring back, even if for a moment, the lost nuances of the father-son bond.

One morning, just as Sarat was about to leave for college, he noticed a large, blue Plymouth car in front of their gate. He recognized the car at once. It belonged to a high level government official who stayed at La Chumiere. As he went inside to inform his father, he saw that Panchtirtha was already dressed in his dhoti, kurta, coat and shoes, with a shawl thrown over his shoulders and ready to leave. He was still wobbling a bit on his left leg. Sarat looked at him in disbelief and asked: 'Where are you going?' Panchatirtha replied with some hesitation. 'There is a sraddha ceremony in Chief Secretary Baruah Sir's house. He will be really offended if I don't go. Since he has sent his car, there should not be a problem.' Sarat retorted with some irritation, 'You aren't well. Why should you go?' Meanwhile, the visitor got out of the car and addressed Haima and Sarat, 'Today on the day of his father's sraddha, our Sir will earn a lot of blessings if he feeds a pundit like him. That's why I have come to pick him up.'

'But have you ever thought what effect such a meal could have on a sick person?' The messenger looked a bit puzzled at Sarat's angry tone. Panchatirtha proceeded with slow steps towards the car, and Sarat went off to college in a huff.

That afternoon there was a meeting of the Asom Sangha at Laban. The winter afternoons were unusually short in Shillong and from around two in the afternoon the sun would begin to disappear behind the haze and the atmosphere would become overcast. It usually didn't rain in winter but with the clouds descending, the temperature would drop sharply. On that day, Haima finished her meal earlier than usual and, with the hope of ending the meeting quickly, started walking towards Laban. As she left, she instructed Sonamon to prepare an evening snack for her father.

The Asom Sangha's programme for the first Republic Day of the country and the role to be played by the women members was discussed at length in this meeting. It was unanimously agreed that the opening song would be Jyotiprasad's 'Triranga Nishan, Bijoyi Nishan'. But there was much debate about which 'national song' was to be sung. One section of women strongly opposed the singing of *Jana Gana Mana* and were in favour of *Bande Mataram*. They argued that since in the first song there was no mention whatsoever of the province of Assam, they could not accept it as their 'national song'. Eventually a compromise was reached and it was decided that the second line of the *Jana Gana Mana* would be sung as 'Kamrupa, Punjab, Gujarat, Maratha', the word 'Kamrupa' replacing the word 'Sindh'.

Although by the time the meeting ended, it was just about four in the afternoon, it was already getting dark. Wrapping her shawl tightly around her, Haima boarded the Burra Bazaar bus for home. Just as she was about to open the gate of her house, she instinctively felt that something was wrong. Lisimon and Keliyan were running through the back lane and had just reached High Wind. When she saw Dr Thomas of the Welsh Mission at the doorstep, Haima's worst fears were confirmed. Some great mishap had occurred. As she walked into the house, she saw Panchatirtha's lifeless body lying on the bed. Sonamon was clutching his hand and crying. Sarat was as still as a statue and looking at his father. The moment he saw Haima, he held her close and cried out aloud, 'Bouti, Deuta left us all without a word! After coming from La Chumiere, he sat down on his chair saying that he was feeling tired and asked Sonamon for a cup of tea. She came with the tea and found him slumped on his chair. By the time I reached, he was no more. Lisimon went and got Dr Thomas.' Haima rested her head on Panchatirtha's chest and was silent for a long while. After that, she literally washed her husband's feet with her tears. All this while, Sarat, Lisimon and Sonamon were mute witnesses to this intense display of grief. Then Sonamon told Haima about her father's last words. Alighting from the blue Plymouth car, Panchatirtha had almost stumbled to a chair in the sitting room and finding Sonamon upset and nervous, he had tried to smile and had said in his Kamrupia dialect, '*Mai, ek piyala chah diyasun. Bor bhagor lagse dekhun.*' (Mai, please give me a cup of tea. I am feeling very tired). As Sonamon tried to recapture her father's intonation, Haima's eyes filled tears again. All his life, Panchatirtha had consciously cultivated the habit of speaking the 'chaste' Assamese or the 'language of the book'. But in his most intimate and unguarded moments, he always slipped into his Kamrupia dialect. Haima tried to recall some of those intensely private moments in their lives when they professed their love for each other, of those sweet and carefree times when he used to share happy moments with the children when they were small. So, in his last words, thought Haimavati, Panchatirtha had expressed his final loyalty towards his 'pargana' roots for which he always had a yearning in his heart.

The cremation took place that night with the help of the Assamese residents of Laban. Bijoy arrived the following day from Dibrugarh. He broke down and told his mother, 'Bouti, if only I had known of the pain in his leg! Actually, in the morning Deuta had a cardiac attack. He shouldn't have gone out and he shouldn't have eaten at an odd hour. He gave his life to keep up social pretences.' Haima tried to console her son. 'Everything is as fate ordains, my son. No one has harmed him intentionally.' But Sarat and Bijoy expressed their ire in strong words, 'Why don't these ministers and bureaucrats bring Brahmins from the plains for all their obscurantist rituals?' However, for Panchatirtha's sraddha ceremony, the Chief Secretary sent his car to bring three Brahmins and all the necessary provisions from Guwahati. For this, he earned adequate praise from the Assamese community of Shillong.

All the rituals had been performed to everybody's satisfaction. But when the matter of disposing of the ashes came up, Haima took a firm stand. Going against the advice of Panchatirtha's Assamese friends who suggested that Sarat and Bijoy should immerse the ashes in the Ganges, Haima declared, 'My husband left this world breathing the air of this place and drinking the water from its springs. One should always consider the place one lives in as sacred. So why should we go in search of a holy river? We will immerse his ashes in our own Umkhra river.' So, Banamali Panchatirtha's last remains were immersed in the dancing waters of the mountain stream and the fast currents carried them down into the waters of the plains.

35

Sarat had been thinking of leaving Shillong ever since his relationship with Lisimon came up against family opposition. Without informing anyone at home, he applied for a job at the newly established Pragjyotish University in Guwahati and was invited to join as lecturer there. After he got the letter of appointment, Sarat sought out Brother McBryde to seek his advice. At first, Brother McBryde seemed surprised and was about to say something, but then he thought better of it and left usnsaid whatever was in his mind. Then, he said a few things which gave Sarat the impression that Brother McBryde was not happy with his decision to leave the college. 'If you continue here then the financial benefits will be limited and there will be little chance of material advancement. In the university, no doubt there'll be more opportunities and promotions. What's more, your social status will also go up. It's true you can't expect all that here. Yet, precisely because these attractions and enticements aren't to be found here, our teachers can pursue their studies in peace. When promotions become the motivating factor, teachers often fall out with each other and come to view their colleagues as competitors, then envy, anger and frustration take over and people start behaving selfishly. In such situations, intellectual progress is also hampered. By the way, do you have any problems on the home front here?'

As Brother McBryde asked this, Sarat felt that the piercing blue eyes of the missionary had invaded his very innermost being and that he knew much more than what he was actually saying. At that point Sarat felt that he should confide in Brother McBryde about all that was going on in his mind. But how would a missionary react to a tale of frustrated love? How would he really explain all this to a person who had probably never gone through such an experience, thought Sarat. So, he decided not to tell him anything. He thanked Brother McBryde and bid him goodbye and a despondent Sarat headed home. It was as if from now on it would be his solitary effort to keep concealed the unruly thoughts that were creating havoc inside him.

Even after the setback in the relationship between Sarat and Lisimon, the rapport between the two families remained intact. Neither family hesitated to stand by the other during moments of crisis. Nevertheless, Haima was always assailed by a deep sense of guilt and sorrow whenever she saw Sarat and Lisimon together. Her heart was burdened by the thought of what the future held for the two of them. That's why she was somewhat relieved when Sarat decided to go to Guwahati. But there were new worries. She cautioned her son about the problems of setting up house all alone in Guwahati. Besides there was also the question of coping with the heat and the dust of the plains. To all these maternal qualms Sarat had a response, 'Don't worry about these things, Bouti. So many people are managing life there and I'll also find my moorings.' But Haima insisted that he should consider certain things seriously, 'Society there isn't like ours here, Barbapu,' she said. 'Here if one wishes one can easily mix with others. But there it's quite different. People will disapprove of your ways and criticise you on the smallest of things. I am afraid that you will never be allowed to live in peace.' Sarat thought for a while and then replied, 'Aren't there similar people here also? Everywhere in this world there is the good and the bad. As long as one keeps one's head, there should be no problem.' Haima was not convinced. 'The environment of a place affects the people a lot. I have always thought that the atmosphere in Shillong is different. When people from the plains come to live here, they have to give up on certain beliefs and practices. Look at me. Before I came to this place, my mind was somewhat cribbed and confined within beliefs and traditions which I now consider to be meaningless. But my world changed after I met and became friends with Kong Keliyan, Rabon Roy, Labanyaprabha and Saradamoni of Brahmopally, Padumi Baideu of Laban, Maheswar Goswami's family and all the other liberal folk. Even people like Ambika have changed and, unlike our Bhabani, they haven't given off their youngest daughter in marriage yet, though she has attained puberty. They have sent her to college and are also allowing her to learn music and dance.' Sarat looked at his mother's worried face and said lovingly, 'I wonder how many mothers there are like you in this world? As your children we'll always be steadfast and strong. Please, don't ever lose faith in us.'

The day before he left, Sarat went to Laban to take leave of Maheswar Goswami. Goswami was busy playing on the khol and teaching Satriya dance to a group of children. A few days later the Finance Commission from Delhi was expected in Shillong and they were to be entertained with traditional dance and music at the Shillong Club. Goswami offered his blessings and wished Sarat well in his new job. But he also sounded a word of caution. 'Here you found a mini London, a mini Calcutta, Dacca, Srihatta, Sivasagar or Barpeta. You also saw how all these came together and created a new mixed culture.

That is the uniqueness of this place. But you will not find this in the plains. There you will have to guard yourself from being hurt in the fights that frequently take place between frogs and mice.' Then he laughed at himself for the colourful image he'd created. But he blessed Sarat and bade him a warm good-bye.

Sarat did not go to Kong Keliyan's house to say good-bye. He had hesitated to go there ever since the family meeting that had taken place there to determine Lisimon's future. Quite suddenly a family that had been so dear to him seemed to have drifted far away. Once the day of his departure was fixed, it was Sonamon who informed Lisimon about it. But she never came to bid Sarat farewell. As he was about to board the taxi that was waiting in front of his house, Sarat cast a side-glance towards the Keliyan house and Sonamon could catch the depth of sorrow in that glance. As the taxi manoeuvred the last curve of the hill, Sarat looked down towards their house and could see Sonamon entering the Keliyan home through the back lane. After that, all the way to the motor station, he tried to forget about home.

In the noise and bustle of the motor station, Sarat didn't have time to think of anything else. But as the bus started moving down the Police Bazaar road, he felt a sharp pang in his heart, as if the umbilical cord with his mother's womb was about to snap. As the vehicle crossed the Burra Bazaar area, Sarat could see Lisimon standing at the front of the small lane that led to their house, her hair completely dishevelled by the strong wind. She had been waiting there with anxious eyes for the bus to pass by. Noticing Sarat sitting by a window seat, she tried a smile and then waved her hand. But Sarat could clearly see tears rolling down both her cheeks. He too raised his hand a little and waved a silent farewell.

36

High Wind was now a quiet place. Every day, after Sonamon left for college, Haima would be assailed by the fear that the home she had built with so much of care was now turning into an empty nest. It was as if the walls of the house still resonated with the songs and music of those lively evenings of the past and Haima would sometimes strain her ears to catch these familiar sounds. One day after trying to remove invisible dust from the chairs and tables, she ventured into the room left behind by Sarat and Bijoy and started going through some of their things. On Bijoy's table there still lay a heap of Russian and Chinese magazines – *Soviet Land, China Pictorial, China Reconstructs*. Haima was captivated while looking at the colourful pages filled with pictures of a new age and a new people. She wondered if these pictures still held the dream of a new world for Bijoy. Pulling open a large drawer, she found some cards, water colours, sketches and paintings in oil on canvas The small paintings had been carefully piled up, one on top of the other, while the canvases were rolled up and kept on top of the book-case. Haima started looking at the paintings, one by one. A few she had seen earlier, but most were new to her. In the midst of these there was a portrait – that of Panchatirtha. Observing the face of her husband, she felt that there was the touch of life in each stroke. She recalled the day when one morning Sarubaapu had made his father sit in front of him and sketched something on a piece of paper. But she didn't have any idea of when he actually drew this lovely portrait of his father. Gazing at the portrait for a long time, Haima put it back with a sigh. She felt sad that Panchatirtha did not realize the worth of such a talented son. Would her Sarubaapu be really happy in life as a physician?

Every afternoon Haima waited for the postman as he passed by High Wind, hoping there would be a letter from one of her children. Bhabani always wrote long letters and her fat envelopes, bursting at the seams were stuffed with pages full of interesting details about her life written in a gripping style. Sometimes, along with all the other news, she added a new song of hers and she regularly updated her mother about her recording schedules. Bijoy, by contrast, was given to writing post-cards. Reading his letters written in a clear beautiful hand, Haima was always left with the desire to know more about his life in Dibrugarh, about the people there and the furious face of the mighty Brahmaputra. But it was not his habit to write in detail about anything. All she knew was that he had passed his final examination, and was now attached to his medical college as a 'houseman'. One day, to her surprise, Haima got a long letter in an envelope from Bijoy. With much expectation, she sat down on the front stairs to read the letter. But the news that the letter carried astounded her. Bijoy had written that right from the first year at the college, he and Nancy Kharkongar had developed a liking for each other. Since the chances of getting approval from the families were slim, they had married through registration at the Dibrugarh court. Seeking his mother's forgiveness as well as her blessings, he was now eager to come home and see her. Haima sat on the stairs for a long while and tried to understand the significance of this development. So, unlike Sarat and Lisimon who had quietly accepted the decision of the elders, Bijoy hadn't even taken the risk of seeking any approval? Haima's heart was torn at the thought of the injustice done to Sarat and Lisimon. But what would she say to Sarat now? She struggled with her thoughts all alone. The following day she wrote to Bhabani and Sarat giving them the news, but carefully avoided expressing her own views on the matter.

About a week later, Sarat, Bhabani and Prashanta and their little girl Uma, came home for the Puja holidays. Bhabani assured her mother that Nancy was indeed a very loving girl and no one could find any fault with her character. Since Bijoy and Nancy loved each other, they were sure to be a happy couple, she insisted. Sarat, however, didn't say anything much. He was reticent even about his relationship with the Kelyan family. No one knew for certain whether he had kept any links with Lisimon after he had moved to Guwahati,. In a rather strange and detached manner he told his mother, 'All these problems will ultimately be solved by time, in its own manner. That which you are finding so difficult to accept right now, will all become easy with the passage of time.' Haima looked at her eldest son and tried to understand what was going on in his mind. But no matter what Bhabani and Sarat said, she was unable to dispel her misgivings about welcoming into her family a girl who had foreign blood in her veins and belonged to a different faith. Eventually she decided she would not discuss this topic any more with her children, silently concluding that the answers to such complicated questions could not be expected from them. As for herself, she had tried all her life to adjust to each of the complicated relationships within the family. She knew that if she adopted a rigid and unyielding stance on sensitive matters, her children could move away from her for good. Haima quietly resolved that like the storm-tossed pine tree in Bijoy's painting, she too would stand firm and detached, unmoved by whatever happened all around her. That alone was the way to get on in life.

On the day of Bijoya Dashami, the last day of Durga Puja, Haima and her family joined the procession that carried the statue of the goddess Durga from the Laban Namghar, for immersion in the Umkhra river. As usual, they walked all the way up to the Police Bazaar traffic point. There, they left the procession and stood by the roadside, watching Durgas from the other parts of the town being brought out in colourful processions. On the way home, Haima bought sweets at her favourite sweet-shop in Police Bazaar, a habit she had developed during her stay at Brahmopally. Everyone was supposed to have sweets on the day of Bijoya so as to overcome the grief of bidding farewell to the goddess. Once home, Haima spread out the sweets on the dining table and asked everyone to join in. Sarat, Bhabani, Sonamon and Prashanta sat round the table with heavy hearts. The immersion ceremony of the goddess always brought with it a feeling of sadness. Added to this was the thought that they would all be leaving home soon after the vacation. As Haima served them the sweets, she turned around and saw Bijoy standing at the door awkwardly. No one knew when he had come in so quietly. Haima looked at her son for a while. There was a trace of joy on her countenance, and then it was clouded over by a fleeting shadow of uncertainty which she could not conceal. 'Oh! You have come!' she said at last, as if it was the most natural thing to say. Everyone was taken aback and it was as if she had broken a spell. Then there followed a few moments of uncertainty when Haima's next move seemed to be assessed carefully by everyone. Haima tried to finish her task of serving the sweets with slightly trembling hands. Then turning to Bijoy she asked in her normal voice, though with a barely audible quiver in it, 'Have you come alone? Where have you left her?' At this unexpected and straight question from his mother, Bijoy answered timidly, 'She is outside, Bouti, waiting in the taxi.'

'Go and ask her in,' Haima ordered. With this, the mood in the room instantly changed and everyone rushed outside towards the taxi. Meanwhile, Haima placed two more plates of sweets on the table and carefully created space for two more persons. By then, Bhabani and Sonamon, holding Nancy's hands, had come in, followed by the others. Haima looked at Nancy as if she had known her for a long time. Then addressing her gently she said, 'Please sit down. The sweets are for you. Have them.'

37

Bijoy and Nancy did not stay for long in Dibrugarh. After having worked at the Dibrugarh Medical College for a year or two, they decided to return home to Shillong. A variety of reasons had prompted them to give up their prestigious positions in favour of posts in the Shillong Civil Hospital. One of these was their desire to be close to their near and dear ones. Soon after their arrival in Shillong, they rented a cosy little cottage at Nongrim Hills and moved in. Meanwhile, matters had been sorted out with the Kharkongar household and Bijoy and Nancy started spending happy days with their two families at Laban and Mawkhar. Nancy's brother, Frank, had just finished his MA in English from Calcutta and was now teaching at the Lady Keane College. He had already become quite popular, especially among the girl students, as an excellent teacher of Shakespeare's plays and many had developed a crush on the fair and handsome young lecturer. But all of a sudden Frank lost interest in teaching after he developed a friendship with an active young man who had also recently joined the college. His name was G.G.Swell.

Swell had been brought up and schooled at the Ramkrishna Mission of Shillong, and had done his Master's in English from Calcutta University. Equally fluent in English, Khasi and Bengali, he was also a fine orator. Once Swell joined the

Lady Keane College, the entire atmosphere of the teachers' common room changed. He started having regular discussions with the Bengali professors on battles for rights among tribal communities in different parts of the world. Although initially Frank was not particularly interested in all this, yet Swell's attractive personality soon drew him closer to his colleague. Finally, at one point, Frank went with Swell to attend the Assam Hills Tribal Leaders' Conference at Tura in the Garo Hills. It was from here that the first memorandum for a separate hill state had been sent to the States Re-organisation Commission.

Meanwhile, Bijoy and Nancy were busy at their new jobs. But even after working the entire day at the hospital, Bijoy would always be eager to talk politics whenever he met Frank and his friends. He had given up visiting his earlier Bengali friends, many of whom had left Shillong for good after the ban on the Communist Party. Others had, after spending several months in Shillong Jail, taken to practising law or had started small business set-ups of their own. They had realized quite early that the Party didn't have much of a future in the hill district. Bijoy, however, would always be a bit embarrassed when he came across his old comrades. Yet, he accepted the fact that change had affected all of them, including himself. He no longer felt it necessary to debate with his erstwhile comrades on the subject of striking a balance between one's political ideals and personal life. But, in his own way, Bijoy had found an answer to this conflict – he would always stand by the poor and the oppressed. In the discussions that took place between Frank and his friends, Bijoy could now hear the voice of the depressed communities in the hills. They had now started a struggle for their rights and Bijoy saw this as quite just and legitimate.

Once, while he was home during the vacation, Sarat met G.G. Swell at the Abdul Ghafoor shop in Police Bazaar. 'Hello Professor,' Swell called out to him and came forward to shake hands. They had known each other as students in Calcutta and Sarat recalled how once Swell had got together the hill students of Assam and organized a debate at the Scottish Church College. He still remembered the topic of the debate: 'Is it Right for the Hill People to Participate in India's Freedom Struggle?' During that debate, Sarat had been spellbound by Swell's oratorial skills. After this, he had made it a point to meet Swell often and discuss the many problems confronting the state of Assam. But the two had not met ever since they left Calcutta. That evening, they had tea at Morello's and recounted their old days and took stock of each other's work. Sarat told Swell about some of his experiences at the university and Swell asked him, 'Are the university students happy with the present situation in the country?' Sarat thought for a while and replied, 'People had a lot of expectations from Jawaharlal Nehru's government and many believed that it would succeed in taking the nation forward. But now it seems that people's hopes are being slowly dashed. The days of trying to build nationalism on the premise of "One Country, One Nation and One Culture" seem to be over. The newly emerging young sections among the ethnic communities are thinking on the lines of a different kind of nationalism and a lot of people have started doubting Nehru's approach.'

Swell was silent for a bit and then he said, 'But Nehru's ideas are quite modern. When he was told about the issues facing tribals here, he was quite sympathetic. The sad part is that the leadership in Assam has not presented him with the correct picture about the tribal situation here. The Assamese leaders seem to think only about their own people and now they are trying to impose their language on us.' Then Swell referred to Reverend Nichols-Roy and said that among all the hill leaders it was he who was the most drawn towards the Assamese people. Just after Independence, he had arranged a meeting of leaders from both the hills and the plains in Shillong so that the friendship and understanding between the two communities would be strengthened. In that meeting there were more than five hundred delegates representing the Nagas, Lushais, Garos, Manipuris, Jaintias and Khasis as well as the tribes from the Tirap, Sadiya and Balipara regions. Following the conference, Nichols-Roy had hosted a tea-party at his home where he called upon the hill tribes to learn the Assamese language and live in friendship with the people of the plains. However, it was the same Nichols-Roy who was now being forced to think of a separate hill state.

After that chance meeting with Swell, Sarat realized that the equations in his homeland were changing very fast. Would the storm signals which he had heard during his interaction with his Khasi friend, finally usher in the tempest that would sweep away his home, hearth and everything before it? The sweet scent of the pines drifting in the breeze made his mind even more disturbed and as he walked through Police Bazaar, the once familiar sights suddenly seemed somewhat alien to him. These days there were crowds of unknown people thronging the bazaar. Sarat felt somewhat lost among them as he walked back home. As he stepped into the sitting room at High Wind, Sarat saw his mother seated in his father's favourite chair and reading a newspaper with great concentration. As usual, he asked her jokingly, 'So, how are the preparations going on for the Matric Examination?' As children, they often teased their mother thus when they found her reading something and

Haima would get irritated at their antics. At that time they thought their mother was annoyed because she was incapable of enjoying a joke. That evening, the moment Sarat uttered those words, he became acutely aware that this was no joke: was it really irritation or was it sadness that was reflected in his mother's eyes? Was it the grief of unfulfilled dreams? He remembered that as small children they had seen their mother carefully preserve her school books and the transfer certificate from her Jorhat school in a large wooden chest which she had brought with her as part of a bride's dowry. Embarrassed at his question, Sarat looked at Haima with some discomfiture. But this time there seemed to be no trace of irritation or sadness on her face and she responded with an easy smile, 'Take a look at this Barbapu. It's printed at Lisimon's press and she comes and gives me these quite often. It's written in the Roman script, but the language is Khasi. I cannot follow Khasi too well, but it looks as if something big is about to happen.'

Sarat quickly went through the pamphlet and discovered that it was an emotional outburst similar to what Swell had told him about some hours ago. The people were being urged to come for a massive gathering. Justifying the demand for a separate hill state, the pamphlet dealt with the long history of neglect, deception and suppression which marked the Assamese political leadership's approach towards the hill people. As Sarat looked up at his mother after reading the pamphlet, she said, 'It seems that the Assamese will ultimately have to leave this place.'

'For a long time now our leaders have been speaking of shifting the capital from here. Once that is done, the Assamese will automatically leave, as most of them are employees. But the Bengalis will never leave because from the very beginning they – especially the people of East Bengal – came here to stay.

They've also set up their trade and businesses in Shillong. The Assamese, however, have never been sure about this place – their connection to this place has been a bit like drops of water on a lotus leaf, untouched and uninvolved, ever ready to drop and disappear. That's why most of them have houses in the plains as well.' Sarat's words were marked by a deep sense of anguish.

'Well, it is only we who have a house here and nowhere else. Your father never thought of setting up another establishment. If we are asked to leave, where will we go, Barbapu?' Haima asked.

'We have not occupied anyone's land by force. Isn't this a part of India? Why are you so worried? We will continue to stay here and be friends with everyone. How can we be seen as foreign intruders? The Khasis had never disliked the Assamese. But once our people got political power, they turned really selfish and inconsiderate. They have even started naming some residential parts of the town after some of the living leaders, Motinagar, Bishnupur, Rupaban. That's the reason the Khasis now look upon the Assamese with suspicion. People should know how to respect the language and traditions of the region where they live. Instead, if we go about proclaiming that our language and culture are the best, why should the local people like us? There are so many Assamese here. But how many can speak the Khasi tongue? And, even if one sees this as a survival strategy, a large section of the Bengalis can. Bouti, do you know that the first modern poet writing in Khasi was actually a Bengali – Amjad Ali? But how many Assamese have ever read a Khasi poem? Has anyone even heard the name of Soso Tham, the first modern Khasi poet?' Sarat said this all in one breath. It seemed that after a long time he had got the chance to unburden his mind. After he had finished, Haima said with a bit of hesitation, 'This time instead of mekhalas, I am weaving muga jainsems in my loom. Lisimon provided the measurements. If it comes out well, then I will teach others too.' The moment she mentioned Lisimon, Sarat changed the topic of conversation and then quietly left the room. Haima felt as if some unknown force had wrenched her heart. She could have taken it more stoically had her son blamed her for his lonely life; but his silence always hurt her the most. She had heard that Lisimon too had happily rejected all proposals of marriage. What were the two of them actually waiting for? This was beyond her understanding.

38

Sarat's meetings with Brother McBryde became scarce after he joined the university in Guwahati. He felt like an alien now to the surroundings of his old college where he had spent so many happy hours. The fond memories of the past which were associated with the college seemed to mock at the new identity he was trying to create for himself in Guwahati. Sarat often felt that the memories of Shillong were totally irrelevant for him now in his efforts to adjust himself to the environment of his new workplace. He had noticed that whenever he referred to his college days in Shillong, the reaction among his university colleagues was quite hostile and derisive. So he avoided mentioning them as far as possible, as if it was a prohibited sphere. Some of his colleagues had openly told him that he was a misfit in their world because he belonged to a different milieu altogether. 'Bhattacharya, people like you who have studied in English medium schools and colleges run by Western missionaries in Shillong will never be able to understand the culture and tradition of Assam as intimately as we do because we went to village schools and local colleges. So please do not try to bring in your ideas of change here.' In the beginning, Sarat tried to reason with them. He argued passionately that the very concept of a university meant a wider, more inclusive space for new ideas; that with teachers, students and researchers from different corners of the country being attracted there, new thoughts would bloom and, in the process, the students would be exposed to a much wider world. This, he told them, would help people to understand and analyse their own history and culture afresh. But, his views were seldom appreciated. Eventually, circumstances compelled him to give up on all this reasoning and adopt a cynical attitude of 'let folly thrive'. Soon after joining the university, Sarat had got together some talented students and made them perform the plays of Bertolt Brecht, Ibsen and Chekov. But gradually the students abandoned this and sought out only Assamese plays and *bhaonas*, much to the appreciation of the audience. Sarat was no longer needed. During class, Sarat would always go beyond the textbooks and try to expand the range of his subject by bringing in the latest theories in social sciences. He would insist on telling his students that history was no mere rendering of the lives of kings and queens or about important dates but it was about the greater processes of social transformation. But when the students did not secure good marks in the examination, the Head of the Department pulled him up, saying he should confine himself to his textbooks and not 'spoil the minds' of the students by talking of other irrelevant matters. It was always more important, the Head declared, to stick to giving notes to students on 'probable questions' which might be set for the examinations.

Once, while visiting Brother McBryde after a long gap, Sarat tried to share his bitter experiences with him. After listening for a while with a puzzled look, McBryde said, 'I can't believe this! It is not at all right on your part to accept all this nonsense. You should protest. Gandhi protested, so did De Valera.'

'How do you reason with a set of people who totally refuse to see the other's viewpoint and regard any difference of argument as a personal affront?' Brother McBryde's blue eyes twinkled with a naughty smile as he said, 'Then, let folly thrive!' And Sarat nodded with a wan smile.

Sarat would sometimes feel envious of Lisimon when he saw that even without him, her busy life seemed to flow on happily like a rippling mountain stream. Her mornings were spent at school and in the evenings she worked at the Ri Khasi Press. She'd completed her graduation, and was now teaching two other subjects, apart from music, at the Pine Mount School. Was she really happy, Sarat wondered? He sometimes felt like asking her about this, but these days both of them avoided those intimate moments when such questions could be asked. Rather, the memories of those intimacies of the past had come to stand as a barrier between them and, whenever they met, they confined themselves to talking about unimportant things. None dared to touch the wound that lay open in their hearts.

One day he met Lisimon in front of his house and asked her casually: 'Well, how are things?' He had expected a formal, civil reply from her. But, Lisimon replied at length and in a serious tone. 'There seems to be some unrest in the school. There is news that the Assam government is about to enact the Official Language Act which will make Assamese compulsory in all schools. If that happens then our Khasi, Naga and Lushai students will have to learn three new languages – English, Assamese and Hindi. Where will they have the time to study anything else except languages? Besides, there are plenty of Anglo-Indians from Calcutta, East Pakistan, and the tea estates in our school hostel and they are all worried about having to learn Assamese now at this stage. In short, there's dissatisfaction all around.' Slightly uncomfortable, Sarat tried to sidetrack and said, 'If the rulers try to force their decisions on the people without thinking about the possible fallout, then there is bound to be trouble. There are several other indices apart from language which are crucial for the progress of the nation. Yet, it is the language issue that seems to subsume everything. I have read the pamphlet brought out by your press. What do you think about the Hill State demand?'

Looking at the distant mist-covered hills thoughtfully Lisimon replied, 'I don't understand a lot about politics. But nowadays Frank, Lakhon and their friends discuss these matters a lot. They say that one day, they will secure their hill state and as long as that does not happen, there will never be peace in this region.'

'How will the common people benefit if the hill state comes about?' There was a touch of anxiety in Sarat's voice.

'At least the tribal people will learn to see themselves as equal to those of the plains and will regain their self-confidence,' replied Lisimon.

'Do they really know about the condition of the poor in the plains? If they did, do you think they'd ever want to be equal to them? It is quite natural for the local Khasi people to be angry with the office-goers and the ministerial class here. But when rich persons like Lakhon and Frank get hold of political power then only will it be clear how it will benefit the poorer Khasis,' Sarat said with some cynicism. To this Lisimon replied with feeling, 'Why are you being so negative even before we have got our hill state? I believe that our people are not totally unacquainted with the idea of running a province. If they get the chance, I am sure they will be good administrators.

The durbars held in the villages bear evidence of this. Everyone participates in them equally to ensure that problems are solved smoothly and effectively. However, we may not have had the experience of sitting in Legislative Assemblies. But aren't our durbars just like the Assemblies?'

'Maybe yes, maybe no. In your durbars women have no voice. But this time four women have been elected to the Assam Assembly. Before that Bonelly Khongmen had gone to the Parliament. If the hill state is realized, then you and other women will have to crow like roosters!' Sarat said jokingly. Lisimon suddenly broke into her usual laughter, 'Why should I crow? Instead, I will give long speeches in my soft and beautiful voice!' She turned to leave, but then she stopped and said in a serious tone, 'These days Amoi looks quite pale. Maybe she is not keeping well. Please ask Bijoy and Nancy to give her a thorough check-up.' Sarat nodded. His mind was filled with gratitude at the thought that Lisimon was still so concerned about their family.

39

Haimavati was gradually feeling more and more like an alien in the small town which she thought she once knew so well. That right in front of her eyes the three small communities living in the place could have undergone such a change was something which Haimavati found difficult to believe. The days she had left behind her now appeared like a dream. When she had first come to this hilly little town, the number of people who lived here was so small that their red tin-roofed cottages nestling amongst the verdant pines seemed to effortlessly merge with the surroundings. Following the earthquake of 1897, the construction of brick structures had totally stopped in Shillong and the British officials lived their quiet and secluded lives in their spacious bungalows made of timber, limestone and thatch, situated in the European Ward of the town. Very few Indians had the good fortune to have a close view of that secluded world. As for the Assamese community, its twenty to thirty families lived primarily in the Laban area while the Bengalis who had come from Calcutta and Dacca had set up their own exclusive Kolkatapara and Dhakapara in specific corners of Laban. Within the town there were just a few old Khasi families and they were confined mostly to areas like Laban, Mawkhar, Riyatsumthiah or Jaiaw. Those who came from the nearby Khasi villages for trade and business in Shillong, usually returned to their villages at night. The demography of the town underwent a major change, however, once the country attained independence. The new government, instead of building sufficient living quarters for its employees, started allotting land to them in different areas of the town so that they could build their own houses. In the areas which had been named after them, influential Assamese ministers now began to encourage kinsmen from their own villages in the plains who had secured government jobs, to come and settle there. Added to this were the thousands of Bengali refugees who came in from Sylhet after Partition and set up their own Sylhetiparas in different localities. These Sylheti newcomers soon outnumbered the earlier group of Bengali settlers who had cherished the icons of Bengal Renaissance in their own small localities of Brahmopally and Kolkatapara. Their language and culture soon got submerged under the onslaught of the Sylheti culture and it almost disappeared when most of the talented people from the younger generation left for Calcutta in search of a better future. Unlike their fellow Bengalis from Brahmopally, refugees from East Bengal came to Assam with their burden of untold misery and they had nowhere else to go. They set up their refugee colonies on the land allotted to them by the Assam government, and these developed into congested localities with houses built almost on top of each other. The inevitable ghetto mentality of these suddenly mushrooming settlements made it impossible for social interaction between them and the Khasi and Assamese communities. As she walked by these localities which had sprung up suddenly on clearings on the hill-sides, Haima often felt that she was no longer a privileged citizen of the capital of Assam.

After the British left, the character of the town changed beyond recognition. The new set of people – the 'brown sahibs' as they came to be known – who came to man the government offices occupied the bungalows that were left behind by the British and began to unabashedly ape the manners and customs of their erstwhile masters. The sprawling bungalows situated by the side of the road which ran behind the Governor's House were occupied by ministers and bureaucrats who had come from the small villages and towns of the Assam plains. Land was also allotted to senior bureaucrats in certain prime localities of the town where they could build big houses and live with their families in their own dreamlands, without ever having to come into contact with the clerks and lower grade government officers. One day, Haima came to know that the Assamese residents from those localities had formed a separate cultural centre and this had nothing to do with their Assam Sangha. She had bitter memories of one of her encounters with the ladies of the new social group. Every year on Independence Day the Lady Governor hosted a party for the leading ladies of the town in the undulating lawns of the Governor's House. Long tables covered with spotless white table-cloths were laid out on the green lawns and a sumptuous tea with all sorts of cakes, pastries, biscuits, sweets and sandwiches arranged on them. On the first few such occasions, Haima went to this special tea party along with some other members of the Assam Sangha. The invited guests considered themselves highly privileged because they were allowed to walk around the sprawling campus of the Governor's House. It was unbelievable that they were intruding into what once was considered to be the very citadel of colonial power. It was at these tea parties that the ladies often felt that they were respected citizens of a free nation. But, as the years rolled by, this too underwent a sea change.

Once, when Haima and her friends from the Assam Sangha were at one such official party, she found that a different group of Assamese ladies was already smugly seated on the chairs placed on the lawns. From their dress and behaviour, Haima could gauge that they were trying to show themselves off as equal in status to the Lady Governor. When Haima picked up a cup of tea and some snacks for herself and was about to sit down beside one of these ladies, the woman who appeared to be some senior bureaucrat's wife, gave her a half-smile and commented. 'Why did they have to invite people who have no idea how to use a fork?' Haima looked at her steadily and calmly retorted, 'The country has become independent now. Perhaps, that's why.' Unable to catch the sarcasm in Haima's comment, the woman again said, excitedly, 'Of course, you are right. Nowadays, the government has started indulging such ordinary folk who lack manners. Because of them, we're also losing our position, right?' Haima could not understand why that uncivil woman thought fit to confide in her thus. Suddenly she started hating herself and, as she moved away, she silently resolved that from then on she would never come for the Independence Day party.

In the beginning, Independence Day had held a totally different significance for Haima. After listening to the speeches of leaders like Jawaharlal Nehru and Subhas Chandra Bose who had visited Shillong on different occasions, she thought she had understood the real meaning of Independence. On the first Independence Day she had asked her sons to raise the tricolor which she herself had woven. Ever since then, she and her family never missed the flag-hoisting ceremony and the military parade which was held either at the Polo Grounds or at the Garrison Ground. They walked all the way to witness the ceremony and, touched by their enthusiasm, many other groups of women in the neighbourhood also did the same. But these days, her enthusiasm had markedly dampened. As it was, after Panchatirtha's death, she had found it difficult to return to her normal routine. And, now when she saw the swiftly changing atmosphere of the town, she gradually lost interest in social activities. The people had become divided on the basis of language, community and status. Who would ever be able to break these barriers that had come up over the years?

Haima began to withdraw from her social engagements in Brahmopally and the Assam Sangha. Since High Wind was situated at a distance from those predominantly Bengali and Assamese localities, it was not difficult for her to keep aloof from the communal turmoil that was brewing in the town. When she saw the harmonious existence of the Khasi families in her neighbourhood, Haima felt that their world was quite stable and contented. At moments like this, she wished things had remained the same, that the world around her would always remain untouched and unaltered .She was reminded of a particular incident that had etched itself in her memory. Several years ago, on the occasion of Independence Day, they were all walking hurriedly towards the Polo Grounds for the flag hoisting ceremony and they passed by a group of Khasi women washing clothes in a nearby stream. They were sitting on the huge stones that lay in the middle of the stream, washing and scrubbing the clothes and spreading them out to dry on the green grass by the side of the stream. Haima recognized some of the girls. One of them worked as a domestic help in her house. That particular day was a holiday for her so, with her tamakhli round her head, she was happily washing clothes. In the golden morning sun the girls looked radiant with droplets of water sparkling on their skins. When they saw Haima and her group all dressed up for the occasion, the girls called out to them, 'Is there a puja somewhere?' Haima shouted back, slightly irritated, 'Don't you know that today is our Independence Day? There is a flag-hoisting ceremony at the Polo Grounds.' The girls didn't seem to comprehend the significance of what they had heard and they went back to their washing with renewed energy. Haima realized that for these ordinary folk Independence Day meant nothing more than just a holiday when schools and offices remain closed and they could catch up with their chores. She'd been a bit irritated at the time at their ignorance. But later, when she looked back on that day's experience, she had a completely different view. She now understood that it was quite natural for a people who had never been touched by the country's freedom struggle, to have a different idea of 'independence'. Even the struggle against the British by patriots like U Tirot Singh had faded away from the memory of the people. Maybe, someday young men like Lakhon and Frank would retrieve these stories and write their histories in a new way and, in doing so, try to regain the self-esteem and identity of their people. But for those women, what could be the significance of 'independence' when one group of rulers had merely been substituted by another? Haima concluded that for the local people there was no greater freedom than that of freely and uninhibitedly enjoying the bright sunshine, the cool breeze, the sparkling waters of the streams and the unending stretches of green in the open fields that nature had given them. Could there be any freedom greater than this?

'How much land do you own?' Haima had once asked Keliyan when she saw bags of potatoes from their fields being stacked in their courtyard. Kong Keliyan had stared at her in bewilderment and answered, 'We grow crops in as much land as is available. No one really knows how much land will be available for whom.' Haima couldn't make sense of this notion of different people cultivating the same plot of land. 'But they all belong to the same family clan,' Kong Keliyan said, trying to explain things to Haima. 'Does land really have any value of its own? Only that which is raised on the land has value. As such, land is community property. Our Durbar decides how much land is needed for each family for cultivation. No one can hand over this land to anyone else without the Durbar's permission.' Haima had slowly begun to understand the significance of these words of Keliyan's. Like the sun, wind, and water, land too belonged to everyone. Yet, it was so difficult to understand this simple thing! Someday perhaps the winds of the new civilization would blow off all these simple precepts and then people like Keliyan would find it difficult to even recognize their own land!

40

There was a time when Haimavati never locked her door when she went out. The only fear was of a sudden blast, and there was a latch outside to keep the house secure from the wind. But now, rumours were rife about thefts in the neighbourhood. So Haima had bought a lock and key. But she always felt uneasy to have to open the lock and enter the house, as if the soul of the house felt stifled when kept locked like this. Instead, she often felt like locking herself within the house, especially given all the news about the increasing incidents of violence all around. Meanwhile, the plains districts of Assam had gone up in flames because of the Official Language Bill and the smoke from these fires was polluting the hills in and around Shillong. Although there had been no violence in the town, there was no doubt that the poison of communal violence was spreading even in Shillong. Local Bengalis took out a procession to protest the possible imposition of Assamese. There was stone throwing and arson and fear became pervasive in the town.

In areas where the two communities had once lived together, volunteer squads started keeping night vigils and, in the process, spread panic all around. But High Wind was quite unaffected by all this. Ominous headlines in the newspapers succeeded in creating an overall atmosphere of despair which affected all the communities. Haima often thought back to those beautiful days of bonhomie and affection at Brahmopally and the long-unseen faces of Subarna, Saradamoni, Labanya and Sisirkana rose up before her. She could never imagine a relationship of hate and mistrust with people like them.

When the flames of violence began to engulf the towns and villages of the plains, some of Bijoy's old comrades came together to form a group and invited Hemango Biswas and Bhupen Hazarika to show them a way to re-establish cultural amity and friendship among the communities. In response, both artistes arrived in Shillong with their collection of inspiring songs. Together they created a song called 'Haradhan Rongmonor Katha' which spoke about Assamese and Bengali culture. They set it to an innovative tune that combined elements of folk from both cultures. As a result, a fifteen-member Shanti Bahini or peace corps was created which worked to spread communal harmony through songs and dances in the different districts of Assam. The group included Assamese, Bengalis, Nepalis and Khasis, and to join it came Prashanta and Bhabani and their daughter Uma from Guwahati. Uma was then just about fourteen and she could sing and dance well. In the first programme to be put up by the newly formed cultural troupe in the Shillong Club, Uma danced to the tune of Bhupen Hazarika's song, 'Nami Aahan Sundarare Sena Silpi Dal'. After a long time, High Wind once again resounded with music and dance. Lisimon too was there participating in the singing sessions just as in the earlier days, but she did not join the cultural group as she was busy with her schoolwork.

On that special day in August, Haima had a busy morning. After everyone had left for Shillong Club, she was overcome by a feeling of tiredness. For several days now, her body had become somewhat rebellious. Sleep would suddenly overtake her at unusual times and her hands and feet would become numb. That day too she was feeling quite exhausted but she called a taxi in the evening and went to the Shillong Club. As she entered the small hall, she felt quite irritated. The first two rows of seats were all occupied by the ministers and bureaucrats with their wives and children. Her anger rose at seeing these people who had come to see the application of balm on the wounds they themselves had inflicted. Seated in a back row, she looked around and saw some known faces of women from Brahmopally and Laban. In the distance she could see Saradamoni and gave her a smile. Saradamoni too responded with a wan smile. The programme began. First, there was a chorus of Bhupen Hazarika's timeless song which challenged the demonic forces of darkness and Uma and her group accompanied it with a soul-stirring dance. Haima watched it with a feeling of exhilaration, her body surcharged by emotion. But as Uma came and joined her afterwards, Haima felt that her entire body was trembling with exhaustion. Clutching her granddaughter's hand and pressing her lips together in pain, she said, 'I am going home, darling. Not feeling well.' Uma looked at her with concern and asked anxiously, 'Shall I call mother?' Haima stopped her and said, 'No, that's not needed. Their programme is not yet over and they will unnecessarily worry. The two of us can go back. They came out of the hall holding each other's hands and boarded a taxi. Once home, Haima just about managed to open the door lock; she went straight to her room and lay down on her bed. Her voice weak, she told Uma, 'Go and call Lisimon. And please phone Nancy.' After that she lost consciousness.

Lisimon came over immediately and started warming Haima's hands and feet as she waited anxiously for Nancy to arrive. Within a short time Nancy and Bijoy came in hurriedly and, when they saw their mother's condition, immediately took her to the hospital. In the meantime, Bhabani and the others had also reached the hospital. When Haima regained her senses after emergency treatment, it was almost daybreak. Bijoy, Prashanta, Sonamon and Bhabani were there standing around her bed. Opening her eyes and seeing her entire family around her, Haima tried to smile and then said in a weak voice, 'Is the programme over?' Bhabani tried to hold back her tears and replied, 'Yes, Ma. Now you can rest quietly for a while.' Haima closed her eyes again. Then the doctors carried out a whole range of tests. After the X- rays and blood tests, it was concluded that she was suffering from severe anaemia. She was given blood transfusion and medicines but there was no improvement. The doctors then concluded that she was suffering from a type of blood cancer. With this declaration, a sudden gloom descended on the family. Bijoy started consulting one specialist after another and each told him that there was no cure for that disease and the best thing to do was to make the patient as comfortable as possible. The doctors prescribed some palliatives and other drugs and the family was advised to try and keep their mother happy and see to it that she did not sink into depression.

After some deliberation, it was decided that they would not disclose her ailment to their mother and that someone or other would always be with her. Sarat, Bhabani, Prashanta each decided to take time off from their jobs and stay in Shillong. High Wind was once again, as Haima had always wanted it to be, filled with concern, love and tenderness.

From her bed by the side of the window, Haima could see the solitary pine tree. It was bent slightly to the north because of the continuous high winds blowing from the south. But it had stood firm through all these years. At night when the wind became stronger and the whining sound of the branches and the leaves could be heard, Haima's mind would often be seized by some unknown yearning. She felt it now too. It was a familiar feeling – the yearning for life.

The days passed slowly. On her return from the hospital, Haima felt much better and it was during this period that Nancy's daughter was born. Haima was filled with happiness as she looked at the newborn, a tiny, rosy bundle. All the members of the Kharkongar family turned up to share the special occasion. They took Nancy from the hospital to her mother's house at Laban. A few days later, Haima was invited to the naming ceremony of the little one. Although Frank and Nancy were Christians, the other members of the family insisted that at least the first ceremony of the child should be held according to traditional Khasi rites and Nancy was happy to do this.

In an east-facing open verandah, a Khasi priest had prepared everything for the ritual. As the ceremony was about to begin, the baby was carefully placed on Haima's lap. For that day's ritual, Haima's role was of utmost importance, because it was the Ka Mei Kha or the paternal grandmother who was supposed to hold the child. Several names were selected and a list of these was handed over to the priest. The priest calculated the auspicious signs and finally picked one name, and that was the one Haima had given, Parbati. At that moment Haima felt that it was God himself who had approved of her blood ties with the child.

For the next few months Haima's mind and body remained quite stable. But gradually the disease renewed its hold on her. In the beginning she could go and sit in the sun in the courtyard. But soon she lacked the strength to do even that. Sarat, Bijoy, Sonamon and Bhabani tried their best to make things appear normal at home. Sometimes they sang songs which their mother loved, or played the piano. But they were cautious as they did not want to disturb her, and she was often in a state of drowsiness. One evening, Bijoy thought he heard Haima say something in her sleep. He called out to her, 'Bouti'. She opened her eyes slightly and said in a clear voice, 'Haimavati, Universe, Milky Way'. Taken by surprise, Bijoy asked, 'What are you saying, Bouti?' This time Haima opened her eyes wide and said with a smile, 'That's my address, right? Just now I dreamt that someone was asking me for my address. Why did I say this?' Holding his mother's hand Bijoy softly said, 'That is everyone's address Bouti! But we tend to forget that we actually stay in the universe which is a part of the Milky Way. Yesterday, you were listening intently to Tagore's song, '*Akaash Bhara Surya Tara*,' do you remember? Maybe that's the reason for your dream. "Haimavati – Universe, Milky Way," what an unbelievably vast and infinite address!' At this, Haima glanced at Sarubaapu and gave him a happy smile.

On another day, she woke up when she heard the voices of her sons and grandchildren in the adjacent room, and she called them near. Caressing Nancy's six-month old baby who was mumbling something, Haima asked, 'Will you all keep calling her Baby, Honey or Maina? Don't forget her real name which I gave her. In school she will be called Parbati.' Uma smiled and said, 'Grandmother has given such a rural name to our Baby! This will not do. We'll have to give her an English name.'

'Something like Queen Elizabeth Kharkongar? Will that do? Tell me why should she have an English name?' asked Sarat teasingly.

'Because when she grows up, she'll speak in English. Since I study in an Assamese school, I can't speak English properly. But our baby will always speak in English,' said Uma planting a kiss on the little one's cheek.

'As it is, you have been speaking so much in Assamese and giving us a tough time! If you start speaking in English, the speed of your tongue will increase tenfold!' said Bhabani, trying to tease her girl. But Uma was not to be subdued. Looking at Nancy, she said, 'Mami, Isn't English your mother tongue? Then that will also be our baby's mother-tongue.' Nancy laughed and shook her head, 'Khasi is my mother-tongue and English happens to be my father's language just as Assamese is baby's father-tongue.' Uma now looked quite confused, 'Then in which language will Baby speak? English, Assamese or Khasi?'

'She will create a language of her own. That will be neither her father-tongue nor her mother's tongue but her own tongue. She will write books in that language,' said Sarat jokingly.

'Then no one will be able to read that book and she will be its only reader,' Uma quipped. Everyone broke into laughter. The baby too gave a cheerful chuckle. Looking at her, Haima smilingly added, 'There, Parbati is trying to say something in her own tongue. Only her mother will understand that language.'

Uma was not to be subdued. Turning to Sarat she asked, 'Tell me, Bormama, when you write books, what language do you use?'

'My own language of course! I create that language for myself. It's not a language borrowed from others,' Sarat said seriously.

'But Mama, do you know that you are speaking in riddles now?' Uma challenged.

'Well let us put an end to the language problem for the time being. As it is all of us are already quite harassed by language.' Prashanta seemed to have the last word.

That evening, as on all other days, Lisimon carefully combed Haimavati's white hair and made her a braid. As she was about to leave, Haima caught hold of her hand and said plaintively, 'Majani, you have been taking so much care of me! In which of my earlier lives were you my daughter?' Without saying anything, Lisimon sat down beside her. Haima spoke again, her voice gentle, 'Before I leave, I wish to leave Sarat to your care. Will you give me your word?' At this, Lisimon laid her head on Haima's bosom and started to cry. Then, controlling herself, she stood up and said, 'I have never distanced myself from this house. I will always be there if you all want me. But ask Sarat about his views.' Wiping her tears, she quickly left the room. Before leaving, Lisimon also had a word with Sarat. He was astonished at his mother's proposal to Lisimon and he asked her, 'Bouti, why have you brought up this matter after all these years? It is better if Lisimon and I stay on as we are.' Haima looked at Sarat sorrowfully and said, 'You have thought about about everyone else all these years, and both of you have forgotten about yourselves. It was a big mistake on our part, son. Please forgive us and come together and set up a family.'

'Have you forgotten about Sonamon?' asked Sarat, trying to change the course of the conversation.

'I haven't forgotten her. She has run the house all these years as my khadduh. Now get her married to the man of her choice. I am leaving that to you all.'

'Does she have anyone in mind?' Sarat asked.

'Maybe, she has. Sometimes she speaks of someone who works in the same bank as her. He is a Bengali boy. I haven't seen him,' said Haima quite casually.

'Bouti, you seem to have forgotten that we're too old to get married now. All that is over,' said Sarat at last, giving voice to what was going on in his mind.

'Take away the idea of age from your mind. Both of you have a long life ahead. Try to think of that. Your love for each other is like pure tempered gold. No one can stop your coming together. Kong Keliyan is growing old. Moreover, those of her family who had opposed your match are gone. Among the younger generation, Lakhon is the seniormost in the family and he will never oppose this marriage. I feel that had your father been alive today, he too would have stepped with the times and blessed your union. He was never a person with rigid views. Only towards the end, he changed a bit,' Haima said with a sigh.

41

Given Haimavati's state of health, Lisimon and Sarat's wedding was held hurriedly. Haima welcomed Lisimon from her bed by applying a vermillion dot on her forehead and gifting her a silk mekhala-chador. The wedding took place at Keliyan's house as per traditional Khasi rites. Dressed as an Assamese groom in silk dhoti-kurta-seleng and a turban on his head, Sarat left High Wind for his Amoi's place where Lakhon and other relatives welcomed him at the doorstep by applying mustard oil on his forehead. The bride wore the silk set her mother-in-law had given her, but in the Khasi style and she pinned flowers in her hair which she had fashioned into a bun. Her soft, beautiful face was glowing with happiness. As soon as the brief ceremony was over, the people from the bride's house came over to High Wind and offered the ceremonial kwai-paan to Haimavati. They also brought with them an assorted tray of delicacies ranging from cakes and pastries to traditional Khasi sweets.

Sarat left for Guwahati just a few days after the marriage. His colleagues at the university were unhappy because he had been away for quite a while because of his mother's illness. They were unwilling to share his teaching burden; but when they heard about his marriage, they were doubly annoyed on several counts. Some of them passed snide comments on his choice of a bride. Sarat had become quite used to such behaviour from his colleagues, but he was also developing an aversion for the entire milieu of the university. Meanwhile, despite several hurdles, he had completed writing his doctoral thesis under the supervision of his former teacher from Calcutta University. Some of his research papers had already been published in well-known journals within the country as well as outside. This gave rise to considerable envy among his colleagues and they conspired to bring some trumped up charges against him. Unknown to him, several of these were now awaiting action from the university authorities.

Thus, shortly after his marriage when Sarat sought permission from the university authorities to go to Calcutta to submit his thesis, his application was turned down on some flimsy ground. Left with no option, he decided to go to Calcutta without permission. He came to know on his return that a week's salary had been deducted and disciplinary action against him was being initiated. A three-member committee was set up to go into his case. After this, whenever Sarat went to the teachers' common room, his colleagues would avoid him as if he was suffering from some contagious disease. Once, on returning from class, Sarat found a sealed envelope on his table. The departmental assistant handed it over to him and asked him to sign on the receipt register. Opening the letter Sarat discovered that it was an official one. For having violated the discipline of the university, Sarat Chandra Bhattacharyya was being asked to appear before the enquiry committee on a particular day at a fixed hour. Sarat looked at the signature on the letter and found that it was of that same person who had, just a few years earlier, been found guilty of an examination scam and disciplinary measures had been taken against him. The same individual was now a highly placed official of the university and was the custodian of the Seal of the University.

Sarat deliberated for a few days whether he should appear before the enquiry committee. He was now completely isolated in the university and he remembered what Brother McBryde had told him once about protesting. Should he protest or just keep silent and accept everything timidly? Even the wise missionary wasn't there by his side now to give him good advice. That broad-minded and liberal missionary had recently left for his heavenly abode after giving his whole life to the service of humanity. He passed away quietly at his workplace in Shillong, thousands of miles away from his homeland. Sarat and Lisimon had visited the graveyard where he had been laid to rest and placed some flowers on his grave .

Ultimately, it was as if some unknown power took that decision for Sarat. For, just the night before the enquiry committee was supposed to sit and decide his fate at the university, Sarat received a call from Bijoy. He was asked to come home immediately as his mother was nearing her end. The next morning, Sarat wrote a letter to his departmental head explaining the situation, and left for Shillong. As his taxi was winding up the hill, his mind was so assailed by conflicting thoughts that he did not even notice that there were no cars moving down from the Shillong side towards Guwahati. As they crossed Nongpoh, the taxi driver expressed his apprehension that something must have happened in Shillong. When they were about to cross the small bridge marking the entry to the town, the driver stopped his taxi. Then pointing to the road uphill, he said, 'The road is closed. I'll go back from here. Please walk the rest of the way.' Helpless, Sarat alighted from the car, bag in hand. Walking up the empty road for a few metres, he found that a group of people were sitting on wooden benches placed in the middle of the road. Most of them happened to be women. As he looked at them, he could hear them singing in chorus, 'We want hill state. No hill state, no rest.' Sarat smiled as he immediately realised that though this song was being sung to a well-known Western tune, it was not that of any cultural troupe. It was in fact a part of the people's movement for a separate hill state. What a refined and unique manner to carry out a movement, Sarat thought. He had been witness to many political processions, strikes and hartals during his years in the plains. Many of these were so emotionally surcharged that the security of the common people seemed to be at stake. But never having taken part in any political agitations before, would these simple Khasi folk be able to achieve their goal through such singing? When violent protests and terrorist activities had become the norm throughout the world, would such peaceful demonstrations really succeed?

Sarat seemed a bit re-assured when he saw a few known faces among the crowd. Just as he was about to pass by, a woman obstructed him and said, 'Today we have called for a bandh. So, you can't go further.' Sarat replied in a surprised but conciliatory tone, 'As far as I am aware, one is not prevented from walking during the bandhs.' This was followed by a murmur among the crowd. Sarat then looked at the known faces and entreated, 'My mother is on her death bed. Please let me go.' After this, no one objected to his crossing the barricade and they made way in a dignified manner for Sarat to pass through.

As Sarat advanced a few steps and was taking the small lane which broke away from the highway and wound up towards High Wind, a small stone hit his forehead. Though it was a pebble, it was enough to make Sarat lose his balance and sit down by the roadside. Feeling his forehead he found that it was bleeding. He pulled out a handkerchief from his pocket and pressed the wound hard. As he stood up he could see some of the women who had been sitting on the benches rushing towards him. They anxiously examined the wound, brought some water from a nearby tap and washed it. They expressed regret and said that some disruptive elements were trying to derail their movement by doing all this. Two young men came forward to escort Sarat to his home and, despite his insisting that it was not necessary, they accompanied him up to the entrance of High Wind. Lisimon had been leaning against the wooden railings of the veranda when she saw the group approaching. She had heard about the bandh and was waiting anxiously for Sarat. Seeing him come, she rushed forward. When she observed the blood on his forehead, Lisimon embraced him in front of the two youths and cried out aloud, 'What's happened? There is so much blood!' Sarat tried to lighten the situation by saying, 'It's just a small stone, certainly not a bullet. Don't be so frantic!' Lisimon retorted in anger, 'If we aren't careful, next time it may be bullets that will fly here.'

Bijoy quickly took his brother inside and put some medicine and a bit of plaster on his wound. 'Now, go and see Bouti.' When Sarat tried to hide the plaster with his hair, Bijoy said sadly, 'That will not be needed. She doesn't know anything now. Ever since the morning, she's been in a sort of stupor.' Sarat approached his mother and, holding one of her pale hands, softly called out 'Bouti'. Instantly, Haima opened her eyes and said with a strange clarity in her voice, 'Have you hurt your head?' Sarat was taken aback and trying to hide his wound once again with his hair, he replied, 'Nothing much, Bouti,

I just hit my head against a wall.' Haima gave a faint smile and said, 'Don't run around like that!' Suddenly Sarat recalled his childhood days. Often, after a football game he'd come home limping, his knee hurt, Haima would reprimand him in the same way. Running his hand over his mother's hair, Sarat looked at his brother helplessly. This was the woman who had ceaselessly fought all the challenges of life and had tried to make her life as well as the lives of others around her as complete and fulfilled as possible. They had never seen her express any regret for what she had missed out in life. Now, even at the moment of her final departure, she appeared so concerned for others! After those words with Sarat, Haima once again lapsed into her stupor. In the evening she awoke for a while and called out to her dead mother like a child. After that she never opened her eyes again and quietly passed away in her sleep.

Following Haimavati's death, many telegrams and letters arrived at High Wind from friends and relatives. Lisimon read out each one to the family. She handed over the letters written in Assamese to Bhabani because both Sarat and Bijoy were busy with performing the rituals for the last rites. But it was one letter addressed to Sarat which Lisimon read quietly and hid in her bag. This was a letter from the Registrar of the university and addressed to Sarat Chandra Bhatacharyya. It was only after all the rituals were over that Lisimon handed over the letter to Sarat. Sarat read the letter and gave a strange laugh. Looking at Lisimon, he said, 'So, justice has been done!' Lisimon caught his tone immediately and completed the sentence in Thomas Hardy's words, 'And the President of the "University" has ended his sport with Sarat!' After that she gave Sarat another letter and commented, 'The university authorities have found you incompetent for teaching and have dismissed you. But go through this letter. Some other people have thought you to be fit for an important assignment.'

Sarat read the second letter and looked at Lisimon quizzically. 'They are thinking of making me the editor of the *Hill Peoples Daily*. Whose decision is this? You must have done something! I don't want to enter into all these intrigues.'

Lisimon gravely replied, 'Please go through the letter carefully. They say that you have been offered the job on the basis of all that you have been writing on the rights of the tribal people. I have no hand in this. But your friend G.G. Swell might have had a hand. The owner of the paper belongs to the All Party Hill Leaders' Conference. It is for you to think about it and decide. I have nothing to say.' There was clearly a touch of hurt in her words.

42

Spring had finally arrived after the long dry winter months. The two azalea bushes in the garden of High Wind were now in full bloom with dazzling deep pink flowers. The grass in the lawn which had dried up because of the winter frost was now once again green, with hundreds of dandelions in bloom. Sonamon was plucking the small yellow flowers and placing them in the little hands of Parbati, or Paru as she was called at home. Nancy would sometimes leave her daughter at High Wind for the day. The little girl was scampering around the grass trying to catch the white fluffy seed-heads like snowballs. Sonamon was reminded of their childhood days at Brahmopally. Those days and those people were no longer to be found anymore. There were new occupants in almost all the old houses. Whenever one came across an old resident, the conversation would invariably be about which houses had been sold and which had been bought by new owners. Listening to such talk, Sonamon was often quite depressed. Moreover, these days Sonamon was both happy and sad at the same time. In April she would be married to her fiancée Pankaj who was her colleague but had now been transferred to Dibrugarh. Sonamon too had asked for a transfer and both of them would be leaving for Dibrugarh after the marriage. This would be the first time that she would be staying in the plains and the very thought of having to leave Shillong made her sad. However, she didn't allow all this to disrupt her dreams of the future.

February's strong cold winds rustled through the tall pine trees of the High Wind compound creating a mysterious music of their own. The branches of the tall, solitary and slightly bent pine tree which was visible from the window of Haima and Panchatirtha's bedroom, were once again swaying violently in the strong wind. Sarat often looked at the tree and found similarities with it when it came to facing the challenges of life. Like so many others, the tree too had withstood all the storms of life and continued to stand firm and erect.

It was after several days that Sarat once again opened the lid of the old piano. As he ran his fingers over the keyboard, he tried to listen to the music of nature outside. The cicadas from the pine branches were heralding the advent of evening with their continuous five-fold tunes, creating a strange resonance. And, from deep within the woods came the mysterious two-fold call of the cuckoo which always reminded Sarat of Wordsworth. He suddenly started playing from memory, a cheerful piece from Vivaldi's 'Four Seasons' at first in a low key, somewhat uncertainly. Then, he opened his music book and started playing to his heart's content. Every wall of High Wind resounded with Vivaldi's composition, the entire house coming back to life at the touch of the vibrant notes.

***

As Jeumon and Arvind alighted from the taxi, they were greeted by a sudden gust of wind which sprayed them with white droplets of water from the drizzle that accompanied it. Jeumon laughed and said, 'It seems your hair has turned grey while listening to my long story!' In an absent-minded manner, Arvind ran his hand over his hair and approached the gate. He looked at the name High Wind inscribed on the wooden plaque and turned his gaze on the house. He seemed to be trying to fix the story which he had just heard from Jeumon into the frame of that house. 'This is my Meikha's house,' Jeumon pointed towards the house, as she drew a deep breath and tried to fill her lungs with the fresh air. 'Who is Meikha?' asked Arvind. 'All this while I was under the impression that this house belongs to your family?'

'Ka meikha's house is the house of my father's family and ka kmierad's house is my mother's. Ka meikha and ka kmierad, both of them were my grandmothers and both houses are our own.'

As they opened the gate and stepped into the compound, they heard a melodious song sung by a mixed group of men and women accompanied by the strumming of a guitar. Arvind stood below the jacaranda tree which was covered with mauve flowers, and tried to listen. Jeumon turned to him and said softly, 'That's my elder aunt's son, Luit, playing on the guitar and with him are my aunt Nancy's daughter Paru and my youngest sister Happymon. On holidays they always get together as we used to do earlier, and have plenty of fun.'

'They are singing one of my favourite songs, John Lennon's "Imagine". Really, if the world could actually have been like the one we dream of, no heaven, no hell, no nation, race or religion but only people with open hearts who would share everything with everyone else...' Arvind said wistfully.

'Perhaps it was because of his unreal imaginings that Lennon was killed,' said Jeumon sadly.

'But don't his dreams continue to sway you, me and so many others, even today? Just as those pine trees are swayed by the wind?'

Holding Arvind's hand, Jeumon slowly walked past the windswept pines into the warm embrace of High Wind.

ACKNOWLEDGEMENTS

Several unforgettable characters associated with the sweet and bitter memories of my childhood and youth have, consciously or otherwise, left their impress on the characters of *Ka Meikhar Ghar* or *High Wind*. First, I would like to pay my respects to all these known and not so well known individuals. Several persons who resided in the Khasi Hills during the first half of the twentieth century have recorded their valuable experiences of Shillong and its nearby areas in the form of memoirs and notes. Apart from these, a lot of useful information about the history and peoples of the Khasi Hills can also be gleaned from the accounts of British officials, anthropologists, historians and researchers. The books of some distinguished Khasi thinkers of the early part of the twentieth century have also, in the meanwhile, been published. From amongst all these books, I would like to make special mention of a few which have especially been of help to me during the writing of the novel. There is a detailed account of David Scott's expedition in the Khasi Hills from 1825 to 1830 in Adam White's *A Memoir of the Late David Scott* (Department of Historical and Antiquarian Studies, Guwahati, 1954). I have specially benefitted from the following three books in Khasi translated into English by Bijoya Sawian (1) *Shaphang U Blei* by Babu Jibon Roy (Ri Khasi Press, Shillong, 2005); (2) *Ka Jingsneng Tymmen* by Radhon Singh Berry Kharwanlong (Ri Khasi Press, Shillong, 2005); (3) The collection of articles by K.S. Marbaniang, Sitimon Sawian and

Wallamphang Roy entitled *The Main ceremonies of the Khasi* (Vivekananda Kendra, Guwahati, 2012) has been of great help to me. My deepest gratitude to Bijoya Sawian for having gifted me these books. Moreover, several books on the old Assamese and Bengali societies of Shillong have also been published in the last two decades or so. I have found a lot of material which I needed from Arun Chandra Hazarika's *Shillongor Purani Asamiya Samaj* (in Asamiya), (Guwahati, 1993) and Shayamadas Bhattacharyya's *Shillonger Bangali* (in Bangla), Kolkata, 2004. The essays written by several distinguished persons in the second mentioned work have been of great help because they give a comprehensive picture of the social, economic and cultural life in Shillong of the late nineteenth and early twentieth centuries. Substantial material on the influence at one time of the Left ideology on the youth of Shillong may be had from Prafulla Misra's 'History of the Communist Movement in Northeast India' (unpublished) and Surama Ghatak's *Shillong Jailer Diary* (in Bangla), (Kolkata 1990). Besides, the centenary volume of the Shillong Club, 'Shatabdi', published in 1996 also throws a lot of light on the social life of Shillong in the early part of the last century. 'Ajo Nityah' (Kolkata 2011) edited by my friend Kasturi Gupta and her sister, the late Kaveri Gupta, presents an enchanting picture of the social and political life of Shillong of those days through the romantic memoirs of their parents, the Sylhet-born late Hemanta Gupta and the Shillong-born Kalpana Baruah. I have benefitted a lot from this book. Finally, I would like to warmly thank Dolly Kikon, student of History and a research scholar at Stanford University for having narrated to me in a captivating and delightful manner the folk-tale of Watlum-Gadapani which is popular among the people living in the region along the Assam-Nagaland border.